ALSO BY KATEE ROBERT

Court of the Vampire Queen

Dark Olympus

Stone Heart (prequel novella)

Neon Gods

Electric Idol

Wicked Beauty

Radiant Sin

Cruel Seduction

Midnight Ruin

DARK
RESTRAINT

DARK
RESTRAINT

KATEE
ROBERT

sourcebooks
casablanca

Published by Sourcebooks Casablanca, an imprint of Sourcebooks
P.O. Box 4410, Naperville, Illinois 60567-4410
(630) 961-3900
sourcebooks.com

Cataloging-in-Publication Data is on file with the Library of Congress.

Printed and bound in the United States of America.
LSC 10 9 8 7 6 5 4 3 2 1

To Sara Douglass.

*You were an instrumental part of my history as a reader,
and I wouldn't have fallen in love with so a cursed ship as
Ariadne and the Minotaur without The Troy Game.*

Dark Restraint is an occasionally dark and very spicy book that contains abortion (off-page, historical), elements of dubious consent, nonconsensual drugging, biting without prior negotiation/conversation, guns, violence, blood, child abuse, and assault (historical, off-page, referenced briefly).

THE RULING FAMILIES OF *Olympus*

THE INNER CIRCLE

ZEUS: (née Perseus) Leader of Upper City and the Thirteen

HERA: (née Callisto) Spouse of ruling Zeus, protector of women

POSEIDON: Leader of Port to Outside World, Import/Export

HADES: Leader Of Lower City

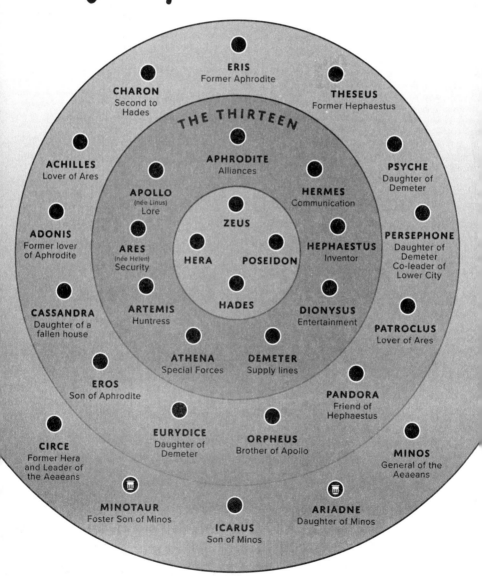

THE THIRTEEN

ERIS Former Aphrodite

CHARON Second to Hades

THESEUS Former Hephaestus

ACHILLES Lover of Ares

APHRODITE Alliances

PSYCHE Daughter of Demeter

APOLLO (née Linus) Lore

HERMES Communication

ZEUS

ADONIS Former lover of Aphrodite

ARES (née Helen) Security

HERA **POSEIDON**

HEPHAESTUS Inventor

PERSEPHONE Daughter of Demeter Co-leader of Lower City

HADES

CASSANDRA Daughter of a fallen house

ARTEMIS Huntress

DIONYSUS Entertainment

PATROCLUS Lover of Ares

ATHENA Special Forces

DEMETER Supply lines

EROS Son of Aphrodite

PANDORA Friend of Hephaestus

CIRCE Former Hera and Leader of the Aeaeans

EURYDICE Daughter of Demeter

ORPHEUS Brother of Apollo

MINOS General of the Aeaeans

MINOTAUR Foster Son of Minos

ICARUS Son of Minos

ARIADNE Daughter of Minos

MUSEWATCH

Previously in Olympus

OLYMPUS'S SWEETHEART GONE WILD!

Persephone Dimitriou shocks everyone by fleeing
an engagement with Zeus to end up in Hades's bed!

ZEUS FALLS TO HIS DEATH!

Perseus Kasios will now take up the title of Zeus.
Can he possibly fill his father's shoes?

APHRODITE ON THE OUTS

After a livestream in which she threatened Psyche
Dimitriou for marrying her son Eros, Aphrodite is
exiled by the Thirteen. She chooses Eris Kasios to
be successor to her title.

ARES IS DEAD!

A tournament will be held to choose the next Ares…
and Helen Kasios is the prize.

…LONG LIVE ARES

In a stunning turn of events, Helen Kasios has chosen
to compete for her own hand…and she won! We now
have three Kasios siblings among the Thirteen.

NEW BLOOD IN TOWN!

After losing out on the Ares title, Minos Vitalis and
his household have gained Olympus citizenship…
and are celebrating with a house party for the ages.
We have the guest list, and you'll never guess who's
invited!

APOLLO FINDS LOVE AT LAST?

After being ostracized by Olympus for most of her
adult life, Cassandra Gataki has snagged one of
the Thirteen as her very own! She and Apollo were
looking very cozy together at the Dryad.

MURDER FAVORS THE BOLD

Tragedy strikes! Hephaestus was killed by Theseus
Vitalis, triggering a little-known law that places
Theseus as the new Hephaestus. The possibilities
are…intriguing.

HEPHAESTUS AND APHRODITE ARE OUT!

Our new Hephaestus and Aphrodite have stepped down unexpectedly! But can a leopard really change its spots? We don't expect Eris Kasios and Theseus Vitalis to fully turn their backs on Olympus politics... even for the love of Pandora and Adonis.

THE WAY TO THE LOWER CITY IS BLOCKED

After a series of attacks in the lower city, Hades has strengthened the barrier along the River Styx! There's no official word on the reasons why, but an inside source says that he won't lower the barrier until the Thirteen present a unified front. We hope he's prepared to wait...

ARIADNE

MY FATHER GAVE ME STRICT INSTRUCTIONS TO STAY IN the house on this afternoon of blood and death. It's the smart thing to do. No matter what else is true, I want to live. I've shared what information I could in the only way I knew how, and it's up to Apollo and Cassandra to figure out the rest. Strangely, knowing that doesn't make me feel better.

But then, I've always been a coward.

Tension seems to bleed into the hot and sticky afternoon air, pressing it against my skin as I slip out the back door and onto the grounds. If I was braver, I would try to warn my father's party guests of what's coming. I would put myself between them and danger.

Instead, I head for the maze. It's a monstrous creation, predating my father's ownership of this house. The previous owner was incredibly eccentric—or *is*, I suppose, since Hermes is here at the party right now. This house and its grounds feel like something out of a novel, a fantasy world where turning down the wrong path can land you in a portal to another realm. I'm far too old to believe in that kind of nonsense, but that doesn't stop me from entering the maze and winding my way through the tall walls of green.

Since my father brought us to the countryside on the outskirts of Olympus, I found myself coming to the maze more and more often. Today, I don't even have to count the turns. My feet know the path by heart. Within minutes, I reach the center.

No one else in my family bothers to come here. My father didn't even notice that I'd absconded with several of the lawn chairs and gone so far as to plant flowers. I doubt I'll be around next year to see them bloom, but gardening calms me all the same. Claiming this space has been the tiniest of rebellions, nothing compared to what I did at the party itself, but I can't help the thrill that goes through me as I sink into my chair. This is as close to private as someone like me can manage. Well, except for...

I hear him well before he finds me. He makes no effort to hide the weight of his footsteps. Even though there's a secret part of me that awakens in his presence, I can't help the shiver of dread. Everything's changed. It was always going to, but knowing that doesn't bring me any peace. My father has had over a decade to put the foundations in place for this plan. To train two unstoppable killers to do his dirty work.

One of them is hunting me right now, tracing my route through the maze as if I've left behind a red string to lead him to me. The truth is far less magical. Asterion comes to the maze nearly as often as I do; even in this refuge, I can't escape him.

Not that I try very hard.

Today of all days, though, I don't want to see him. Not when he's finally enacted the plan my father crafted him for. Taking the life of one of the Thirteen so that he can slide into that position and claim the title for himself. Somewhere on the grounds, Theseus is doing the same. All in service of the destabilization of Olympus. With two of my father's household sitting among the most powerful positions in the city, the real reign of terror can begin.

I can't make myself look up as *his* shadow falls over me, blocking out the sun. The Minotaur. A presence so fearsome that my father doesn't refer to him by name. No one does. According to most who have cause to brush against him, he's more monster than man.

He's always been Asterion to me. At least until today.

I might be a coward, but I can't sit here and ignore the truth indefinitely. I drag in a breath that feels hot and sticky on my tongue and look at him. I understand why everyone fears him. With his massive body, his scars, and the blank look in his dark eyes, he *is* terrifying. He's also beautiful in his own way: long, dark-red hair and medium-brown skin, strong hands that are just as capable of building things as they are of holding a weapon, and his mouth... sensual and decadent.

His eyes aren't blank right now. They're so hot, I'm surprised I don't burn up on the spot. I may have been studying his form the way I always do when it's just us, but he's doing exactly the same thing—drinking me in as if he might never get another chance. There's a level of desperation to the chemistry that snaps between us. It can never be.

He is my father's perfect weapon, and I'm the perfect daughter, destined to be married for the family's political gain. In no world would my father give my hand to a murderous orphan, part of his household or no.

I lick my lips without meaning to. "Is it done?"

"Ariadne." His voice is just as scarred as his body, rough and jagged. He takes one slow, stalking step toward me and then another, eating up the distance between us with long strides until he can lean down and plant his hands on the arms of the chair to either side of me. I'm not a small woman; what my body lacks in height, it makes up for in plentiful curves. I'll never be the delicate little doll my father wishes for, but I've never felt anything less than desirable when staring into Asterion's eyes.

He's so close. I can see the sweat dampening his skin and making his dark shirt press firmly against his carved torso. Gods help me, but I inhale deeply, chasing the scent that is him and him alone. "Answer my question," I whisper.

"I let her get away." He releases the chair with one hand to clasp it loosely around my throat. "For you. I will weather your father's rage. *For you.*"

I can't catch my breath, and it has nothing to do with him restricting my airflow. He's not. But in all the years we've known each other, he's been incredibly careful never to touch me. Not like this. Not with intent and...possession. "You can't talk like that."

"Can't I?" He leans closer yet, until he blocks out the very sky. Until his cheek brushes mine as he speaks directly into my ear. "Now we've both betrayed him."

He knows.

But that's impossible. There's no way he could know that I left information for Apollo to find. Now is the time to push him away, to demand he remember his place. To retreat to a safe distance with the reminder that I will never be his.

I don't move. I don't speak. I can barely seem to breathe at all. Because he's right. I have betrayed my father at this party. I will likely do it again and again in the coming conflict if I think it can mitigate the loss of life. But betraying him now? Like this? It's nothing less than selfish.

I don't know that I care.

"Tell me no, Ariadne."

"What?"

"Tell. Me. *No*."

I don't realize his other hand has released the chair until he grips the front of my dress. His rough knuckles press against the delicate skin of my breasts, sending a jolt of pure need through me.

Understanding dawns, bringing with it conflicting emotions of fear and desire. "We shouldn't." I'm protesting for the sake of protesting, but it's the truth.

My father may look the other way when it comes to how Asterion watches me, the strange almost friendship that has cropped up between us, the way we seem to gravitate toward each other again and again. But he won't forgive this. If we cross *this* line, he'll slit Asterion's throat. I'm afraid to think of what he might do to punish me. "We *can't*," I force myself to say.

"We *can*. What's one more betrayal?"

"Asterion—"

"Tell me no." The rumble of his voice makes me press my thighs together. "Or I'm going to rip this dress off you."

Now's the time to do exactly that. If I say no, he'll stop. Asterion may be a monster in so many ways, but not with me. Not like this.

What's one more betrayal?

I don't tell him no.

He pauses for one beat, and then another. I expect him to rip my dress down the center, to send the line of vintage buttons flying. Instead, he thumbs open the top one. And then the next. And then the next. Exposing me, inch by agonizing inch. All without moving away or putting any distance between us. It's just as well; if either of us had a chance to think this through, surely common sense would reassert itself. We would remember who we owe everything to. Me by blood, him by circumstance.

By the time he bares me to the waist, I'm shaking so hard that I rattle the metal chair against the gravel. Asterion drags his knuckles up the center of my body to catch my chin. He still has ahold of my throat, still not doing more with his grip than claiming me. Now, finally, he moves back so that he can capture my gaze. "You've been mine from the moment I saw you. Your father might have been dangling you in front of the Olympians like a particularly tempting fruit, but we both know the truth. You are mine, Ariadne."

My stomach flips and I want to hate what he's saying, to reject yet another man claiming to own me. I've never belonged to myself, not from the moment I was born. I never had a chance. No matter what else is true, being claimed by Asterion will change everything. "You're wrong."

He drags his thumb roughly over my bottom lip. "I'm not." He reaches down without breaking my gaze and shoves up the bottom half of my dress. "But if I am, then tell me no." He slips his fingers beneath the band of my panties and wraps his fist around the fabric. "Because if you don't tell me no right now, I'm going to take what we both know is mine."

No one has ever touched me like this. Other people my age interested in sex have done plenty of exploring, whether it's out in the open or in secret. My brother certainly has, leaving a trail of broken hearts in his wake. Not me. Not Minos's precious, innocent daughter. According to him and people like him, my value hangs on a hymenal thread. I think it's bullshit, but when it comes to my life, I'm not the one who holds the power.

Except... Right now it feels like I am.

I may be shaking and overwhelmed, but there's a fine tremor in Asterion's hand where his knuckles press to my pussy. All it will take is one word, two little letters, and this all stops. *What is power, if not that?*

I reach up with a tentative hand and fist the front of his shirt. Agreeing to this will damn us both, but I'm not sure I care. We were damned the moment my father decided to bring us to this place. Any deaths that happen today are only the beginning. That blood is on my hands by proxy. "You didn't kill anyone today?"

"I didn't."

Maybe I'm a fool for believing he did that for me. So be it. I drag in a breath. "Don't stop."

He doesn't ask me again. He rips my panties from my body with a violence that makes me jerk. And then his mouth is on mine, his fingers tightening around my throat ever so slightly as he marks me with his tongue and teeth.

I may have been a passive passenger for most of my life, but I'm choosing this. I'm choosing *him*, even if it's only right here, right now. It can't be forever. But I don't say that as he breaks our kiss to pull off his shirt and shove down his pants. His cock is big enough to make a thread of fear dampen my desire, but Asterion drops to his knees and buries his face in my pussy before I can decide if I really *do* want to say no.

The first drag of his tongue through my folds makes my brain short out. I've read about this. I've bought toys that are supposed to mimic this. What a joke. There's nothing like the feeling of his tongue on the most intimate part of me. His fingers dig into my hips, pulling me several inches off the edge of the chair so that I can spread my legs wider for him. I don't make a conscious decision to shove my hands into his hair, to lift my hips and seek more, but my body has overridden my brain. His broad shoulders make a perfect perch for my thighs, and he licks me as if he'll never get enough.

What we're doing is strictly forbidden, and we don't even have the decency to do it under the cover of night. The sun bears witness to my orgasm cresting, to Asterion pressing his palm to my lips to stifle my cries as I come all over his face. He gives me one long lick, and then another. There's a pause, as if he might keep going, might not stop until I'm coming again. As if he might *never* stop.

But then he turns his face to my thigh and bites me. Hard. I shriek against his palm, the pain getting mixed up in pleasure. It confuses me. That feeling only gets more complex when I look down to see blood. He bit me hard enough to break the skin. A lot.

He rises and wraps a giant fist around his cock. "You might have been tempted to forget this. Now you won't." He angles his cock to my entrance and looks at me, tracking the tear that leaks from the corner of one eye. Asterion shifts his hand away from my mouth long enough to say, "Tell me no. Tell me no right fucking now or I'm going to take this virgin pussy and claim it as mine. Forever."

"That's not how virginity works." I don't know why I say it. My thigh is one throbbing ache, and no matter if I'm already feeling empty and yearning for more pleasure, I can't pretend my orgasm has washed away all the reasons we shouldn't do this. His bite made sure of that.

"It is with us."

Some instinct overtakes me, and I dart forward to set my teeth into the space between his thumb and forefinger. He watches me as I bite down, his dark eyes intense. Instead of pulling away, he presses his hand more firmly into my mouth, against my teeth. At the same time, his cock breaches my entrance. He doesn't go fast, but there's no time to adjust to the sheer size of him. It hurts. Oh *fuck*, it hurts.

"You can take it." He slips one arm behind my hips and pulls me closer, pushing himself deeper. "Leave a mark, sweetheart."

I bite down in sheer desperation. The coppery taste of his blood hits my tongue just as his cock hits the end of me. Pain and pleasure dance together, confusing my senses. It's only as pleasure takes the lead that I realize he's not moving. That he hasn't moved from the moment he sank fully inside me.

My tension turns into pure need as I shift restlessly against him. Only then does he begin to move. Long, harsh thrusts that hit something inside me that makes everything go hazy. I've orgasmed plenty on my own. I've used toys and techniques and explored my body to find out what works for me.

Nothing has ever felt like *this*.

This time, when my orgasm rises, it feels world-ending. There's no taking this back. I don't want to. I couldn't stop for anything. I bite harder on his hand even as I grab his hips and pull him deeper into me. He growls, the fierce rumble vibrating through his body and into mine. That's what makes me come. My orgasm goes on and on, driven to new heights I didn't think were possible. And then he grinds into me, starting the whole process over again. It's only as he stills that I realize he's following me over the edge.

He tugs his hand free and replaces it with his mouth. Our kiss tastes of blood and sex and a promise that I'm not certain I can follow through on. In this moment, nothing matters. Nothing but *us*.

He thrusts into me one last time and then withdraws. We both look down to where his seed leaks out of my pussy. Distantly, part of me is screaming that I'm going to regret this. We didn't use a condom. It didn't even occur to me to ask for one. Even if it had, I don't know if that would have been enough to stop me from wanting him with nothing between us.

Nothing but the impossibility of us.

Asterion grips my thigh over his bite and squeezes hard. "You're mine, Ariadne. This is a promise. When you start questioning that, look here. Remember." He takes the time to button up my dress as I stare at him. Then he pulls on his clothes in quick, efficient moves. One last claiming kiss and he's gone, striding out of the maze the same way he came in.

He took my panties with him.

What the fuck have I done?

THE MINOTAUR

TWO WEEKS AGO

I KNOW SOMETHING'S DIFFERENT THE MOMENT I WALK through the door. I'm not one to jump at shadows or let nebulous feelings override reality, but I know Ariadne's not here. This place feels empty without her. Dead.

Icarus is nowhere in evidence as I walk down the hallway to Ariadne's room. At first glance, it's exactly the same as it was yesterday. I've given her space since that day in the maze. It obviously freaked her the fuck out even as it settled something inside me. Minos can keep acting like she's up for grabs. She knows she's not. That's enough for me to wait until she makes her peace with it. My girl's been skittish as fuck, and giving her time to settle is a small enough sacrifice.

I look around her room. It's as familiar as my own, even if I haven't spent as much time in here lately. Ridiculously soft mattress, four-poster bed, clothes and random shit scattered everywhere in

what she's strongly protested is not a *mess*. She knows where everything is. Gotta watch my step.

But the room is missing *something*. I move on instinct to the
closet and shove the clothing aside. Sure enough, the prepacked bag
she keeps hidden in there is gone.

Which means *she's* gone.

She's too smart to have left anything to track her with, so I head
to my room. I'll need my shit before I go after her. I stop short at the
glimpse of pale-purple paper shoved under my pillow. She didn't
bother to hide the note well, but she knows no one comes in this
room except me. Not even Minos.

I stare at the thing like it's a fucking snake. I knew something
was wrong with Ariadne. She's been acting strange for days. Stranger
than normal, anyway. Even more skittish, jumping at shadows and
hunching her shoulders like she expects a blow. As if I wouldn't rip
the arm off anyone who tried.

I thought the change was because she's been sneaking around
with Eurydice Dimitriou, slipping information to the other side.
Ariadne has too much heart, too much guilt. She's too fucking good
for this world and sure as shit too good for this fucking family. Her
old man has no idea what she's up to. It doesn't matter to me. I have
no dog in this fight, and I don't give a shit about the city or any of
the people in it. Except her.

And now she's gone.

I pull the note from underneath my pillow and read through it,
each line stoking my disbelief and rage. I knew the shit at the party
fucked with her. I knew better than to let my control slip its leash in
the maze. But this thing between us has been simmering for most of

our lives, and she wanted it just as much as I did. We have forever; I haven't been in a rush to corner her again. I thought she'd come to me on her own timeline. She likes to think about shit until she turns herself into knots, but I knew she'd reach the same conclusion I did years ago.

She's mine. I'm hers. Nothing else matters.

But that's not what this fucking note says. I read it again, as if this time, the words will change into an order that makes sense. They don't.

Asterion—

You deserve more than me telling you this in a letter, but if I say it to your face, then I won't be able to do what's necessary. I know the loyalty you hold for my father. I respect you too much to ask for you to choose between us, but I can't stand by while more people die for petty politics and the illusion of power.

No. That's the truth, but it's not all of the truth.

The real truth is that I'm scared, Asterion. I'm fucking terrified. I'm sitting in the bathroom staring at two pink lines, and I can't do this. If he finds out I'm pregnant, what little choice I have will be gone. And as for you...I might care about you, but I have no illusions about the kind of man you are. You'd lock me away from the world in order to protect me, but you might as well kill me instead,

because my soul would wither away to nothing
as a result. I can't risk that. Not even for you. I'm
getting an abortion, Asterion. I'm sorry. I don't
expect you to forgive me for this or what I'll do
afterward.

I know this makes me your enemy now. And
I'm just selfish enough to ask you for mercy that I
don't deserve if we ever meet again.

Goodbye,
Ariadne

I sit on the edge of the bed and I let the knowledge roll through me. She's gone to them, to the Olympians. She wouldn't trust Icarus with this; and as much as her brother loves her, he's no match for me and her father. Even now, she's trying to protect him. My girl's got too good a heart. Can't stand the thought of innocents dying. She'll try to work with the Olympians to save people. I could have told her it's a lost fucking cause. It doesn't matter what information she hands over; it's too late to stop what's coming.

The Olympians have no reason to honor their promises to her. No matter what their origins, powerful people think the rules don't apply to them. How long has Minos been dragging out his promise to me? He says it's because I haven't fulfilled my part of our bargain, but the truth is that he's never going to allow me near his daughter. The Olympians sure as shit aren't going to stand aside and let me come for her.

I crumple the note in my fist. I don't give a shit about her being pregnant or about her getting an abortion. That's her choice. It's always been her choice. But she's running from me, from us, and that I won't forgive.

Ariadne knows me. She should fucking know better than to ask for mercy. I meant what I said in the maze all those weeks ago. She's mine. I'm never going to let her go.

Even if I have to hunt her down to prove it to her.

ARIADNE

NOW

FROM THE MOMENT I AGREED TO MY BARGAIN WITH Hades—giving him all the information I have in exchange for sanctuary and an abortion—I knew I was damned. I didn't expect the Olympians to keep their word. What motivation did they have to protect the enemy? My only value is in being a captive, but my father will happily watch me burn once he finds out I walked into enemy arms willingly.

There is no forgiveness when it comes to Minos.

However, I didn't expect the care taken by Eurydice and the others in the wake of my abortion. They have no reason to show me kindness, and even as I attempted to keep my guard up, it faltered. I'm so tired. I feel like I've been running and resisting for years, even though it's only been a few weeks. When I made my deal with Eurydice, I didn't expect to survive it.

I still might not.

That thought should fill me with determination to fight, but I hold no power here. I don't think I ever have.

My current circumstances only drive that point home. I'm sitting in a room with two of the Thirteen facing off over my future. Neither of them asked *my* opinion, because they don't care. I'm a pawn to be moved at their whim. A political prisoner who handed myself over willingly.

Aphrodite is a petite person with medium-brown skin and short black hair, with the kind of features that would be perfectly at home on a magazine cover. They pace back and forth, every movement rife with fury.

The source of their anger sits next to me, the very picture of studied apathy. Hera is a stunning white woman with long brown hair and the kind of energy that I would actively avoid if I had a choice. She's dangerous in a way that reminds me of Asterion.

But I can't think about *him* now. I've done what I had to do, and in the process, I cut off any chance of us having a future together. Now we're on opposite sides of the coming war, and I have no one to blame but myself. I miss him like I'd miss a limb. I didn't expect that. Our chance of being together was always nonexistent, but that doesn't seem to matter to my heart. It's a foolish organ, wishing on stars.

Gods help me, but I'd do it all again without a second thought.

"This isn't the plan, Hera." Aphrodite spins to face us, their dark eyes furious. "I have a list of acceptable suitors, just like Hades asked of me. Every single one of them would put her safely in the countryside. *That* was the agreement."

"Consider the agreement changed." Hera examines her long nails, black with golden tips and sharp enough to impale someone.

"I expect you, of all people, to understand exactly how vital a weapon marriage is when it comes to political adversaries. Ariadne is the daughter of our enemy. What better way to showcase the fact that she's on our side now than to marry her to someone beloved by the people?"

Perhaps I should care more about who they intended to marry me off to, but I can't work up the energy. Too much is happening in too short a time, and I haven't had the opportunity to process any of it. From the moment I saw that positive pregnancy test, there was no going back. It's bad enough that Asterion and I betrayed my father in that maze. But to bring a baby—*Asterion's* baby—into the world to be just another pawn my father uses to ensure we do what he wants? Less than a pawn. A *prisoner*. Unthinkable.

Marrying someone that the Olympians choose will likely mean children, but I can't think about that right now. I can't think about anything. It's all I can do to put one foot in front of the other and not scream my despair to the skies.

Aphrodite looks like they want to throw something at Hera's head. "It doesn't matter what your ambitions are—and don't think I mistake this for anything other than a power grab. He'll never agree to it."

"He already has." Hera drops her unimpressed act and narrows her eyes at Aphrodite. "Let's stop wasting time and do away with all your petty protests. The only reason you're upset is because *I* arranged this, not you."

"No, I am—"

"Which is why *you're* going to be the one to announce it. You're Aphrodite, after all. Marriages are your bread and butter. It only makes sense that you would be the one to arrange this coup. Marrying off Dionysus, who has managed to dodge past every single Aphrodite's attempts for the last decade, impossible to ignore. Even with the constant assassination attempts, it will get people talking."

Aphrodite props their hands on their hips. "Why would you let me take credit?"

"I have my reasons." Hera pushes slowly to her feet. I tense without meaning to, responding to the threat I can't unsee. She shoots me an amused look before returning her attention to Aphrodite. "It's as simple as this: I give you this win and you owe me. A favor of my choosing at a time that I determine."

It's brilliantly done. I've studied Olympus politics along with the rest of my family for years now. There's been more changeover of titles in the last six months than there has been in the last decade. This Aphrodite is a new addition, although they worked for the last two people who held the title. They're looking to make a splash. Arranging a marriage with one of the most beloved members of the Thirteen—a man who swore he'd live and die a bachelor—would do exactly that. What's an open-ended favor when it comes to securing their position so fully?

This moment also showcases exactly how dangerous the new Hera is. The last three people to hold her title were little more than placeholders, spouses to the previous Zeus. He killed two of them, and it wasn't for lack of trying with the third. He should've finished the job. Now, all of Olympus will pay the price for his failure.

Circe is coming for them, and she will have no mercy.

Aphrodite only considers Hera for a moment before they nod. "Fine. An open-ended favor. Consider it done."

"Lovely. It's been a pleasure doing business with you." She turns to me, and although there is no mercy in her hazel eyes, they're not unkind. "Dionysus is a mess, but he's not a bad man. My sister is keeping her word to you—and so is Hades. You'll be safe with your new husband, and he won't expect the marital privileges that others might."

Marital privileges. She means sex. The thought makes my stomach twist. I've already betrayed Asterion in a thousand different ways, so what's one more? When I agreed to marry someone of Olympus's choosing, I knew sex would be part of the bargain. Children, too. Both so often are included with these types of things. That was a problem for a future me who might not even survive long enough to deal with it.

But if Hera is telling the truth… If Dionysus won't expect that of me… Even though I know better, a tiny kernel of hope takes root in my chest. I drag in a deep breath. "Thank you."

"We'll be seeing each other again very soon, Ariadne." From her, it sounds like a threat.

Aphrodite and I are silent for several seconds after she leaves the room. They finally curse softly under their breath. "She's a menace."

"I think I like her." I don't mean to say it out loud, but once I do, there's no taking it back. She scares the shit out of me, but most people do these days. I'm used to it. I wipe my sweaty palms on my jeans. "What happens now?"

Their phone pings, a jaunty, merry tune. Their perfect brows draw together as they read the text message. "Apparently, your betrothed is here to see you."

Fear flickers through me, and I don't think I do a good job of hiding it. It's just as well that Aphrodite seems distracted. I clear my throat. "Oh. Great."

I don't have time to do more before a white man with messy dark hair and a truly impressive dark mustache walks through the door. I didn't talk to Dionysus much during the party my father hosted ten weeks ago, but to the best of my knowledge, he was drunk the entire time. When his guest, Pan, was attacked and hospitalized, Dionysus didn't leave the party with him. Aside from that, all I know is what the rest of Olympus knows. He was given his title roughly a decade ago in the last great shift of the Thirteen, and he specializes in alcohol, drugs, and any number of things best left unsaid. He also keeps secrets just as well as Hermes does, which is saying something.

He looks like he hasn't slept since I've seen him last. He's lost weight, and he was already rather thin to begin with. His eyes are sunken, his features standing out from exhaustion. He barely gives me a glance as he crosses the room and drops into the seat next to me. "My assistant sent over the prenup. I expect you'll have some thoughts on it, Aphrodite. Let's make this quick."

They flip through their phone, their frown deepening. "This is highway robbery. You can't seriously mean to agree to this. I know you play the fool, but no one is actually *that* foolish."

At first I think they're talking to me, and I open my mouth to tell them I'm in no position to argue with anything. I'm not marrying for money, and I have no other choice in partners. I'm certainly not bringing a dowry to this union. I've already given away my only bargaining chip—information.

But Dionysus is the one to answer. "If we're both going to be forced into this union, the least I can do is ensure that it's even."

Aphrodite curses again and hands their phone to me. "You might as well read it over. I don't expect *you* to protest."

As contracts go, it's a simple one. A single page of text. My horror grows as I read through it and then go back to the beginning and start again. Aphrodite is right. This is a disaster. Or a trap. Either way, I can't agree to it. "This is too much. You're giving me a house?"

"Two houses, actually. One in the city proper, and one out in the country. I expect there will be events that will require both of us to be in attendance, but you might as well be comfortable in your own space. Just like I will be comfortable in mine."

This can't be real. My life has been relatively privileged, but I learned at a very young age that nothing good happens in a vacuum. Everyone has an angle they're playing, something they want from you in exchange for their *generosity*. "You're specifying that sex is off the table."

He raises his brows. "You have a problem with that?"

"No, of course not." I flush. "I just didn't expect to see it in the contract itself." A contract that, if violated, results in a massive amount of money being deposited into the victim's account—and the termination of the marriage. If this contract is binding—and all signs point to it being binding—he's not bluffing. Which means Hera was telling the truth when she said I wouldn't be expected to participate in *marital privileges*.

"Of course, I don't expect you to go without if that's something you require. Should you want to take a lover, all I ask is that you communicate with me so we can ensure a unified front for the public."

I understand how important it is to go into a negotiation from a position of strength, but I feel like the ground is crumbling beneath my feet. Nothing about this is what I expected, and certainly not from a member of the Thirteen. To hear my father—to hear Circe—speak of it, they are the worst of the worst. People completely corrupted by the power they wield. Monsters willing to crush anyone who gets in their way. By all rights, they should have thrown me into a cell and forgotten about me for the next several decades.

They should've *killed* me. My death would hurt my father. I'm not foolish enough to think it would stop his plans; things have gone too far to stop now.

"Reread the contract all you want, but ultimately you don't have much choice." Aphrodite still sounds pissed about Hera backing them into a corner.

They're right, though. This contract could have required any number of things from me and I would still agree to it. I'm out of options. "How do I sign this?"

"Give me two minutes to print it out." They grab the phone from my hands and walk out of the room, leaving me and Dionysus in awkward silence. He doesn't seem keen to break it, so I stay still with my hands clasped and wait for the other shoe to drop.

Aphrodite returns with the contract and an expensive fountain pen and passes both to me. The pen feels strange in my hand. I sign my name on the dotted line before I can think better of it. Maybe after this, I can rest. From the moment I found out I was pregnant, I've been in a state of panic, rushing through the motions with no thought for the long-term future. I am tired. Really, really tired.

Dionysus gives me a long look, but he accepts the pen from me and signs his name as well. Aphrodite snatches the contract from the table as if they think one of us will set it aflame. They glance over our signatures and nod. "While I understand that you plan to live in separate residences, you know how this works, Dionysus. I need you together up until the wedding, at least."

He looks like he wants to argue but finally shrugs. "Very well." He stands and extends a hand, his fingers covered in rings. "Shall we?"

No choice. No choice. No choice. I was never going to be happy. I've known that from a very young age. Ultimately, this man seems preferable to anyone my father would've chosen. He might not be who *I* would choose, but... No use thinking about that now. I just hope whatever fondness Asterion had for me is enough to keep him from hunting me down and cutting out my heart.

At this point, I'd almost welcome it.

At least then maybe I would stop hurting from the loss of him.

THE MINOTAUR

"THAT LITTLE *BITCH!*"

I don't flinch as Minos grabs the nearest lamp and hurls it across the room. Icarus, on the other hand, looks like he's about to bolt. His narrow shoulders are hunched and his skin has gone gray with fear. All these years, and he's never learned to hide his terror of his father. He should know by now that fear only incites Minos to further violence.

I'm feeling pretty violent myself currently.

She *left* me. Not so she could leave this cursed city. That, at least, I could forgive. I know how Ariadne longs for freedom, that her dreams have always gone far beyond her current circumstances. Back in Aeaea, she'd had a secret notebook filled with magazine clippings of all the places she wants to visit. She'd even gone so far as to create itineraries. It made my fucking head hurt, but she'd get this dreamy look on her face when she'd walk me through the fantasy trips.

Except she didn't run away to live out those dreams. If she had,

I would have finished my tasks here in Olympus and then gone to find her. She never explicitly invited me along, but what are all those damned itineraries if not an invitation?

But no, she only ran far enough to cross the River Styx. To deliver herself into the hands of her father's enemies. Even that, I could've forgiven. But not this. I stare at my phone screen as if hating the words I'm reading is enough to change them.

LOVE IS IN THE AIR!

Our new Aphrodite has arranged a marriage between Dionysus and Olympus's newest addition, Ariadne. More details to come!

Marriage. To one of *them.* To someone who isn't *me.*

Minos drags his hands through his hair. He's a big fucker, almost as big as me, and age hasn't diminished his strength. The living room is in ruins, except for the chair Icarus huddles on and the couch I lean against.

He exhales slowly. "We have to assume she's told them everything she knows. It shouldn't be enough to sink us. Not when we already have people in the city. Circe is amassing her navy, so all that's left is to take out the barrier. My traitor of a daughter doesn't know how we plan to do that."

I'm not sure that *Minos* knows how they plan on doing that. His benefactor has been tight with information every step of the way. Considering how things have gone, I don't blame her for that; even in a party of five, information leaks like a sinking ship—and we're losing allies fast. Theseus switched sides, taking Pandora with him. Neither of them knew enough to hurt us, but Minos is severely underestimating his daughter. He always has.

Not that I give a fuck. Not anymore. I slip my phone into my pocket. "What's the plan?"

He spins to glare at me, his dark eyes furious. "And what, pray tell, makes you think I would rely on you for the next steps? You've done nothing but fail me. You failed to take Ares. You failed to kill Artemis. In the weeks since, you haven't made a move on a single member of the Thirteen."

I won't pretend the loss of the Ares title was anything other than a catastrophic failure. If I had possession of the armed forces in the city, the last few months would've played out significantly differently. Yes, as Ares, I would've had to deal with Helen as my wife, but wives are easy enough to neutralize. The last Zeus all but set a precedent.

Saving Artemis was my choice, and even with the current clusterfuck, I don't regret it. Ariadne never would've given herself to me that day in the maze if I came to her with blood on my hands. But that's the key—she gave herself to me. She's mine. She has no fucking business running off to marry some asshole. "I'll kill Dionysus."

"He is not on Circe's list." Minos shakes his head sharply. "It won't matter in the end. Ariadne can marry him, but it won't protect her. Olympus will fall, and she will fall with it."

I may be so furious at Ariadne that I can barely think past my rage, but that doesn't mean I'll let anyone else touch her. I have no intention of the punishment she fucking deserves being fatal. She's *mine*. "I'll take care of it."

"You don't get to make that decision." He turns and kicks a piece of broken lamp viciously. "Now that the way across the river is closed, we'll have to focus our efforts on the upper city. Meet with Aeacus and discuss options. I want a full report by tonight."

I consider him. "And Ariadne?"

Minos sneers. "Fine. Have it your way. If you want to be the one to do it, then consider this an order. Kill my traitorous daughter. Make an example of her."

At that, Icarus surges to his feet. It's about fucking time he grew some semblance of a spine. "That's bullshit! She only ran because she's afraid of you, Father. This is your fault. You don't get to punish her for *your* failures."

The look Minos gives his son is so full of hatred that it affects even me. Icarus actually takes a step back. His father's sneer grows more vicious. "You have been a failure from the moment you first drew breath. Don't think you sharing my blood is enough to protect you if you keep talking to me like that. Get out of my fucking sight."

Icarus manages to hold his ground for a single heartbeat, and then he turns and rushes from the study. If history is anything to go by, he'll hide in his room and lick his wounds. The man is not a threat, and he never has been. If he was, Minos wouldn't have gone searching for two violent, vicious orphans to serve his purposes. Not that it's worked out well with Theseus. But then Theseus was always fickle. All it took was Theseus's new wife applying pressure to his beloved Pandora for him to crumble.

My only weakness is trying to run from me and marry another man.

As if sensing my thoughts, Minos turns to me once more. "Don't get any funny ideas, Minotaur. My daughter is a traitor, and if you fail to fulfill my orders, I have half a dozen people more than capable of taking care of her."

I could kill him right now. He's not as strong as he thinks he is, or as capable. He taught me and Theseus everything he knows, but he'd be a fool to think that my education ended there. I've always known that when push came to shove, he would stand in the way of my taking what I want. *Who* I want.

It would be simple enough to remove Ariadne from her new fiancé and dodge Minos's people. None of them are as good as I am. The problem is that we're currently trapped in a city filled with enemies. Without safe harbor, it's a numbers game. Eventually they'd catch us.

But once the barrier protecting Olympus falls?

That's a different game entirely. I can bide my time until then. I've always been a patient hunter. But I'm not about to let Ariadne think she escaped me. I'll let her new fiancé play the part of keeping her safe from Minos, but that doesn't mean she's safe from *me*.

I let the silence stretch out until a tic starts next to Minos's right eye. Only then do I respond. "I understand."

"Get out of my fucking sight."

I go. As I walk down the hall, I catch sight of Icarus frantically shoving clothing into a backpack. He freezes when he sees me, his dark eyes defiant. Both he and his sister share their father's coloring, medium-brown skin paired with dark eyes and dark hair. But where she is soft in every way, he's all sharp edges. He's looking particularly brittle right now.

Icarus raises his chin. "Don't try to stop me from leaving."

He won't stay gone. He's surrounded by enemies with no

resources of his own. He might as well walk around the block, because he'll be back here by nightfall. I continue down the hall to the room I keep here. It's not my only residence in Olympus, but Minos is easier to deal with when he thinks he has perfect control of a situation.

It's quick work to change into nondescript dark clothing and arm myself with several guns and knives. Tonight, once I get a better read on the situation, I'll let Ariadne know she hasn't escaped me. In the meantime, it doesn't hurt to continue to dance to Minos's tune. It's time to track down Aeacus and see what he has to say.

I need the barrier to come down, after all.

ARIADNE

LIKE SO MANY OTHERS AMONG THE THIRTEEN, DIONYSUS keeps a residence in the city proper. Unlike the others, his apartment is at approximately an equal distance between the warehouse district and the center of the upper city. He leads me inside, rattling off the security code as if he's truly unconcerned I might use it against him. I normally don't have a problem getting a read on people, but he's always avoided me before. I honestly can't tell if his carefree personality is a mask or simply him.

He wanders into the kitchen and pulls down a very expensive bottle of vodka. "Drink?"

I normally don't drink. My father disapproves, and even if he didn't, I can't afford the loss of control that comes with being drunk. But there's no one here except my new fiancé, and I've already spilled most of my secrets. At least the ones that Dionysius might be concerned with.

I move closer, watching as he pours clear liquid carelessly into two tumblers, spilling alcohol onto the counter in the process. "Does drinking really make you forget all your problems?"

"Sometimes." He shrugs. "Sometimes it just makes them all seem so much worse. It's a gamble." He nudges one of the glasses toward me. "But you've had a rough go of things, especially recently, and I'm a master of escape. If the alcohol doesn't do it, I have plenty of other party favors up my sleeve."

It's entirely possible that he's getting me drunk to take advantage of me. That the contract we signed was all bullshit designed to put me at ease. But...I don't think so. He seems just as miserable as I am, and that old saying about misery loving company is far too true. I reach out hesitantly and pick up the glass. I expect the alcohol to burn my throat the same way it has in the past when I let Icarus convince me to indulge, but it goes down so smooth that I actually startle. Warmth starts in my stomach and spreads outward. "Oh wow. This is actually good."

"Only the best for Dionysus." He hops onto the counter and drains his glass. "Look, we could dance around this and I could pretend to be mysterious and let you dangle in the wind, but I'm not interested in doing that."

I still don't trust this "honesty," but I'm not about to cut him off and risk alienating him. He might have a contract that says we essentially live our lives separately once we're married, but we'll be in close quarters until then. "Okay."

"So cautious." He smirks. "Olympus is faltering. You and your family are to blame for that, but you wouldn't have been able to destabilize us within a matter of months if we weren't already teetering on the brink. I know Aphrodite wanted to tuck you away safely in the countryside, but Hera's right—you're more useful here, front and center, wedding planning for Olympus's favorite bachelor."

"*Are* you Olympus's favorite bachelor?"

"Darling, you wound me." He presses a hand dramatically to his chest, but the move is missing the flamboyant energy he normally possesses. "Apollo and Zeus being paired off has ensured the field is wide open. People adore me because I'm nonthreatening."

I take another drink, the warmth spreading through my chest and chasing away the chill that's hounded me since I saw the two lines on that pregnancy test, a chill that only got worse when I took the steps to end the pregnancy. At some point, I'm going to have to deal with the emotional fallout waiting in the wings, but I don't have the luxury of a breakdown right now.

To distract myself, I study Dionysus. He's attractive in an eccentric kind of way, though his purple suit looks like he slept in it, his bow tie is crooked, and there's a crack in the right lens of his glasses. Not to mention his mustache is…drooping. "Are you okay?" I don't mean to ask. The words just sort of pop out.

"Nope." He pours more alcohol into his glass and toasts me with it. "Not even a little bit."

Why do I find that reassuring? The man I met at my father's party back in August was just as polished as the rest of Olympus's elite, his mask effective at hiding his true feelings. I'd watched him unravel under the stress of being there…of being even partially attached to my father's plans. It all came to a head when his guest, Pan, was attacked.

Was attacked. What a neat little use of passive voice, designed to skirt the truth. My brother attacked Pan. He almost killed him, and for what? It wouldn't have furthered my father's goal to have members of his household installed as one of the Thirteen. Pan was just a guest. The attack might have been intentional, but the victim wasn't. It was Icarus's desperation that led him to make that mistake, and in the wake of it, I watched Dionysus drink more and more. He might say that alcohol doesn't provide an escape all the time, but during the remainder of the party, he was obviously running from his guilt over Pan being hurt.

"Do you want to talk about it?"

He smirks. "Absolutely not. We might be in this sinking ship together, but I'm not a complete fool. You've changed sides once. It wouldn't take much to change right back. If Circe's coming for us, she has all our secrets already, so I don't know what you could learn that would tip the balance, but there's no reason to tempt fate."

I drain my glass and nudge it closer until he pours more for me. "I've had my fill of secrets. I just want some peace."

"Peace is one thing we won't have." He watches me with bleary blue eyes. "War is coming one way or another. Just gotta hope you picked the winning side."

War.

I knew it was on the horizon. This has hardly been a bloodless coup, and that's only going to get worse. I would love to say I won't shed a single tear should my father finally see consequences for his actions, but I know better. He might be a monster, but he raised me. In my own way, I'm just as monstrous as he is. But my brother? Or...

Gods, I can barely bring myself to *think* Asterion's name. Part of me expected to hear from him somehow after leaving that note, but I should have known better. He's always been a silent hunter. If he decides to come after me, I'll never see him coming.

"I'm tired," I say abruptly. "Where am I staying?"

"Second door on the right." He waves a hand in the direction of the hallway. "Get your rest while you can. Aphrodite has something to prove with this wedding, and they'll be putting us through our paces." Dionysus peers down into his glass. "I suppose I'll be dodging more assassination attempts in the process. It'll be *fun*."

He doesn't believe that any more than I do, but I don't challenge the statement. "Then I'll see you in the morning."

"Good night, fair Ariadne. I hope you dream sweetly."

I walk away without answering. What is there to say? These days, every time I close my eyes, only nightmares await me. Tonight won't be any different.

I step into the room and stare. There are two familiar suitcases sitting next to the bed. But that's impossible. I fled my father's apartment with only a backpack full of necessities, and he's more likely to burn every single thing I own than he is to pack a suitcase for me. I love my brother, but I doubt it would occur to him to do it, either. And Asterion...

I really have to stop thinking about Asterion.

I'm feeling too fragile to go back out and ask Dionysus about them. If he did this as a nice gesture, it *is* nice, but it only leaves me more off-center. This whole thing feels too good to be true, which means it's a trap. It has to be.

When I move closer, I see a small envelope tucked into the handle of the tallest suitcase. Inside is a bright-green note. My eyebrows climb as I read the careless scrawl.

You've performed your role beautifully. Such
things deserve a reward, don't you think?

Cheers!
—H

H can only be Hermes, but... "What the fuck is she talking
about?" The only *role* I've acted out is that of traitorous daughter.
Hermes might play at being magical, but she's just a human. There's
no way she could have anticipated my ending up here. I certainly
didn't.

Before I can talk myself out of it, I grab the phone Hera provided
and dial my brother. I owe him an apology, but maybe I can get some
information when I'm doing a bit of groveling for his forgiveness.

He answers immediately. "Hello?"

"Icarus." My throat tries to close, but I push past it. "It's me."

"Ari. Thank fuck you're okay." His voice goes tight. "I am so
mad at you."

"I know. I'm sorry."

"You should have told me you were going. I would have—"

I cut him off before he can lie to himself and me. "No, you
wouldn't have. I don't doubt for a second you would have tried to
help me, but you're still too tied up in *him*. You would have faltered,
and I couldn't risk it."

He curses. "You don't have much faith in me."

I know how much that hurts him. I would spare him that if I
could, but my brother's feelings ultimately matter less than ensuring
I didn't have anything standing in the way of doing what needed to

be done. There's no point in secrecy now, though. It's finished. "I was pregnant."

"You were…" His voice trails off, and silence descends. I wait him out. My father might call my brother a fool, but he's not. He is reckless and wild, but he grew up in the same household I did. He's more than capable of following things to their logical conclusions. "You should have told me," he finally says. "I wouldn't have sacrificed you for our father's ambitions, Ari. I'm not so desperate for his approval to stoop so low."

"I know," I say gently. "But this isn't our city, and I needed to make sure no one knew I was pregnant before it was taken care of. If we went somewhere in the upper city, Father would have heard about it. He might have even stopped me."

Icarus curses again, but softer this time. "I should have been there for you. You shouldn't have had to go through that alone."

This is the part of my brother that my father can never exorcise. At his core, Icarus is a good man who just wants what's best for those around him. My heart wobbles in my chest, and I have to sit on the edge of the bed to steady myself. "It wasn't as bad as all that." Mostly. In some ways, it was worse. I spent a day or two in a small apartment in the lower city with Medusa and Calypso, who were kind enough in their own way, but the distance between us was clear. They didn't treat me as an enemy to be destroyed, but their warmth was only surface level. I don't blame them for that.

At least I wasn't alone.

"Ari."

I sigh. "Okay, at some point, I'm going to have a very long and intense cry over it. Not with regret, but just… It's a lot."

He's silent for several long moments. "It was *his*, wasn't it?"

No point in pretending I don't know who he's talking about. I've never spoken aloud about my fascination with Asterion, but Icarus is too smart not to pick up on things. He's made comments over the years, but they've been lightly teasing, invitations to confide in him that I've never taken him up on. Talking about my feelings threatened to make them real in a way I couldn't take back.

Joke's on me. What happened in the maze isn't something I can ever take back. In my heart of hearts, I don't know if I *want* to take it back. How unforgivably selfish of me. "Yes. It was his."

"No wonder he's been such a fucking monster since you disappeared," he says slowly before his tone sharpens. "You need to be careful, Ari. Father came in today ranting about your wedding to Dionysus. He wants you dead."

I stare at the intricately patterned wallpaper and wait for the words to penetrate. Surely he didn't say what I think he just said. I knew my father would never forgive me for betraying him, but... "What?"

"Dead, Ari. Like six feet under. There was no way to misunderstand him." He hesitates. "He told the Minotaur to do it. And the Minotaur, well...he agreed."

THE MINOTAUR

AEACUS IS ONE OF CIRCE'S MEN WHO SNUCK THROUGH the barrier on a shipping container a few weeks ago. He's a short man with medium-brown skin and a shaved head. He's older than me by about a decade, and he's got a weathered look that says he's seen some shit. Half his crew were murdered by Hades two weeks back, right before the secondary barrier between the lower city and the upper city became impenetrable. No matter how Minos blusters, I know damn well that losing so many people wasn't part of the plan.

Aeacus points me to a map spread out on the table in the dingy apartment where he and his remaining team are living. "Here." He touches Dodona Tower. "This is the next target. It will take some time to get things in place, but it's the heart of the upper city, and Circe wants it crushed."

A solid move. It's where the rich and powerful gather, wanting to see and be seen. They think they're sharks, but in reality they're a bunch of peacocks. Zeus and Hera even have thrones that they perch on, pretending they're royalty. Taking down that building will be as big a blow as any we've managed so far.

I don't particularly like the way he's looking at me right now, though. Intently. Expectantly. "What do you want me to do about it?"

"You still have access, don't you? I need blueprints."

Whether I have access is up for debate. I haven't tried to enter the building since the assassinations started. There was a small chance I'd maintained clearance while Theseus was a member of the Thirteen, but since he defected, he took what little protection Minos's household maintained with him.

There is more than one way to skin a cat, though. And this is just the excuse I need to put things into motion without Minos questioning it.

I turn for the door.

Aeacus clears his throat. "Where are you going?"

"You need blueprints, I'll get you blueprints. I'll be back when I have them." I walk out the door. He shouldn't let me get away with that, especially not in front of his people. All it takes is one sign of weakness, one kernel of disrespect, and a hierarchy comes tumbling down. I don't know how long he's been the team leader, but I doubt he'll maintain the position for long.

That isn't my problem.

It only takes a moment to orient myself on the street and start making my way toward my destination.

Minos and the rest of them believe I'm all brawn and no brains. I've given them no reason to think otherwise. But I've spent half my life watching how Minos operates. He's a mean bastard, especially to those he decides aren't worth charming, but he never attacks when coercion can accomplish the same goal. It's a lesson I've considered countless times over the years. It seems like a waste of energy when the thing you want is right in front of you, but maybe he has a point.

I'll never be charming, but no one expects *me* to be duplicitous.

Ariadne thinks too much. It's all she fucking does. It's made her an impressive weapon, but it also means she'll never take something at face value, even from me. If I go to her and tell her to toss the fiancé and that I'll get us out of Olympus, she won't believe me.

So I'll come at this from another angle.

It's a short enough walk to the building where Dionysus lives. I stop on the sidewalk across the street and study it. It's got a bit more character than most of the buildings in the upper city, though there's plenty of steel and glass involved. Based on Minos's information, Dionysus owns the entire top floor.

Security will be a bitch to get through, but most of the Thirteen use Ares's people, which means they all have the same protocol—the same flaws in said protocol. I can get to Ariadne any time I want, but charging in there and tossing her over my shoulder, while satisfying, just ensures she'll bolt the first chance she gets.

She'll have to come to me instead. I just need to soften her up first.

I pull out my phone and dial the one person she would still be in contact with. It rings long enough that I think Icarus won't pick up, but his wary voice finally comes on the line just as I'm about to hang up. "Yes?"

"I need your sister's new number."

"Absolutely not."

I fight not to grind my teeth. It's inconvenient as fuck for him to try to grow a backbone now. Thankfully, Icarus's weak point is practically a neon sign flashing above his head. "Do you want her dead?"

"What the fuck kind of question is that? Of course I don't." He curses. "Not like what *I* want matters, though."

Under normal circumstances, he'd be right. I have few qualms about doing what needs to be done. But Ariadne isn't one of Minos's many enemies. Not that Icarus is savvy enough to recognize that. "If you don't give me a chance to talk to her, I'll slit her throat the next time we come face-to-face." I deliver the statement mildly; there's no need to yell. I've never hurt Icarus, but the possibility has always stood between us. It has ever since his father brought me home at fourteen. And that's enough to fool Icarus into thinking I could ever hurt *her*.

He might dig his heels in out of sheer perversion when it comes to Minos's orders, but he genuinely cares about his sister. A single threat against her, and he's always folded like wet paper. Just like he does now. "You are such a bastard."

A fact he never lets me forget.

I don't say anything in response, and a few moments later, he curses again and rattles off a phone number. I hang up without saying goodbye. What's the point? The only thing that bonds us is mutual loathing. I'm the man his father wants him to be, the constant reminder of all the ways he'll never measure up. Not tall enough, not strong enough, not vicious enough. Sure as fuck not ruthless enough. If he was, he would've called my bluff.

But then, being a ruthless bastard means there's no guarantee it *was* a bluff.

I type the number into my phone without hesitation. There's no point in wasting time. Within seconds, Ariadne's throaty voice is in my ear. "Hello?"

I let the connection wash over me for single moment before I force myself to focus. "Come downstairs and go to the coffee shop on the corner across from your building."

Her shocked inhale irritates me. Did she really think I wouldn't come for her? I meant what I said back in that maze. She's been mine from the moment I saw her. It might have taken me fifteen years to claim her, but I'm sure as fuck not going to let her get away now.

"Don't make me wait."

"I can't meet you, Asterion. I can't see you ever again."

She really believes that, which only makes me angrier. I don't expect her to tell me about the things bothering her. Her father made damn sure that she doesn't trust anyone enough to do that. But I'm not just anyone. *We* are not just anyone.

She should have come to me the moment she knew she was in trouble. "Get your ass down here right now. You won't like what happens if you make me ask again."

"No." Her voice firms up. "I know my father sent you, and I'm not going to play into his hands. Goodbye, Asterion." She hangs up.

"Son of a bitch." I almost call her back, but it won't change a single damn thing. As long as she believes she's safe in that tower, she's not going to cooperate. Stubborn woman.

So be it. I'll ensure she knows that I can get to her anytime I want. We'll see if *that* changes her tune.

Part of my and Theseus's training back on Aeaea was doing missions exactly like the one I'm conducting tonight. Infiltration. It's a good thing Aphrodite set up Ariadne with Dionysus, because I already have the specs for his building and dossiers on the security team. So I know the solo guy they have on monitors for night shift likes to sneak his boyfriend in every night right around...now.

As if on schedule, a tall white man wearing jeans and a light jacket walks around the corner. He doesn't see me in the shadows across the street. Neither does his boyfriend, who unlocks the door for him and hurriedly ushers him into the building, both of them laughing under their breath. Judging by the information I have, there's a solid thirty-minute window where he won't be watching the monitors too closely.

Perfect.

I circle the building to the delivery entrance where there's a single guard at the door playing on their phone. They never see me coming. I cover their mouth with my hand and stab them a few times in the chest. They go limp almost immediately, and I ease their body to the ground and grab their badge.

Rich people are all the same. Even when they're bolstering up their security, they focus on the front-facing elements, the bits they can see. The same can't be said for the spaces the *help* occupy. Gotta have those creature comforts.

I take the service elevator up to Dionysus's floor. A whole fucking floor. Ridiculous. But it has a little foyer right as the elevator opens, and that's where I find the two security guards. I throw one knife the second the doors open, taking the left guard in the throat. They fall with a quiet gurgle, clutching at the blade and instinctively yanking it out. They'll be dead within a minute or two.

The other has a chance to go for their gun, but I slam into them before they can draw it. I barely manage to keep us from hitting the wall and potentially alerting Dionysus and Ariadne and stab them enough times for them to stop fighting me. I drop them on the floor and walk back into the elevator, retracing my steps to the delivery entrance and out onto the street.

The whole thing took maybe fifteen minutes.

Once I'm a few blocks away with no sign of trouble, I pull out my phone and dial Ariadne again. She answers after a few rings. "Asterion, you have to stop—"

"Check your front door," I cut her off.

Silence for a beat. "No…I don't think I will."

"Do it. I left a present for you."

She's a smart woman. She knows I didn't go through all that trouble to drop off some chocolates. She sucks in a sharp breath. "You didn't. Tell me you didn't."

I don't bother to answer because I can hear her moving around. She's going to check.

A few seconds later, she gasps. "Asterion, what the *fuck?*"

"A reminder that I can get to you anytime I want. Tomorrow, Ariadne. Meet me at the coffee shop across the street." I could threaten to do this again as many times as it takes until she does what I want. I could tell her that all these people's blood is on her hands for denying me, even though that's bullshit. But my woman has a big heart, and she hates unnecessary loss of life.

I don't do either. There's no point. That big brain of hers is already saying all that and more.

When she speaks again, her voice is thick. "Fine. I'll be at the coffee shop tomorrow. Just don't kill anyone else. Please."

"Nine sharp." I hang up.

ARIADNE

I can't breathe. I don't remember falling, but I'm on my knees staring at the dead bodies of the two guards who were stationed outside Dionysus's door. Two people killed by Asterion, just to prove that there's nowhere I can run, nowhere safe enough, to protect me from my father.

From him.

I am such a fool.

I press my hands to my chest and slump back onto my ass. Now's the time to scream, to call for help, but it's too late. They're dead and Asterion is already gone. He wouldn't have called me to alert me of his little *gift* if he was still in the building and in any danger of being caught.

Shakes work their way through my body as I watch the pool of blood expand. I need to move. At the very least, I need to get up and tell Dionysus what happened, but I can't seem to make my body obey my mind's increasingly shrill commands.

What's the point?

What's the fucking *point*?

Of betraying my father? Of fleeing to the Olympians?

Somewhere in the back of my mind, I wanted to be free, but that was never an option. It doesn't matter what side of this conflict I end up on. I'm a pawn to be moved about at the whim of others. To be knocked off the board entirely when I fail to serve my purpose.

A pawn can't even mitigate loss. I failed to alert Apollo in time to save the last Hephaestus. I don't have the information or power to stop Circe from invading. I sure as shit can't stop my father from continuing to stir chaos and violence in Olympus.

Useless. All I am is *useless.*

"Ariadne? What are you… Oh." Dionysus stops a few feet away, his attention falling on the murdered guards. His already pale face goes a bit gray, but he gives himself a shake. "Come away from the door."

"He killed them," I whisper.

"Yes, I can see that." He leans down and catches me under the elbows. I totter to my feet with his help, but the room feels hazy in a way that suggests I should sit down and quickly.

I watch with disbelief as Dionysus gently shuts the door. "What are you doing?"

"They're both gone." He comes back to me, once again taking my elbow and guiding me deeper into the penthouse. "Right now, I need to make some calls, and you need to lie down. I'll take care of this."

Take care of this? What a laughable concept. There is no *taking care of this.* Not the dead. Not Olympus. Most definitely not Asterion. "But—"

"Rest, Ariadne. You can't do anything to help right now." He says it kindly enough, but it stings nonetheless. Because he's right.

I allow Dionysus to urge me into my bedroom and watch as he closes the door softly between us. The wood is thick and sturdy, but I can still hear him raising his voice as he calls someone to demand more security and a cleanup.

If he'd asked me, I could have told him it's no use. Two people or twenty, no numbers are high enough to stop Asterion from getting what he wants. And what he wants is me dead. There's no stopping him.

My throat tries to close, and I swallow thickly. At least two people are dead tonight because I resisted him. His hand might have held the weapon, but it was my denial that set him on this course. My betrayal that made my father give the order for my death.

Standing by and letting more people be killed to protect me is the height of selfishness, especially when it won't make a difference in the end.

I lie down on the luxurious bed and stare up at the dark ceiling and wait for dawn.

THE MINOTAUR

THE NEXT MORNING, I'M AT THE COFFEE SHOP WELL ahead of time. It's unnecessarily fancy, all chrome and stained glass. Feels like walking into a fucking church. The barista cringes when I step up to the counter. I'm used to that sort of shit. People see me coming and get the fuck out of the way. It's what I prefer. I order two coffees and take a seat at the small round table near the back.

Exactly five minutes before nine, Ariadne walks through the door. I chose my position well. She doesn't see me at first. It gives me a chance to drink in the sight of her. She looks like shit. I'm pretty sure she's lost weight from stress, and the way she carries herself is brittle, as if she's afraid that one sharp movement will shatter her. She's wearing leggings that hug her thick thighs and wide hips and a sweatshirt that I'm slightly mollified to recognized as one of my old ones from back when we were teenagers. I doubt she remembers it was mine—she's been wearing it for a decade—but I'll never forget. Every time I see the faded blue fabric on her, it feels like she's declaring my ownership.

She finally notices me and heads over to sink into the chair across from me. Her eyes are a little puffy from crying, and her voice is hoarse when she finally speaks. "Are you here to kill me?"

It's irritating as fuck that *that* is her first question. As if I couldn't have killed her last night if I wanted to.

I stare at her until she lifts her coffee mug and takes a nervous sip. Her eyes flutter closed, and she makes a surprised sound. "How did you remember my order?"

It's not like it's hard. She drinks the same damn thing every time she orders: a white mocha with oat milk and enough extra pumps of syrup to make my teeth ache.

But even if she hadn't ordered it more times than I can count, it's her favorite. It has been for years. I don't have to understand why she likes the drink; all I need to know is that she does. Instead of answering that question, I circle back to the first one. "If I was going to kill you, I could have done it last night."

She takes another sip, and while she doesn't exactly light up, something seems to relax in her. "You aren't usually one to play with your victims. I don't understand why you made a point last night of getting close enough to fulfill my father's order but then didn't go through with it. I'm not sure I care at this point. I'm tired, Asterion. So freaking tired. If that's what you're going to do, then just do it."

Alarm bells peal in my head at the resignation she exhibits. Where the fuck is my sunshine fighter? The one who will bend but never break? The one who survived two and a half decades under her bastard of a father's thumb? I don't move, but my voice is harsh when I speak. "So that's it, then? You're here to offer me your throat? The perfect little sacrifice."

"If you were anyone else, I'd fight you to the bitter end. Maybe. Probably." She takes another sip of her coffee. How the fuck is it not scalding her tongue? I have to clench my jaw to keep from telling her to slow down. Ariadne shrugs. "But you're not anyone else, are you? You're the Minotaur. You always get your target."

She's not wrong. I've been one of her father's fixers since I was sixteen years old and he sent me to kill a rival. I can't remember what the man had done to earn Minos's wrath, but ultimately it didn't matter. I wasn't brought into the household to think for myself or question his orders. I was brought in to kill. "Not today."

She stares at me for a long moment. "Does that mean I'm not your target...or that you're just not killing me today?"

If I were a better person, I would reassure her that I have no intention of killing her ever. But I'm not a better person. As much as I enjoy the sight of her before me, I can't fully divorce it from the anger simmering just below the surface. She *left* me. She didn't give me a chance to even fucking talk to her. She didn't turn to me when she needed help. She snuck off in the night like a fucking thief.

So no, I will not be reassuring her right now. "I need the blueprints for Dodona Tower."

"So go get them."

I lean forward, and I like that she doesn't shrink in her seat in response. "You know it's not that easy. You, however, have the skills necessary to acquire them for me."

She picks up her mug and starts to take a sip before she realizes she's drained the entire thing. Ariadne sets it down with a clink. "This is the part where you're supposed to threaten me. Tell me what happens if I don't do what you're demanding."

"Ariadne." I wait for her to look up and meet my gaze. Only then do I speak. "I don't need to threaten you. Last night, you saw what I'm capable of when I don't get my way. Get me the blueprints. I want them in my hands by tomorrow night."

Her mouth drops open. "You're asking too much. Do you have any idea of the security they have around—" She clamps her mouth shut, but it's too late. She's given herself away.

"You've already tried it."

"I haven't tried to get the blueprints, no."

It's a dodge, and not even a good one. I'm curious about what she was searching for, but there's plenty of time to get the answer to that later. I pull out my phone and text her. Even though we're sitting right across from each other, she checks it and frowns. "What is this? An address?"

"Be there tomorrow at midnight." I rise slowly, letting my shadow fall over her. "If you don't come to me, I'm going to come to you. Again. I don't give a fuck what extra security they have in that building. If I have to cut every single one of them down, that blood is on your hands." She's too good of a person to let that stand. I'm counting on it.

She glares. "Why are you doing this? You don't normally toy with your prey."

"I told you before. The rules don't apply to us. Be there, Ariadne. On time. You won't like what happens if you try to call my bluff." It kills me to walk away from her. We're so fucking close; it would take nothing at all to toss her over my shoulder and haul her out of here. She's mine. She should be with *me*, not some flouncy fuck in his high-rise apartment. She doesn't have his ring on her finger yet.

Maybe that should reassure me, but I saw the headlines. I know what she intends.

Even so, taking her now would be a mistake. I don't have an exit plan in place. I might be formidable, but in the end, I'm only one man. If both Minos and the Thirteen rally their forces, there's nowhere in the upper city or countryside I can hide with her. I need to be able to leave the city, and for that to happen, the boundary has to come down.

We'll play this little song and dance to completion. In her heart of hearts, she knows I won't hurt her, or she wouldn't have come this morning. No matter how defeated she looks, I believe that. She'll get me those blueprints, and Aeacus will do what Aeacus does best and bring down Dodona Tower.

In short order, I'll have everything I've spent my life pursuing.

Ariadne and my freedom.

ARIADNE

I CAN'T STOP SHAKING. I SIT IN THAT COFFEE SHOP FOR nearly an hour after Asterion walks away, staring at my empty cup and replaying his words. My brother said he intends to kill me. The dead guards last night were a clear enough threat to confirm it. Asterion didn't contradict any of it. He might be a monster in so many ways, but he doesn't lie—not to me. If he had no intention of following my father's orders, surely he would've said as much. Surely he wouldn't have made a point of proving that he could get to me even through Dionysus's formidable security.

He really intends to get what he wants from me and then fulfill my father's order. Dodona Tower is a bastion of the upper city. An attack on that will crumble the power of the Thirteen even further. I know I'm capable of acquiring the blueprints, for all that the cybersecurity in Olympus is formidable. But just because I *can* doesn't mean I *should*.

I changed sides. I'm marrying Dionysus. If I were a true ally, I would go straight to him with the information I have and let him know the address and time I'm supposed to meet Asterion tomorrow. All it would take is a couple of Athena's strike teams and Asterion would be no more. I would be safe, or as close to it as I'm capable of being. Being married to Dionysus is hardly my idea of a perfect future, but at least I'd be alive. I might even be safe.

Gods help me, but I can't do it.

If it was anyone else... If my traitorous heart didn't keep getting in the way... If, if, if.

Asterion isn't bluffing. If I don't go to him tomorrow night, he'll come to me again, and he'll kill more people to do it. The statement about blood on my hands was blatant emotional manipulation, but even recognizing it doesn't mean I'm immune. I don't want anyone else to die.

No, damn it, that's not the full truth. The *full* truth is that I want Asterion alive, and I'm willing to let others fall to make it happen. He's not asking for the blueprints of this building to plan a surprise party. It's obviously part of my father and Circe's continuing attack on Olympus. It's only a matter of time before they bring down the barrier.

Then she'll come and we'll probably all die. I wish I had more faith in Olympus at this point, especially since I've changed sides, but they've been a step behind her this entire time. They're too fractured, even now, when their only chance is to cooperate with each other.

"Fancy meeting you here."

I jolt as a familiar woman drapes herself across the chair that Asterion vacated. Hera. She looks as good as always, her long dark hair slicked back and her lean form draped in loose menswear that looks intentionally rumpled. She peers into Asterion's mug and then uses one sharp-nailed finger to slide it away from her.

"What are you doing here?"

"I was just in the neighborhood and thought I'd stop by."

I blink. Surely she doesn't expect me to believe that. There's no such thing as coincidences, especially now. Which means... "You're having me followed."

"Of course I am. I took a risk bringing you across the river and setting up the marriage with Dionysus. I would be a fool if I didn't check up on my investment. Especially after that little scare last night."

If that's true, then she knows what I'm doing here and who I met. I search her expression, trying to divine what she's thinking. Is she about to turn me in? Maybe she'll kill me herself. For all her polished exterior, she seems the type who's not afraid to get her hands dirty. I press my hands flat to the table and strive for calm. "What do you want?"

"A lot of things." She taps her sharp nails on the table. "But from you? You're perfectly positioned to further my goals. The Minotaur wants the plans for Dodona Tower? I'm more than willing to sit back and let it happen...for a price."

This table is situated back from the others. Asterion and I spoke softly enough that no one should've been able to overhear what we were talking about. I fight down a shiver. I don't know how she managed to get that information, and I doubt she'll tell me if I ask. I sit back. "Everything has a price. Do you think I don't know that? There's no point in playing coy. Tell me what you want, Hera."

"I like you." Her smile is downright predatory. "I won't stand in the way of you getting the blueprints for your...friend. In exchange for my silence, your father's people won't try to kill anyone—except Zeus."

Zeus. Her husband.

"Why do you want him dead?"

"He's more than capable of taking care of himself." She shrugs a single shoulder. "But if he's not? Well, then, he deserves his fate. He's the most powerful person in the city, and his choices are bringing us to the brink of ruin."

Wasn't I just thinking the same thing earlier? Zeus shouldn't shoulder the full blame, not when the rest of the Thirteen continue to indulge in backstabbing and selfish ambition, but he's the only one who has a chance to unite them—and so far, he's failed spectacularly. I wouldn't necessarily condemn him to *death* over it. *Circe will, though.* I swallow hard. "But what about the succession? If he dies, someone else steps into the role of Zeus, and whatever your purpose, it will be chaos. He has no children—"

"Doesn't he?" She leans back and presses a hand to her stomach. "You're right, at least in part. If he died with no children, the title would pass to one of his siblings; Helen, in this case. She'd have to give up the title of Ares, and it would be an unmitigated mess. But in the event that one of the legacy titles dies and their spouse is pregnant?" Her smile widens. "Well, that spouse becomes regent."

Which means Hera.

Her ambition leaves me breathless. I won't pretend to be an expert in Olympus's laws, but I've never heard of this one. She must have gone looking for it, which means she's been thinking about murdering her husband for some time. It would be shocking under normal circumstances, but considering the threat crouched just beyond the city limits, it's downright suicidal. "Zeus is the one defining leader in the city right now." Or at least he's trying to be.

"Only because our people are used to looking to Zeus above all others. Hades is a better leader. My mother has a better track record of taking care of her people. Even Poseidon rules his little shipyard kingdom with efficiency and care." She shrugs. "Things are already changing. There's nothing wrong with wanting to ensure they change to favor me and those I love."

Ultimately, I have no loyalty to Zeus. I have no loyalty to anyone. I don't know if Asterion will really kill me, but I know he's capable of it. Maybe it's no more than I deserve, but... The hopeless feeling inside me wells up until I can barely breathe past it. I could deny Hera, deny Asterion and likely end up dead within a few days.

And nothing will change.

My father's people will still find a way to bring down the tower, likely with a massive loss of life. Hera will still play her games and achieve her goals of becoming a widow. The only difference will be that more people will die.

It's entirely possible—probable, even—that I won't survive the coming conflict, but I don't think I can sit by and let people die if there's a chance to help. I swallow hard. "Does Dionysus know what you're up to?"

"He knows what he needs to." Hera nudges a bag across the floor with her spike-heeled shoe. She must have brought it when she came to sit down. "I'm told this will have everything you need to accomplish your goals."

I glance down into the bag, and my heart beats harder when I recognize the computer. Historically, I prefer to build my own, but this is a nice model and far more expensive than it has a right to be. It'll do what I need it to do. "Are you setting me up?"

"If I was, it wouldn't be very smart to tell you, would it?" She chuckles. "But no, I'm not setting you up. I have no need to. You walked right into the palm of my hand when you delivered yourself across the river. I understand why Hades didn't keep you, but the lower city was the only chance at safety you had."

She's not saying anything I don't already know. In my own way, I'm just like Icarus. I've never been the child my father wanted. Never pretty enough, thin enough, docile enough. Too smart, too willing to meddle where I'm not wanted. Teaching myself the ins and outs of computers was pure rebellion at first, but eventually it became something I loved for what it represented. *Freedom.* The internet served as a reminder that while my own world may be claustrophobic and confined, freedom exists for other people. Once upon a time, I believed I might be able to experience that freedom for myself. I know better now.

Marry Dionysus. Hope that Asterion doesn't kill me. Survive the inevitable downfall of Olympus. Three tall orders that seem nearly impossible individually and incomprehensible when combined.

No, there will be no freedom for me. The best I can hope is to negotiate for a more appealing cage. "If you want me to play doting fiancée, I'm going to need the proper tools." I've had a chance to go through the clothing in the suitcases left by Hermes, but what she considers appropriate and what I do are worlds apart. At least everything she provided was the right size, but dressing entirely in glitter pants and graphic T-shirts doesn't exactly convey the right image. "Clothes, for one. Cosmetics. Some invitations to those little parties your people insist on throwing, even though war is on the horizon."

"War is already here. It has been for a long time." She pushes slowly to her feet. "Meet the deadline and you'll have everything your heart desires. Materially, at least."

This woman and Circe aren't so different. Not just because Circe was once Hera before the last Zeus attempted to kill her, but because they're both determined to make the world choke on their rage. And they're both powerful enough to make it happen. I dread the moment they come face-to-face. At this point, it's all but inevitable.

I didn't quite tell the Olympians everything. They don't need to know that Circe is beautiful and charming and fury personified. They don't need to know that she scares me beyond all reason. They know that she's coming; that's enough.

I expect Hera to leave the same way Asterion did, but she motions for me to stand. When I raise my brows at her, her lips curve in a way that feels like a threat. "Olympus isn't nearly as safe as it used to be. You and your father made sure of that. I'll walk you home."

Home. What a joke. Dionysus doesn't seem to be a complete monster, but his penthouse will never be home to me. Despite everything, I find myself missing Aeaea. It's just as corrupt as Olympus in its own way, but there were happy times there in my childhood.

I'm not naive enough to ignore the fact that those memories were with Icarus and not my father. How we used to play prince and princess of the castle, racing about in games of pretend as we explored the villa. The way old gardener Doris showed the patience of a goddess in teaching us how to garden. Icarus wandered off after only a few days, but I found peace with my fingers in the dark earth. In watching the seeds I planted grow into vegetables that nourished the body.

I doubt I'll have much time to garden in my new life.

It's only as we exit the coffee shop that I notice Hera's personal guard. There isn't a single man among their number, and they fall into ranks around us with military precision. I study them on our trip across the street. Their black uniforms could be mistaken for Athena's or even Ares's, except for the patch on their shoulder. A crown and two peacock feathers. Hera's crest.

I'll look into them when I have a little time, but I would wager a significant amount of money that these people came from Demeter's ranks or perhaps from the countryside that surrounds Olympus. Hera seems too smart to surround herself with people who are loyal to anyone but her.

I wonder what Zeus has to say about that. He's not a fool; surely he realizes that his wife hates him. If he doesn't... Well, I have enough to worry about.

We stop outside the doors to Dionysus's building. The wind picks up Hera's long dark hair, giving her an otherworldly appearance. She studies me. "You've come this far, Ariadne. Don't falter now."

There's a threat beneath her words, but I'm too tired to force her to speak plainly. Instead, I make myself meet her gaze. "If I do this, you will also promise to protect my brother. Not with the Thirteen, not with some half-baked security squad. You personally, Hera."

"He's hardly my domain." She shrugs. "I'm not in the habit of kidnapping folks. The best I can promise is that I will extend him an offer of protection. It's up to him whether he decides to take it."

Icarus will take some convincing. Even then, Hera's protection is hardly all-encompassing. There are no guarantees. If Olympus falls, I'll have to think of something else to keep my brother safe. A problem for another day. This is as good a deal as I'm going to get. Honestly, she could just demand I do what she wants and I wouldn't have a choice. I have no power here; a pawn being moved back and forth by Asterion and Hera, subject to the whims of people more powerful than me. Just like I've always been.

I extend my hand. "You have yourself a bargain."

THE MINOTAUR

WITH TIME TO KILL AND NO DESIRE TO FACE OFF WITH
Minos again, I spend the next day stalking Dionysus. He's the one
among the Thirteen who I never paid much attention to. He was
ordered off-limits at the party and therefore beneath my notice. The
few interactions I've had with him have done nothing to convince
me of his worth. He's a thin white man who dresses in inexplicably
fancy clothing and always seems to be in an altered state of mind.
At the party, it was alcohol, but in the time I've spent following
him today, I watched him take no fewer than three different kinds
of drugs.

Or at least I assume the pills he's been popping are drugs. I *am*
certain the line he snorted is.

It doesn't seem to affect him, though. He bumbles through his
meetings with a carelessness that aggravates me. This is one of the
thirteen most powerful people in this fucking city, and he doesn't
seem worried in the least he might be a target for assassination or
that the city itself is about to be under siege. Not that he would

know that last bit, but the rest of the Thirteen walk around as if they have targets on their backs or with a fierce bravado, daring someone to try them. Dionysus does neither.

As best I can tell, his meetings today in the dingy bars of the warehouse district are regarding the importation of the substances he's testing. Publicly, his prestige comes from the entertainment he offers. He's partners with several of the largest businesses in the upper city and a handful in the lower city and has exclusive distribution to said businesses when it comes to alcohol. I've tasted his vintages, and they're fine. I'm not really a wine guy, though.

There's nothing about him that's impressive. There's sure as fuck nothing about him that's worthy of Ariadne.

I'm under strict instructions not to murder any of the Thirteen until the barrier comes down, but I'm tempted to defy that order here and now. The final bar we've ended up in is the most threadbare of the bunch. The floors beneath my feet are sticky, the barstools appear to be in danger of collapsing under the next patron, and the booths near the back are bathed in shadows that invite shady dealings. It's one of those booths Dionysus has retreated to. I can't see him from my current position, but I can see the back door. He won't get away without my knowing it.

The bartender—a short, plump person with a bald head, pale skin, and star freckles tattooed across the bridge of their nose—stops in front of me and sets down a tall glass of beer. I frown at them. "I didn't order this."

"Compliments of the owner." They jerk a thumb toward the booth Dionysus disappeared into.

Son of a bitch. To not drink is cowardly. To drink is foolish.

I've witnessed how many substances this man has access to. Surely some of them are deadly. While I've been considering taking him out, he might have been watching me watch him and thinking the same thoughts.

Only one way to find out.

I pick up the beer and walk to the booth where Dionysus is slouched. He doesn't flinch at my presence, but judging from how dilated his eyes are, that might be because he's incapable of sensing the danger he's in.

"So. It *is* you. I thought I saw a hulking monster shadowing my steps. Very spooky."

"It's me." I survey him just like I've been surveying him all day. It doesn't matter what angle I come at this from. The truth is that I don't understand him. As far as I can tell, he's the personification of all of Olympus's vices. Selfish and indulgent and completely oblivious to the danger all around him.

Dionysus heaves himself forward and braces his elbows on the table. He seems to be making an effort to study me back, but he keeps getting distracted with other things. The hazy light hanging over the booth. The spill of some liquid near his elbow. His nearly empty glass. Finally, he sighs. "Have you come to kill me?"

If I were a different person, everyone's willingness to believe I'm there to murder them might irk me. But I've spent my entire life cultivating a reputation that is not to be fucked with. When people think you're too dangerous to cross, they don't cross you. Even Minos, who has held my leash for half my life, hesitates to yank it too hard. That's just the way I like it.

"Well?"

The truth is I don't know why I'm here. I might not like him, and I certainly don't understand him, but as long as Ariadne is engaged to him, I know exactly where she's at. It gives me leverage that I fully intend to use. "I'm not going to kill you...yet."

"How comforting. Cheers." He raises his glass and drains the dregs. I have to fight not to wince at how thick they look. Surely that can't taste good, but it doesn't seem to faze him in the least. He raises his dark brows. "You haven't touched your drink, friend. For someone who doesn't seem to have much respect for me, you sure act like I'm a threat."

"I'm not your friend." I can't tell if he's provoking me with the intention of making me look like a fool or if he really has poisoned me. No, I'm thinking like an Aeaean, not like an Olympian. They fight their battles with words and public perception, not with knives and poison.

At least they do since the last Zeus died.

I hold his gaze and drain my beer in a single drink. I'm mildly irritated to discover it's the best beer I've ever had. This man might be a fuckup in a number of ways, but he knows his alcohol. I set the glass on the table with a clink. "You're set to marry Ariadne."

"That's what they tell me."

I wait for some kind of gloating or pride or even lust, but he seems completely indifferent to his pending nuptials. "You act like you didn't choose it."

"I didn't. If I had my way, it would be the permanent bachelor life for me. Don't have much interest in marriage or relationships in general, and Dionysus isn't a legacy title, so there's no need for me to procreate." He shudders delicately. "Thank the gods."

"Then why do it?" I don't know why I'm asking him. It doesn't matter why he's doing it, only that he is. If he doesn't want to get married, perhaps that'll save Ariadne from being put in a position where she has to sleep with him. I don't know what she would do if that choice was before her. I sure as fuck don't like thinking about it. "If you try to force her—"

"Going to stop you there. No one is forcing anyone to do anything." He frowns. "Well, there is a marriage bed, but this is Olympus. Marriages of convenience are the rule rather than the exception. At least these days." He leans forward even farther, peering up into my face. "Why are you so invested? Is it because of her father?"

"He wants her dead." I stare into his dilated pupils and find myself speaking the truth without having any intention of doing so. "He commanded me to kill her."

"That's going to be a problem."

Again, I speak without having any intention of doing so. "It really won't. I'm not going to kill her. She's mine. She has been from the moment I saw her."

"*Interesting.*" His brows wing up. "That's not very enlightened of you."

"It has nothing to do with enlightenment and everything to do with fact. I'm hers. She's still in denial about that, but she won't be for long." I snap my mouth shut and shove back. I've never said that shit aloud. I wouldn't have said it to *him.* "What the fuck did you put my drink?"

"A little of this, a little of that." He waves a hand leisurely. "Since you've spent so much time haunting my steps today, I thought it important that we have a frank conversation. You seem like the strong, silent type, so I took it upon myself to give you a little...lubrication."

"You motherfucker."

His body language is still relaxed, but the dazed look in his eyes melts away. It's enough to make me wonder if he took any drugs at all today or if that was all a show for my benefit. The better to underestimate him.

Dionysus waves over the bartender, who delivers two fresh drinks. "Let's chat. I have a number of questions requiring answers."

"With all your brilliant planning to pull me in and drug me, did it ever occur to you that I could just kill you once I realized what you'd done?"

He nods solemnly. "The thought did cross my mind. Especially after the attack last night. That's why I brought them." He nods and I follow the movement to the booth across from us. Two nondescript people sit there, draped in shadows. They weren't with him earlier or I would've noticed. I sure as fuck would've noticed the guns in their hands, pointed casually in my direction. Dionysus takes a long drink of his beer. "Let's not dirty ourselves with meaningless threats. You might end up killing me today—I'll give you that. But if you did, you wouldn't make it out of this building alive."

Entering the booth was a mistake. The few seconds it'll take me to slide out are enough to pump me full of bullets. He chose his trap well. I consider the people in the booth across from us and then turn back to him. "You'd still be dead."

"I absolutely would. But you would be too, and that's what I'm betting on. You seem like a man with a plan, and men with plans aren't suicidal. So why don't you drink your beer and we'll have a nice little chat and then go our separate ways at the end, both healthy and whole."

Clever motherfucker. I lean back, pointedly not touching the new beer. "There's nothing I can tell you that your fiancée doesn't already know." It's the truth, more or less. At least it's true enough to satisfy the drug in my system. Ariadne knows about the barrier coming down and she knows about the pending attack on Dodona Tower. Whether she told him—and I know she didn't—is not my problem.

"I see. What are your current orders?"

I debate not speaking at all, but curiosity is a powerful thing. He isn't acting like I expected, which means my father's—and Circe's—information has holes. "Kill Minos's daughter."

"Yes, you mentioned that already." He blinks slowly. "He's really not one to let sentimentality hold him back, is he?"

"You've met him. What do you think?"

"Ah, ah." He waves his finger at me. "No getting around the drugs by answering a question with a question."

I shrug. "His children have always been disappointments. Ariadne betrayed him, but more than that, she betrayed Aeaea. He's not going to let that go. Not even for a blood relation." Which is why I have to get her out of here. Eventually he'll figure out that I have no intention of harming her, and he'll send someone else to do the job. Maybe Aeacus. I don't have strong bonds with any of Minos's men, but I've trained with them and I know their strengths and weaknesses. I can beat them, but it will have a high cost. It's better to avoid that particular confrontation.

"How Olympian of him." Dionysus sits back. "When will Circe attack?"

"I don't know."

"Make an educated guess based on the information you currently possess."

Again, I debate not answering, but I suspect he already knows the answer. If not him, then another among the Thirteen with more battle prowess. There are stages to these things, and Circe and the council are moving through them like clockwork. "It will be soon. She already softened you up. It didn't take long for the city to turn on you or for Hades to erect the barrier, cutting the city in two. You're divided and you're weak, and she's too smart not to take advantage of that."

Dionysus twists the edge of his mustache into a perfect curl. "There is the barrier still in play."

Not for long. "The barrier continues to fail. I wouldn't stick my hopes on that."

"On that, my murderous friend, we are in agreement." He drinks his beer. "You have a plan to bring it down."

"Minos does."

"Thought as much." I expect him to press me on that, but he just contemplates his glass for a few moments. "Where is Hermes?"

"I would think you'd know. You two were attached at the hip." When he just stares, I finally shrug. "I have no idea. As far as my information goes, her deal with Minos ended at the party." I have no loyalty to either Minos or Hermes at this point. Dionysus doesn't seem inclined to murder me and toss my body in a dumpster, so there's no point in dodging this series of questions. It's not like it will make a difference in the final outcome.

"Ah well. Hope springs eternal, and she owes me some answers.

Now for the less delicate business." His dark eyes go hard and his body language firms up, until it's like looking at a different man entirely. "You're more than welcome to keep following me if that suits your fancy, but Ariadne is now my fiancée, and she will be my wife. I have no great love for the woman, but she *is* under my protection, and I won't see her harmed. If you continue to be a threat and murder my people…" Again, he waves to the pair in the booth across from us. "Well, you get the idea."

"If this wasn't an ambush, they wouldn't stand a chance. They sure as fuck didn't last night."

"Perhaps. Perhaps not." He glances meaningfully at the beer in front of me. "You're in Olympus, old boy. Everything you eat comes from Demeter. A good portion of what you drink is courtesy of me. You've been in the city too long to be running on food you brought in with you. All it will take is a little bit of this, a little of that, and *you* won't be a threat to anyone."

ARIADNE

THE COMPUTER HERA PROVIDED IS MORE THAN SUFFI-cient to meet my needs. It took about an hour to get it set up to my specifications, and then I spent another hour checking on the various forums to see if anything new has popped up since I've been offline. It's been remarkably quiet. There's something big stirring in Europe and a handful of revolutions across the globe, but it's startlingly silent when it comes to what's going on here.

Part of that is because Olympus operates on its own server, of sorts. With a barrier keeping it walled away, it's reached almost mythological status to the rest of the world. They know it exists, but it's not real to them. Not like it was on Aeaea.

I reassure a few of my online friends that I am, in fact, still alive. It's tempting to sink into that, to catch up with them, to check the fan fiction sites that I spend so much time on, to do anything except my task.

I'm all but assured to be walking into a trap tomorrow. The question is why bother to set a trap to begin with? It's not Asterion's style. He prefers blunt honesty, sometimes to the point of cruelty, so one never wonders where they stand with him. He was right yesterday—if he wants me dead, he has no reason to play the long game. He could've just done it.

He's only disobeyed one of my father's orders. Because of me. I'd be a fool to believe he'd disobey a second time. Any fondness he holds for me will have burned up with my betrayal.

But Hera wants him to have those blueprints, which leaves me little choice.

If she wanted to make this easy on me, she could've accessed the information on her own instead of sending me on this wild-goose chase. "But that might get her perfectly manicured hands dirty. We can't have that," I mutter under my breath as I get to work.

The cybersecurity in Olympus isn't terrible, but it's somewhat out of date. These days, hacking technology advances almost faster than the defense can keep up. Good for me. Bad for them. I suppose they haven't had to worry about it much since the most interest they get is from conspiracy theorists wanting to prove they don't exist… or that they do.

I barely register the time passing and the light changing in the room. It's not until the front door shuts softly that I snap out of it. I close the laptop just as Dionysus walks into the room. He doesn't appear to have slept since I saw him last, but there's a bounce in his step and he's humming under his breath.

He stops short when he sees me. "Oh. You're here."

"I…do live here now."

"Right. I kind of forgot." He drags his hand through his thick dark hair. "I have some things I need to take care of this evening, but how about brunch tomorrow?"

I blink. "Brunch?"

It's hard to tell, but I think he might be blushing. "Yes, well, I'm almost never awake in time for a proper breakfast, so brunch is the way to go. Plus, brunch comes with a flight of mimosas and the best food money can buy."

If I didn't know better, I might think he's nervous. It's such a strange experience that I almost don't recognize it. Very few people even notice me, let alone consider me someone worthy of being nervous around. I don't know if I like it.

But he's making an effort, so I can too. I try for a smile. "Brunch sounds lovely."

"Oh. Great. See you then." He hurries out of the living room without another word.

It's not a good idea for me to do sensitive work while he's in the apartment, so I use this as an excuse to log on to my favorite fan fiction site and read the most recent update from one of my favorite authors. They write the most deliciously angsty hurt/comfort, and they branched out into fandoms that aren't mine, but I still read every fic they write. This one is absolutely agonizing, and I soak up every feeling.

About an hour later, Dionysus reappears. He's changed into a mustard-yellow suit with a floral-printed vest and shirt of the same color beneath it. It's downright outrageous, but he manages to pull it off, just like he pulls off everything he wears. He's obviously showered and combed his hair, and his mustache is looking particularly perky. This time, he doesn't jump when he sees me. "Feel free to order yourself food or whatever you need. One of my people in the lobby will bring it up to you. After the...incident...the other night, the service elevator is locked down, and I've focused my people on the perimeter rather than having two stationed up here at the door. It's best you don't leave after dark, but if you need to, just let someone know, and some of my security folks will go with you."

In other circumstances, I would appreciate that he's not trying to box me into a corner. He's obviously as uncomfortable with the situation as I am. Unfortunately, the first thing I'm going to do once he leaves is betray him. It kind of sours the whole experience of him trying to make me feel welcome.

Still, I attempt a smile. At least no more of his people will die because of me. "Thanks. I appreciate it."

"It's the literal least I can do." He edges toward the door. "We'll talk in the morning."

"At brunch."

"Yep, at brunch. Good night, Ariadne."

I wait to hear the front door close, and then I wait several more minutes before I pull up the program I was working through. The address Asterion gave me isn't particularly far from here, but I'll have to take precautions so no one is aware I've left the building. A quick check of the security cameras shows they're not on a closed network. It's child's play to schedule a loop for the time when I intend to leave. I'll need to program another one for when I get back, but that's a little bit harder to gauge. If I miss the window, my return will be in plain sight.

To distract myself from all the things that could go wrong, I finish crafting the back door into Dodona Tower's network. It's incredibly tempting to nose around in other files, but I force myself to keep on task. It's only thirty minutes later that I realize I messed up. The blueprints are nowhere to be found, which means they're probably filed at a completely different location. "Fuck."

I look at the clock and curse even harder. I have less than an hour to get out of here and make my way to the apartment. Not enough time to hack an entirely new system. This was a foolish mistake, and one I wouldn't have made if I wasn't so stressed out. Unfortunately, I don't think Asterion is going to be sympathetic. Or Hera, for that matter, but Asterion is currently the larger threat.

I hold my breath and dial the number he called me from yesterday. He makes me wait several long rings before he answers. "You better be calling to tell me you're on your way."

"I fucked up." Desperation makes my voice harsh. "I spent all day hacking into Dodona Tower, when I should've been hacking into the Olympus clerk's records. I don't have the blueprints. If you give me another day—"

"Ariadne." He waits for me to stutter to a stop before he continues. "You have the address. You have the time. I expect you to be there." He hangs up.

I stare at my phone. That motherfucker just hung up on me. I immediately call back, but he doesn't answer. His voicemail is the generic one that comes with the phone, and it's everything I can do not to curse it out. He knows me well enough to anticipate that I could probably argue my way out of this if given half a chance—so he's not giving me a chance. Damn it.

I could just not show up. But if I don't, he's likely to follow through on the threat to come to me. The thought makes my stomach do strange things that I refuse to examine. I stand and stretch and have a weak moment where I consider changing into more flattering clothing. Fuck that. He's forcing me to come to him, so he gets what he gets. I throw my hair up into a ponytail and pull on my boots. I only packed a light jacket, and it does little against the chill of the night air when I finally make my escape.

Even with Dionysus's extra security, it's pathetically easy. Once the cameras are on a loop, I just take the elevator to the second floor, descend the stairs to the first, and take a side door out to the street. Between my escape and Asterion's attack, Dionysus should fire his entire security team and start over from the ground up.

I've been in Olympus long enough to note the changes that my father's plans have brought. When we first arrived, there was a boisterous nightlife in the center of the upper city. Even on weekdays, from my window I could hear people partying and giggling and chatting as they walked down the street in groups. These days, people seem to retreat to the relative safety of their homes with the setting of the sun. Even the streets seem colder in a way that has nothing to do with the coming winter. The few people I see out walk with their heads down and shoulders hunched as if bracing against a freezing gale-force wind.

It's...eerie. I don't have another word for it. I haven't traveled much—my father has always kept me close at hand—but I've never seen a city voluntarily locked down like this. It makes my skin crawl.

It takes longer than expected for the car I call to arrive, and by the time I show up to Asterion's address, I'm ten minutes late. I pull the thin coat tighter around me and press the buzzer for the appropriate apartment. Asterion doesn't answer, but a few seconds later, the door clicks open. There's nothing to do but go up.

I'd like to pretend Hera is invested enough in my safety to ensure

I leave this place alive tonight, but I know better. I'm only one small component, and I failed in my task today. She's obviously playing a deeper game, and she's not going to show her cards before she's ready.

I'm on my own.

The apartment door is unlocked, and I step inside to find a room bathed in shadows. This isn't a building I've been to before. My father keeps two apartments in a building a few blocks away. I wonder if he's aware Asterion has another residence. I suppose it doesn't matter. "Hello?"

No answer.

I frown and take several steps into the living room. It's not like Asterion to play games. "Asterion?"

Large hands come down on my hips, planting me in place even as I startle and shriek. He jerks me back against his body and then his rumbling voice is in my ear. "You don't have the blueprints."

I open my mouth to speak, but the feel of him overwhelms me. It's been months since that day in the maze. Months since he touched me even in passing. This isn't incidental; he's plastered against my back with his lips brushing my ear. Gods help me, but I close my eyes and melt against him.

I *missed* him.

No. Damn it, *no*. This man is under orders to kill me. Nothing he feels for me will be enough to stop him from following those orders. "Let go," I manage. Barely. "If you're going to…hurt me… the least you can do is look me in the face when you do."

"Ariadne." He says my name roughly, as if it's a curse. As if *I'm* the curse. "You were put on this earth to drive me out of my mind."

He still hasn't let me go. I should step away. I need to. Asterion might not be hurting me right now, but he's going to. I failed to bring him the blueprints. More than that, I left him. Betrayed him.

I start to lean forward, but his grip tightens on me. Still not hurting me, although I almost wish he would. It would make it easier to think. He's so damn *warm*, chasing away the chill of the night, the fear that seems to plague my every step. It's absurd that I should find comfort in his touch, but my body isn't on the same page as my mind. I clear my throat. "You killed those guards."

"Yeah."

"You were ordered to kill me, too."

"Mmm."

Is that agreement? I can't tell. I need to see his face to be sure.

"Asterion, you need to let me go." The sentence has so many layers. I'm not even sure if I mean right now or in a larger sense.

One of his hands moves to my stomach, holding me against him. The other trails up to cup one of my breasts. "Tell me to stop."

It's the same thing he said to me all those weeks ago. Suddenly, I can't bring myself to speak, but it's not the same thing, is it? I'm not telling him yes. I'm simply not telling him no. That small, reasonable voice inside me is shrieking in dismay, is trying to remind me what happened the last time we went down this path.

Maybe it's grief that takes the wheel now. Maybe this is the only way I know how to process the complicated emotions that have arisen after the events of the last couple weeks. Maybe I simply want to take something for myself in this world that demands everything of me.

I don't tell Asterion to stop. Instead, I lick my lips. "Do you have a condom?"

THE MINOTAUR

I SHOULD HAVE KNOWN THIS SHIT WOULD HAPPEN THE
moment I got my hands on Ariadne again. I'm so furious at her, I can
barely think. Not because of the godsdamned blueprints but because
she still seems to truly believe I'm going to hurt her. Kill her. I don't
know what it says that even with that, she's pressing back against
me, writhing as if she can't wait to fuck.

But if she thinks she's getting my cock again after the shit she
pulled… Well, shit, she might just be right. I can't think clearly with
her big ass pressed against me, with her melting against my body in
a way that speaks of trust even if she'd never admit it.

I've played the waiting game, and all it did was ruin me in the end.

Maybe it's time we just flat out fuck.

This doesn't really count as her coming to me, but damn if I can
remember that right now. I pull a condom out of my back pocket
and hold it up in front of her face. "This what you want?"

"It's not about *want*." She reaches back and palms my cock. "It's
about *need*. It's like a fever I can't quench. You touch me and…"

"Yeah." It's like she pulls the words right out of my head. But better. Always better. There are a thousand reasons to stop, to remind her of all the shit she has to answer for. I don't. I tilt my hips forward, letting her feel how much I need her, too. The promise of more. "After this, we talk."

She huffs out a laugh. "About what? I failed to get what you wanted, and now you're going to kill me." She hardly sounds like herself, her voice low and ragged. "I should be running and screaming, calling for help. Or at the very least I should be telling you no."

"You aren't telling me no." I don't quite manage to remove the threat from my voice, but then, I never do.

"I never seem to, even when I should."

Because we're meant for each other. Because she recognizes me the same way I recognized her when I was thirteen years old. I had nobody. I slept where I could, and people ran me off regularly. The only food I had access to was what I stole or climbed into dumpsters to get. And when times got really rough, I crawled into whatever bed I had to, did whatever acts were required of me, just to live another day.

Until the morning I saw Ariadne.

I was begging in the square, tempting the wrath of the cops that liked to hang out there and pretend to work. And there she was, a vision in blue, fresh-faced and innocent in a way I long since stopped believing in.

Until that moment.

Until she slipped away from her dour-faced security guard and crouched in front of me, all innocence and goodness that I no long believed in, and pressed a hundred dollars into my hand. But she didn't stop there. She noticed I was shivering, noticed that my clothes had seen better days. Noticed that I didn't have any gloves to stop my fingers from turning into fucking ice blocks. So she slid off her gloves, as easy as can be, and pressed them into my hands, too. I don't think I've ever been so speechless in my life, not before that moment and not since. The feeling only grew after she left and I got a good look at the gloves. They were a thick wool, knitted and embroidered, imperfect in a way that speaks of handcrafting—of an item made with love.

These were gloves that *meant* something to her—and she'd given them to me without a second thought.

I decided right there and then that if the gods existed, they'd sent her to me. If they didn't, it didn't matter, because I was going to take matters into my own hands. I was going to marry that girl.

It took me two weeks of carefully asking around to find out her name—to figure out who her father was—and another three to catch wind of the whispers that he was looking for the kind of muscle he could train up into being *his*.

I'd sold my soul for less. It didn't take much to bring me to his attention. I already had a mean streak and a vicious temper. Now after seeing Ariadne, I also had something to fight for.

Three days after I joined up with Minos, I found out that those gloves she gave me were a gift from her late mother. They're priceless and she gave them to me without hesitation because she felt I needed them more than she did.

She claimed me that day without meaning to, and I've spent the rest of my life trying to claim her right back.

Not that she remembers the day we met. If she did, she'd never believe that I'd actually kill her. The fact that she keeps insisting on clinging to that bullshit only pisses me off.

It makes me want to punish her.

It feels like I'm punishing *myself* to step away, but I do it all the same. "Take off your clothes."

She jumps. "What?"

"Don't make me repeat myself."

She turns slowly to face me. She's worrying her bottom lip the way she does when she's doing something she thinks she shouldn't. She did the same thing in the maze. The memory feels like acid under my skin. It was the realization of everything I'd ever wanted, a physical promise of a future together...and then she left me.

Now she's engaged to another man.

"Has *he* touched you?"

She props her hands on her hips, anger overriding her caution. "Does that seriously matter? He's my fiancé. Even if he wasn't, would you really see me as less valuable if I had sex with someone else?"

She doesn't get it. She never fucking gets it. "No one else matters but us. No one has ever mattered but us." I drop onto the couch. "But you forget; I know you. You wouldn't have chosen it—not with him. If I need to kill the motherfucker..."

"Stop." She shakes her head sharply. "No one has touched me. Dionysus even wrote a clause into the marriage contract that takes sex out of the equation."

Relief threatens to bow my shoulders, but I force them straight. *Thank fuck* she hasn't been harmed like that. "Good."

That takes some of the steam out of her sails. "Yes. Well. I thought so. He's been very kind, actually."

"I'm done talking about him."

Ariadne rolls her eyes. "Great. Wonderful talk."

"Ariadne." I wait for her to look at me. "Take off your clothes."

She shrugs out of her jacket and lets it drop to the floor. Then she reaches for the bottom of her shirt with shaking hands and pulls it over her head.

The maze was a frenzy. This is something different. No matter what else has happened, I relish this moment of freedom between us. She might be engaged to someone else. I might be under orders to kill her. But right now, there is only us.

We have all night.

She doesn't stop, removing one piece of clothing after another until she stands before me in only her underwear. I was right. She's lost weight. I don't comment on it, but I file the fact away, along with a determination to feed her soon. I knew the stress of the situation in Olympus was getting to her, knew it was taking a physical toll, but I thought there was still time to deal with it...at least until she left.

Even so, her body is still lush, her soft belly making me want to sink my teeth into her all over again. Her thighs have dimples, and there are stripes of paler stretch marks over her hips.

In short, she's fucking perfect.

"Show me."

She sinks slowly onto the chair across from me and tentatively spreads her thighs. She's wearing cotton panties, and I can actually see how wet she is from here, but I'm just as interested in the scar marking her thigh.

I have a matching one on the fleshy spot between my thumb and forefinger.

I want to ask her if she thinks about the maze just as often as I do. I want to sink to my knees and taste her again. I fucking *want*.

Not yet.

"*You left.*"

To her credit, she doesn't look away. "I didn't think I had any other choice. I'm not sorry I did it, but I'm sorry it hurt you."

We stare at each other for several beats. I hadn't planned on having this conversation now, but maybe it's best to get it all out in the open before we move forward. Or at least part of it. "You could have told me you were pregnant."

"I thought you might stop me."

Again, she underestimates me. I lean forward. "One of these days, you'll see the truth of me." I hesitate. "Are you okay? Did it—"

"I'm fine." She clears her throat. "Mostly fine. I've recovered physically, but it rocked me a little more than I expected." She lifts her chin. "I don't regret it."

"Good." I'm not sure if I believe her about the recovery, though. It's only been a couple weeks. Surely it takes longer than that.

So. No penetration tonight. There are other options. Guess I'll get on my knees for her again after all.

I hook my foot under her chair and drag it to me. Her little yip of surprise feeds my soul. The way her dark eyes light up when I move to kneel between her legs adds ten years to my life.

I press a light kiss to the scar on her thigh. "No biting tonight."

"Are you promising not to bite or telling me not to bite *you*?"

I nudge her thighs wider. "I'm never going to tell you not to bite me. Wearing your scars is sexy as fuck."

"*Oh.*" Her lips part and her legs shake against my palms. She's quivering like a fucking leaf, but she meets my gaze steadily. "I like you wearing my scars, too."

Gods, but I love this woman.

I lean down and press an open-mouthed kiss to her pussy through her panties. She's so soaked, I groan against the thin fabric.

How can you miss something you barely had to begin with? It doesn't matter.

She sinks her hands into my hair without hesitation, lifting her hips to meet my tongue. I lick her until the fabric is drenched, until she's moaning and thrashing. Only then do I nuzzle her panties aside and allow myself unrestricted access to her pussy. She's slick and soft and all mine.

Her first orgasm catches both of us by surprise. She makes a surprised little sound, and then she's trying to take my head off at the neck with her thighs. An honorable way to go if there ever was one.

I give her clit a long lick. "That's a good start."

Her hands in my hair get more insistent. "Come here."

"I'm not done."

"Asterion."

Does she know what hearing my name on her lips does to me?

She's the only one who calls me by that name. I went by the Minotaur in the ring, and that's who Minos brought into his household. The brutal killer. That's all anyone sees when they look at me, and I've never mourned that truth.

But not Ariadne.

"Asterion."

I finally lift my head. Only then does she continue. Her eyes are heavy-lidded with the pleasure *I* gave her.

"You aren't, by chance, denying me your cock because you're worried about hurting me, are you?"

My skin heats even though I have no reason to be embarrassed. But in a world where every soft part of me has been systematically carved out, it feels almost like a flaw. Ariadne, on the other hand, always puts others first. She wouldn't think twice about hurting herself if it made others happy... If it meant a little pleasure for her.

She needs someone to look out for her.

Instead of answering with words, I stand and scoop her up, moving us over to the couch. That will be more comfortable for her. She sinks back, opening her legs for me once again. Her mouth might say she doesn't trust me, but she gives me her body readily. I settle back into place and drag my tongue over her center. She melts a little bit for me in response, and I reward her by slipping inside. Just a taste. Soft. Gentle. Fucking sweet.

After that, Ariadne doesn't have the breath to argue with me. Not for a long, long time. At one point, I allow her a small break and she promptly dozes off, snoring lightly. It gives me the opportunity to wake her up with my tongue, to tease her into an orgasm when she's still got sleep clinging to her. We were supposed to talk, but fuck if I want to stop long enough to start fighting again. Making my woman come is an addiction I have no plans on denying. Not tonight.

The sky is lightening with the first hint of dawn when I finally tug her clothes back on her languid body. She's practically drunk from all the orgasms, and she's sweetly trusting as I urge her to her feet and guide her down to the street where the car I called is idling.

I tuck her into the back seat and grab her jaw. "Ariadne."

She blinks those big eyes at me. "Yes?"

"You have three days. Get me those blueprints."

She licks her lips. "Uh...okay."

"Good girl." I kiss her lightly and then straighten and slam the door.

I head upstairs and strip the second I get inside. My cock is so hard, I'm surprised I haven't passed out from the lack of blood to my brain. I stalk to the primary bedroom and into the shower. Only then do I allow myself to wrap a fist around my cock. With the scent of her orgasms all over my face, it only takes three rough strokes before I blow, my orgasm so intense, my knees buckle.

Three days before I see her again is too fucking long.

ARIADNE

I WAKE UP FEELING LIKE THE NIGHT BEFORE WAS A FEVER dream. Surely that didn't happen. Surely Asterion didn't spend hours worshipping me with his mouth. I failed to get him the blueprints. That should have made him finally fulfill my father's command to kill me.

It's almost enough to make my foolish heart believe that he cares about me more than he cares about my father's approval. Almost. Too bad that sort of thing—the monstrous hero falling in love with the sheltered, nerdy heroine—only happens in fan fiction. If this were one of my favorite fics, he'd scale the building to get to me, whisper some sweet nothings in my ear, and then spirit me away to his penthouse, courtesy of some independent wealth I never knew about. We'd live happily ever after.

I laugh bitterly. That's how I know it's fiction. There's no such thing as happily ever after. We're all just struggling through this life as best we can with the tools allotted to us. I may be sheltered, but I'm as much a monster as my father. How else to explain my changing sides with so little hesitation? I may not have been able to hand the Olympians every detail of my father's plans, but I gave them enough for them to prepare for the coming attack. It means more Aeaean people will die. It might even mean my father will die. I knew that, and I didn't let the knowledge stop me.

How else to describe that but monstrous?

But...Asterion didn't do the expected. I'm still nearly certain he avoided using his fingers or cock because he was worried about hurting me. That level of care doesn't align with him wanting me dead. Nothing about what happened last night does.

I still don't have any answers by the time Dionysus swans into the living room. I feel like an absolute disaster compared to his pristine appearance. He's wearing a remarkably mundane gray suit with a purple pin-striped shirt beneath it, but then I see that his glasses have jewels encrusted on the frames and I almost laugh. "Good morning."

"Almost afternoon. Hence why I enjoy brunch so much. Shall we?"

I keep waiting for the silence between us to grow uncomfortable as we take the elevator down to the parking garage and climb into the back seat of a nondescript black town car. It doesn't. Dionysus seems lost in his own world, which allows me space for my own thoughts without having to worry about missing something important. It's...nice.

Even so, I fight not to think about Asterion. The knowledge that I'll be seeing him soon makes my stomach erupt into butterflies. It doesn't matter that I know he's no good for me. Being around him makes me feel like I'm in bloom. Like I'm more than the daughter who never measures up or the traitor who doesn't have enough information to actually make my betrayal worthwhile. When Asterion looks at me, I can almost believe that he thinks I'm perfect.

But then, I've already made peace with my rose-tinted glasses. They won't be enough to save me when reality comes calling.

We stop in front of a charming little shop on the outskirts of the upper warehouse district. I shoot Dionysus a questioning look and he shrugs. "There will be plenty of time for fanfare and playing to the public later. Brunch should be enjoyed, and Dolores has the best around. There's also the benefit of privacy. We won't be bothered here."

I examine his words for some kind of insinuation, but as best I can tell, he's being honest. Truth be told, I wouldn't mind getting to know him a little better. He's made it abundantly clear that he has no intention of being a true spouse to me, but if we get married, we'll still be partners of a sort. It doesn't hurt to make sure we're on the same page.

Though I can't be entirely honest, can I? Not when I'm actively betraying him...

I shove the thought away. The place is entirely empty as we walk through the front doors and are greeted by a petite woman with light-brown skin who looks to be approximately a hundred years old. Her white hair is almost completely gone, and her face is covered with age spots and wrinkles that indicate a life well lived. She smiles brightly when she sees Dionysus. "Hello, stranger. I thought you were getting too important to come visit little old me."

"I'll never be too important for you, Dolores." He takes her hand, bowing over it as if he's some kind of royalty, pressing a perfectly polite kiss to her knuckles. "You're looking as beautiful as ever. Is your husband treating you right? If not, I may have to marry you and take you away from all this drudgery. You'll cook only for me, and I'll treat you like a queen."

Her laughter fills the room. "You're a lovely boy, but you don't hold a candle to my Rufus. Besides, I hear you already have a wife, or near enough." She turns that happy smile on me, and I can't help grinning right back. There's something about her that's so warm and welcoming that I want to just stand here and soak up her presence. "Come, come, let's get a look at you."

I should probably feel like a horse at auction as she circles me, clucking her tongue and muttering under her breath. But her examination is so obviously done out of love for Dionysus that I can't quite hold it against her. Especially when she stops in front of me and smiles even wider. "Aren't you the loveliest little thing. Treat my boy right. He's a terrible flirt, but there's no harm in it."

"I'll keep that in mind."

She turns back to Dionysus. "Sit, sit. Food will be ready shortly."

It takes another fifteen minutes to get settled and served, and then I'm left staring at a table piled high with more food than two people could ever possibly eat in a single meal. And that's not even getting into the flight of mimosas for each of us. I glance at Dionysus, only to find him blushing.

"Dolores means well, but she's certain I'm starving myself whenever I'm not here. Don't worry about the food going to waste. She's got seven children and more grandchildren than I can count. On any given day, there's at least half a dozen teenagers passing through here, looking for food. They'll make short work of any leftovers."

I almost comment on the fact that he knows this family so well, which is similar to how Hades runs his territory in the lower city. It's not how the rest of the Thirteen have historically operated. I guess that's changing now. By all accounts, Ares runs a tight but respectful unit. The current Poseidon keeps his head down and seems beloved by the people under his command. People fear Demeter, but she takes care of her own. The list goes on.

I take a long sip of the first mimosa. Pomegranate, I think. "I still don't fully understand why you said yes to this marriage, but I'm beginning to realize I've gotten incredibly lucky."

"I wouldn't go counting your luck just yet." He picks up one of his drinks but sets it down without taking a sip. "I don't know how to tell you this, love, but you have a stalker."

Of all the things I expected him to say, that wasn't on the list. "Excuse me?"

"The Minotaur. He's got quite the fascination with you, bordering on obsession. He spent all of yesterday following me around, so I thought it important that he and I have a chat."

None of those words makes sense in the order that he put them in. "He doesn't chat." At least not with anyone who isn't me.

"Yes, well, I may or may not have dosed him with a little something to loosen his tongue."

I blink. "You *drugged* him?"

"Only a smidge." He holds up his thumb and forefinger with the barest width between them. "It wore off within an hour, with no long-term side effects. I can't speak for his blood pressure, though. He wasn't very happy with me when he realized what I'd done."

I can only imagine. Asterion doesn't like to be out of control. He drinks, but never to excess. I don't think he's ever done drugs in his life, or at least not in the time I've known him. "I'm surprised he didn't kill you."

"He thought about it." Dionysus sounds entirely too gleeful. "Despite all appearances to the contrary, I'm not a fool, so I didn't give him a chance to act on his more violent impulses. But we're getting away from the point. While he's still appearing to dance to your father's tune, he has an unhealthy obsession with *you*."

There's a part of me that knew that to be true. Don't I feel exactly the same way? From the moment I saw him, I felt an instant and unexplainable connection. I still don't know how to define it. It's as if there's a vibrating cord that connects my heart to his, and every time I see him, it thrums in my chest. I knew he wanted me. But he owes everything to my father. More importantly, I betrayed Asterion. If there was ever a chance of him choosing me over my father, I killed it with my own choices.

I clear my throat. "My father commanded him to kill me."

"I see." Dionysus finally picks up his mimosa and drains the first glass. I'm not quite sure how he manages that with the bubbles. I'd be impressed if I didn't feel so twisted up inside. He nudges a plate piled high with pancakes toward me. "I won't pretend there's nothing to fear. We're experiencing a scary moment as a city, and it's only going to get scarier as time goes on. But I'll protect you from him."

It's sweet that he offers, but it's an impossible task. Asterion proved on the first night that he can get to me anytime he wants to. The only reason I'm alive is probably because he still needs those blueprints.

I don't know if Dionysus knows about the blueprints, though.

So instead of answering, I just smile and take a bite of my pancakes. They're the best pancakes I've ever eaten, but I can't really enjoy them because it feels like they turn to lead in my stomach. I feel pulled in a thousand different directions. No, that's a lie. The only pull I feel is for a man I can never have. One who's dangerous, not just to other people but to *me*.

"I have to be honest with you, Ariadne. While I did want to chat about your stalker problem, this is a bit of an ambush." He must see the panic on my face because he holds up both hands. "That was a poor choice of words. You're not in any danger. I promise. But it's been brought to my attention that you were tasked with providing the Minotaur with something specific. Since Hera has chosen to intervene, that means you've been co-opted into our little..."

"The word you're looking for is *coup*."

For the second time in as many days, Hera's appearance startles the shit out of me. This time, I can't keep my reaction locked down. I slide all the way to the end of the booth and nearly hit the wall. Because she's not alone.

At her shoulder stands a massive white man with a shock of red hair and shoulders even wider than Asterion's. *Poseidon.* I recognize him from my father's files; he looks even bigger in person, as if he could cart around shipping containers with his bare hands. He doesn't seem particularly happy to be here.

Hera flicks her wrist, and Dionysus slides farther into the booth to make room for her. Unfortunately, that leaves Poseidon to sit next to me. I can't help cowering a little. He looks different from his pictures, more worn down and haggard. He's attractive enough in an earthy kind of way, but everything I read about this man says that he prefers to keep to his shipyard and avoid politics. As one of the legacy titles, he never had to jockey for a position. He might have inherited it unexpectedly when his uncle and cousins died from some kind of sickness—the details escape me—but he was always part of that family. He always had power. The fact that he's *here* doesn't bode well.

Hera, of course, looks immaculate. She's wearing tailored slacks and a lace top that's just shy of inappropriate. Both in black, of course. She eyes the spread of food before us and then plucks an untouched mimosa from Dionysus's flight. "You've brought her up to speed. Good."

The shock of their appearance slowed me down, but I'm just beginning to register what she said. *Coup.* I already knew she wanted her husband dead. But for her to be saying as much here, in the presence of two other members of the Thirteen? They have to be in on it.

Guess I'm not betraying Dionysus after all.

"I was just getting to the important part." Some of Dionysus's glow seems to dim, and he turns serious dark eyes on me. "You see, for the moment it appears that your father's aims and ours are in alignment. While we have no intention of telling *him* that, there's no reason not to use it to our advantage."

I glance at Poseidon again, but he's glowering at my stack of pancakes as if it insulted him personally. I clear my throat. "You as well?"

"I don't have to explain myself to you."

"Poseidon." Hera's tone is almost cheerful…as long as you don't notice the sharp edge beneath it. "Play nice."

He sighs and his big shoulders drop. "This mess isn't figuring itself out. Following Zeus has gotten us to this point. It's time to make some changes."

"You met with the Minotaur last night."

I search Hera's face for some indication that she knows exactly what I spent hours doing with Asterion in that apartment. If she's aware of how quickly I folded without any kind of actual pressure from him. If she is, she keeps it to herself. I lift my mimosa with a shaking hand and take a quick sip. The bubbles burn my throat. "Yes."

"Did you convey my message?"

Shit. I completely forgot. I want to say it was panic that made it happen, but the truth is that as soon as Asterion touched me, I wasn't thinking about anything but him. I take another hasty sip. My head feels just as full of bubbles as my stomach. "No. I wasn't able to get the blueprints. It was a rookie mistake, but I was looking for them in the wrong place." I debate leaving it there, but if she's following me, then she'll figure it out anyway. "I have a meeting with him in three days—two now, actually. I'll have the blueprints by then and be able to deliver them with your message."

"Three days," Hera says slowly. "That fucks our timeline."

"It will still work. We'll miss the scheduled sweep of the building, but we can come up with another reason to get everyone out." Poseidon shoves to his feet, nearly taking out the table in the process. "Are we done here?"

Hera's gaze sharpens and she lifts her face slowly until he wilts in response. "We're done when I say we're done, Poseidon. But yes, scurry off to your shipyards for now. Just be ready to move as soon as he's dead."

"I've got it. You'll have your way." He turns and stalks out of the restaurant, but I don't miss the fact that he pauses just long enough to make sure he says goodbye to Dolores. He might be scary, but apparently he does have some manners.

I turn back to find Hera watching me. It's easy enough to connect the dots. Zeus dies, Hera declares her unborn child the next Zeus and herself regent, and Poseidon steps up as one-third of the legacy roles to take over leadership. "Is Hades also in on this?"

"No. My brother-in-law has enough to worry about with Persephone pregnant."

Dionysus snorts and pours enough syrup on his waffles to drown them. "Not to mention he's too nice to plot cold-blooded murder. Otherwise, he would've taken care of the last Zeus years ago. Then maybe we wouldn't be in this mess to begin with."

Hera shakes her head. "He doesn't need to be part of the initial planning because he'll do the right thing once Zeus falls. For the first time in Olympian history, the three legacy titles will be in agreement. With us standing together, we have a decent chance of not crumbling the moment Circe knocks at our door."

I don't like the idea of cold-blooded murder, either. But knowing what I do of Olympus and the Thirteen, I can't say she's wrong. The rest of the Thirteen might indulge in petty conflicts and social backstabbing, but they take their guidance from the three legacy titles. With Hades essentially a boogeyman until recently and Poseidon having chosen to abstain from any kind of politics, that only left Zeus. And the last Zeus was heavily invested in the Thirteen being as fractured as possible so as to not challenge his personal power.

This Zeus, however, seems interested in unification.

Unfortunately, he doesn't have the charisma to pull it off. The fault lines go too deep. But Hera? Along with Hades and Poseidon? She might actually make it happen.

I just don't have the heart to tell her that it might not be enough to save them from Circe.

THE MINOTAUR

MINOS ISN'T AROUND WHEN I STOP BY THE APARTMENT that afternoon. It's just as well. I don't have anything to report, and he's not likely to take that kindly. Since I'm not in the mood to kiss ass, it would be a confrontation I don't want to deal with.

Unfortunately, it seems I don't get a choice in avoiding confrontation entirely. I'm in the middle of throwing clothes into a bag when I hear movement behind me. I turn to find Icarus standing in my doorway. I've never had much use for him, but Ariadne cares about him, so I don't go out of my way to make his life more miserable than it already is.

He doesn't quite tremble as he forces himself to meet my gaze. He's learning. Not fast enough, but I guess it's better than nothing. "Leave my sister alone."

"You heard my orders." I say it mostly because I'm curious about what he'll do. How far he'll push this.

"Yeah, I did." He actually steps into my room and closes the door behind him. He's a slight guy, almost delicate. I could crush him with one hand tied behind my back. The fact that he's willingly shutting us in a room together is mildly impressive. He leans against the door, but his posture is too tense to quite pull off the intimidation he's attempting. He lifts his chin. "But I also know your little secret. I know that you had sex with her in the maze at the party. Just like I know that she ended up pregnant as a result. What do you think my father will do if he finds out?"

Despite everything, my reluctant admiration for him grows a little. I cross my arms. "If Minos finds out, he'll punish me and kill her. She's dead either way." Or at least she is if I let him have his way. I don't intend to give him a chance. Fuck, now that I'm thinking about it, it would be smart to take Minos out before we leave the city. Circe will be too busy bringing Olympus to its knees to worry about us. Minos is a different story. He has a vested interest in removing evidence of Ariadne's disobedience. In this case, that means removing Ariadne—and me—if he finds out the truth. It's a complication I don't want to deal with.

"Maybe. Or maybe he can be convinced that the only reason she betrayed him is because she's afraid of you."

It's a bold move. If I was anyone else, it would even work. I'm not interested in bringing Icarus into my confidence. The only allegiance he holds is to Ariadne, but that doesn't mean he won't buckle and break under his father's pressure. He wants to be strong, but he's not. He never has been.

I cross the room slowly and get right into his space. "That's a risk, and not one you're going to take."

"Oh?" He swallows hard. "What makes you so sure I won't?"

This is a bit of a gamble on my part but one that needs to pay

off. I lean down, and I'm just asshole enough to enjoy the way he
flinches back against the door. "Because your father definitely wants
your sister dead. No amount of manipulation will make him retract
that order. Not when he thinks doing so will make him look weak.
Me, on the other hand? You don't know where I stand. Yet."

"Don't I? You're a fucking monster. A murderer. A brutal beast.
You might want my sister, but you're not a complete fool. You have
to know that claiming her will break something in her forever. She
wants to be *free*. That's all she's *ever* wanted. Being with you is a
chain closed around her throat. She'll suffocate." He shoves me, and
it's surprise more than strength that has me taking two steps back
and allowing him to leave my room.

He's wrong. I think. If Ariadne knew me, trusted me, the way
I do her, she never would've doubted for a second that I mean her
no harm. She wouldn't have run from me in the first place. She
would've come to me and asked me to help her get out of the mess
it took both of us to get into. She wouldn't melt in my arms with a
submission that feels like giving up.

I don't like the direction my thoughts have taken. I don't like
the implications of their potential truth. Most of all, I don't like the
fact that it changes nothing.

I leave my room without my change of clothes. I don't have
any specific plan on where I'm going, but I find myself outside
Dionysus's building just as Ariadne walks out the door with Hera
and Psyche in tow. The Dimitriou sisters couldn't look more different, for all that they share the same dark hair and pale skin.
Hera is a weapon. Psyche? Well, her weapon is walking two paces
behind her and surveying the street as if he expects a threat to pop

out at any moment. I step back into a doorway before he looks in my direction.

I have no desire to tango with Eros.

Ariadne is fine. Following her is a risk at this point, and even as I tell myself not to, my body moves without permission. I shadow them for several blocks until they slip into a boutique with a bunch of frilly clothes in the window.

I almost follow them right inside before my common sense takes hold and I turn into the bar and bistro next door. It's barely open, the place empty this early in the day. It's not positioned properly to see the entrance of the boutique, but stepping inside feels like waking up from a strange waking nightmare.

What the fuck am I doing? I have shit to take care of. At the very least, I should be going through the motions to ensure Minos doesn't decide to micromanage me. If he realizes he no longer holds my leash, it will...complicate things.

"Can I help you?"

I look down at the little server, and I have to fight the urge to growl. No one can help me right now. I need to get out of here. I start to turn for the door when a voice stops me in my tracks.

"I know you take your reputation seriously, but maybe we could draw the line at terrorizing the staff?"

I twist to watch Hera walk through the door. I check the space behind her, but she appears to be alone. Not that I trust the appearance. I thought Dionysus was alone, and look how *that* mess ended up. I take one step back, putting the wall behind me. If Eros is coming in the back door...

"The big, bad Minotaur, skittish around little old me? What a compliment." She turns to the server and her smile becomes slightly less sharp. "We'll have two beers."

"I'm not drinking." I snap out the words before I can think better of it. I regret them instantly. The last thing I want is these Olympians to think that I'm scared of them. *They* should be scared of *me*. I could snap Hera's neck in an instant, and there's not anyone close enough to stop me.

"Thinking about murdering me?" She laughs softly and walks right past me to take a seat on one of the barstools. "Maybe you could toss my body on the ground at Ariadne's feet like a cat displaying its hunting skills—the same way you did with Dionysus's guards."

So she knows about that and doesn't seem bothered. Despite myself, I follow her. Curiosity really is a bitch. "The thought did cross my mind."

"I'll just bet it did." She grabs a beer and takes a sip and then slides it over to me. If I needed confirmation that she knows what happened with Dionysus, there it is right in my face. She seems to know a lot of shit she shouldn't. Hera snorts. "See. Not drugged. Feel better?"

"Hardly." But I take a seat and take a long drag of the beer. It's another of Dionysus's brews, and while I'm not an IPA guy, even I can appreciate the way the taste brings to mind a crisp fall day. "You want something. Let's hear it."

She takes a long drink of her beer. "You're going to attack Dodona Tower."

I shutter my expression. "What makes you say that?"

"You asked Ariadne to get you the blueprints. I may not be someone with active combat experience, but I know how to draw a straight line between one point and another." She cuts me a look.

"And no, Ariadne didn't tell me. I watched that cozy little meeting you had the other day in the coffee shop. Honestly, it was very shortsighted of you to do that right out in the open where anyone could eavesdrop."

There hasn't been any one close enough to eavesdrop...or so I thought.

I glance over my shoulder at the door, but there is no security waiting to snatch me up the moment I walk out. Which begs the question—why? What does she want from me? "If you knew this a couple days ago, then you know where I've been in the meantime. Easy enough to snatch me up."

"Yes, it would be—if I wanted you to fail." She traces the rim of her glass with a sharp nail. "I'm willing to offer you a deal, Minotaur."

Now *this* is interesting. "I'm listening."

"I won't stand in the way—of any of your plans—as long as the only person you kill in Dodona Tower is Zeus himself."

The high lady of the upper city, intent on the murder of her husband? This is the kind of information Minos would kill for. This is the potential ally Circe dreams of.

Too bad I'm not going to get her in touch with either of them. "I'm not the one you should be making deals with."

"And yet I think you're exactly that person. Everyone believes it's Minos who holds your leash, but that isn't the truth, is it?" She finishes her beer and pushes it gently away. "She's made her own bargain, you know. She will ensure you get the blueprints without any interference from me, in exchange for the safety of her brother. Isn't that sweet?"

I'm not remotely surprised Ariadne would make a deal like that. She knows her brother's weaknesses just as well as I do. Without a strong protector, his chances of surviving what comes next are minuscule. Before today, I would've said Hera doesn't fit the definition of a strong protector. Now, I wonder.

"That's what you offered *her*. What motivation do *I* have to do what you want?"

"Beyond your life?" I'm sure she doesn't move, but she seems closer. Menacing. "Who do you think arranged for her marriage to Dionysus? Who could just as easily pressure your precious little Ariadne into a marriage with someone less…safe?"

I clench my fists and then force myself to loosen them. "It won't matter who she's married to when they're dead."

Her laugh is downright musical. "You Aeaeans love your threats of violence."

"And you Olympians love your little power plays that ultimately do nothing."

"Not this time."

No. Apparently not this time. If this is legit and she really means to kill Zeus, that will do more to further Circe's goals than anything else we've done so far. The city's already destabilized. Bringing down Dodona Tower is as much about symbolism as anything else. To then kill Zeus in the process? Minos will be beside himself with joy.

"Why tell me any of this? You could've just sat back and let me do what I intend to do."

"Because I don't want anyone dead except my husband. I want your word." She flicks her hair over one shoulder and stands. "Do this for me, and Ariadne is yours. As long as she'll have you."

I watch her walk to the front door. She glances over her shoulder, her expression once again blank, the way it is in every photo of her. "In fact, if you want a little taste…Eros is quite distracted right now with my sister. It would be nothing to slip in and have a little *chat*."

I don't like her offering up Ariadne as a prize. It's exactly what Minos did to win my loyalty as a teenager. But I'm not a teenager anymore. Despite myself, I can't stop Icarus's words from ringing in my ears. He's wrong. He has to be. I will not be the death of the very thing that's kept me going all these years. There's only one way to be sure, though. One way to guarantee that he's wrong and I'm right. That she's mine and I'm hers.

Ariadne has to choose me.

And the only way for *that* to happen is for me to ensure she remains safe to make that decision. "You have yourself a deal, Hera."

"I thought I might." She holds open the door for me. "You have fifteen minutes. Make them count."

ARIADNE

I DIDN'T BELIEVE HERA WHEN SHE TOLD ME THERE WAS A store with fashionable clothing in my size. Online shopping has been my best friend since I hit puberty, because the plus-size clothing offered on the rack tends to be hideous, without much selection. But then, Hera's younger sister Psyche would know. She's about my size and an influencer with amazing style. The boutique they take me to is so new that I swear I can smell the fresh paint on the walls. And it's a wonderland in variety.

Or at least it is until I see the first price tag. I reluctantly hang the dress back on the rack. "This is too much." Not something I ever really had to worry about before, but my father has frozen my accounts, and not even I am good enough to hack into a bank's electronic system to unfreeze it.

"It's courtesy of my sister." Psyche grabs the hanger and presses it back into my hands. "I promise it's okay. Zeus's bank accounts are practically limitless, and he gives her a ridiculous monthly budget to use for whatever she wants. She won't even notice what you'll spend today. But it'll make you feel better, and that's what's important."

I stare at her, waiting for the barb to follow the sweet words. Except it never comes. She stands there, this beautiful woman completely at home in her body, and smiles at me in perfect understanding.

It feels a little silly to say that clothing is important, but what is clothing but another kind of armor? I will never have the waifish body that my father is sure would secure me a powerful husband, but I can dress in a way that makes me feel good. That makes me feel...powerful. It might be an illusion, but it's one I'll accept gladly.

"I took the liberty of placing a few options in the dressing room. I think the owner may have a new shipment in the back, so I'm going to go snoop while you try the first set on." She smiles without any hint of artifice. "I know things haven't been easy, but don't worry. We'll take care of you."

I don't know if she's a better liar than most or she has no idea about Hera's plans. Ultimately, it's not my business. I need new clothes, and Psyche is making the experience of acquiring them as painless as possible. In another life, maybe we could've been friends. I'm not naive enough to think that's an option in this one.

So I simply smile in response. "Sounds good. Thank you."

The dressing room is larger than I anticipated, another welcome surprise. There's plenty of space for the massive selection of clothes that Psyche somehow managed to slip in here when I wasn't paying attention. A large floor-to-ceiling mirror is positioned perpendicular to the door, across from the bench seat. Everything, of course, is the height of luxury, from the thick carpet beneath my feet to the gilded edges of the mirror itself.

I strip quickly and pull on the first dress, one of Psyche's selections. I'm only mildly surprised to find that it fits perfectly. I turn to look at myself in the mirror and...it's not necessarily something I would've chosen for myself, the print a little too eccentric and the cut fitted enough to give my father a stroke. But I love it. I skim my hands down my hips and twist to look at it from the side.

Clothes really *are* powerful. In this moment, I almost feel something like hope. That I have a future. That someday I might live a life where I can choose the things that make me happy without worrying about pleasing other people.

It's a lie.

I peel off the dress and place it back on the hanger. I don't care if it's false; I want the promise this dress gives me. I try on a pair of jeans that also goes into the keeper pile, and then a flirty short skirt that's entirely impractical for the coming winter. Who knows if I'll live long enough for the season's return. It's a depressing thought.

No. I'm not going to be defeatist. I'll pick out a cute top to wear with this skirt, and I *will* wear it this spring when the flowers begin to bloom.

The door opens behind me and I spin, skirt swirling around my thighs, to see the last person I expect. Asterion. "What are—"

He's on me in a moment, his big hand plastering over my mouth and cutting off my words. His other arm goes around my waist and then I'm pressed to his chest and, oh gods, but it's happening again. Touching him makes something short out in my brain. My survival instincts demand that I scream, fight, do anything to draw the attention of the other people in the store. But those demands are quiet whispers in the face of the inferno flaring inside me.

He looks down at me with a forbidding expression on his scarred face. Like *I'm* the one who's done something wrong…who's done *him* wrong. His fingers tighten on my face ever so slightly. "Don't scream."

I nod slowly. Just as slowly, he lifts his hand from my mouth, shifting down to grip my jaw. Not tight enough to prevent me from speaking. I lick my lips, achingly aware of how he follows the movement, of how he *always* follows the movement. "What are you doing here?"

"You can't trust Hera."

I blink. "Might as well tell me that the sky is blue. *I know.* Everyone in this godsforsaken city has their own agenda, Asterion. Even you. I can't trust anyone."

He glares at me as if I said something wrong when all I've done is confirm exactly what he came here to claim. He opens his mouth but seems to change his mind about what he's about to say at the last moment. Instead, his dark gaze flicks over my head to the mirror behind me. "What are you wearing?"

What kind of question is that? It's pretty obvious what I'm wearing. "It's a skirt."

"It's a tease." His grip on my jaw tightens again, and he moves away, pulling my torso forward while keeping the bottom half of my body in place with a hand on my hip. His glare intensifies. "Barely bend over and you're flashing your panties. Did you pick this out for your husband?"

I'm not the one who picked it at all, but suddenly I am a

thousand percent done with his shit. He was sent to kill me. Yes, he hasn't done a single thing to intentionally hurt me to date, but that doesn't change the fact that he owes my father everything. No matter what I feel for Asterion, I am intensely aware of where I stand in the hierarchy of his allegiance.

I've done what it takes to survive, and I'm sorry if it hurt him, but he doesn't get to play the jealous lover when *he* is the most dangerous person to me right now. I glare right back up at him. "I already told you that Dionysus doesn't want that from me. But you know what? He kindly informed me that I am more than welcome to take a lover as long as we discuss it first. I'm wearing it for *them*, Asterion. And when I do, there won't be panties underneath it."

His grip on me becomes almost painful. "Show me."

I shove at his chest, but all it does is guide him to sink on the bench across from the mirror. Even as I tell myself that this won't be the time I melt for him, my hands find their way under my skirt and hook the edges of my panties. One good jerk and they reach my knees so I can shimmy out of them.

Then my traitorous hands find his thick thighs. He's big enough that I can brace my elbows just above his knees and my fingers barely touch his hips. The new position folds me in half, and no matter how reserved this motherfucker is, I hear his shocked inhale right down to my soul. I can feel the air of the changing room on my exposed pussy. This is dangerous and one more mistake to add to my list, but that doesn't stop me from shifting my legs farther apart.

I turn my head until I can see his face, but he's not looking down at me. He's looking at the obscene display I've created for him in the mirror. Because it is for *him*, regardless of what imaginary lover he's decided I'm taking.

My breath feels harsh in my throat. "Do you think they'll like it?"

"Yeah." He shifts his grip, one hand finding my elbow and the other sinking into my hair. "You look wet, Ariadne. You like imagining them?"

Them. The thought is laughable. There's only ever been him, and I'm not at a place in my life where I can picture being with anyone but him. It's too big of an ask. But I have my pride, and I'll die before I admit that I'm wet because I'm putting myself on display for him, because of the way his eyes go dark and hot when he looks at me. As if he's barely controlling himself. As if he wants to devour me whole.

"Of course I do." I clear my throat. "They're gentle and selfless and give me exactly what I need."

He huffs out a ragged chuckle. "Liar." His hand in my hair goes tight enough to hurt, surprising a moan out of me. "You want every experience too desperately for *soft* to ever satisfy you."

"How would you know?" I snap. "All you're capable of is violence."

"Maybe." The amusement is gone from his voice. "Want to prove me wrong? Show me what that pretty pussy needs, Ariadne."

"W-What?"

"If soft is what you're craving, then show me how you come so much harder when you touch yourself softly. How much better your orgasm is without my *violent* hands on you."

Now is the time to tell him to fuck right off. He keeps pushing me. It's not enough that I'm not telling him no. It's not enough that

I'm a willing participant with him guiding me. No, I have to play out my poor decisions without any prompting from him. My pride demands I stand and walk away. But my panties are on the floor and my clit is pulsing in time with my racing heart.

And there's a fact that Asterion's cock is a hard imprint against the front of his jeans, mere inches from my face. It looks painful, and I'm surprised by the vindictiveness that rises in me in response. It feels almost like power.

In his apartment, I orgasmed more times than I can count, but he never took pleasure for himself. Not like he did in the maze. And now, again, he's denying himself. All to focus on leaving me unbalanced and at his mercy.

It makes me want to punish him.

If I'm to be a victim to my own foolishness, then he damn well will be, too.

I straighten abruptly, and he barely has time to get his hand out of my hair to keep from hurting me for real. He opens his mouth, but I don't give him a chance to say a single word. I turn around and sink onto his lap, right on top of his hard, trapped cock. Again, he makes that intoxicating sound, a hissed exhale that would be too soft to notice if he wasn't doing it against my ear.

I widen my stance, spreading his legs in the process, and lean back against his broad chest. He's tall enough that he has a perfect line of sight to where I delve my hand between my thighs and stroke my clit. Softly. Slowly. As if I can't feel his coiled violence at my back.

The shock on his rough face is almost enough to make me orgasm right then and there. It's not often I surprise this man. It's not often I get the upper hand in any situation. I have it now, though.

He grips the edge of the bench, his knuckles white. It only drives my desire higher. I keep circling my clit with my middle finger, and though I've touched myself to countless orgasms, I've never watched it happen in a mirror. Never seen the way my pussy blooms with need. Never watched my fingers grow slick with desire.

It's still not enough.

My orgasm hovers at the edge of my awareness, but no matter how I touch myself, it skitters away. I don't want him to be right. I desperately want to put him in his place. But... "Asterion."

"Tell me what you need." His voice is barely a whisper in my ear.

We're in a dressing room in the middle of a public boutique with three dangerous Olympians on the other side of the door. Now is the time to stop this. To let reason take the reins again.

But reason never had a foothold when it comes to me and Asterion.

"Fuck me." I don't mean to speak the words, but I don't take them back once I give them voice. I see the immediate denial on his face, so I keep speaking. "Please, Asterion. I need your cock. I need you to fill me up and make me come. I might die if you don't."

He closes his eyes and, for a moment, I think he'll actually tell me no. It would be the smart thing to do. But if my need for him is a sickness in my blood, then it's a trait we share. He urges me up so he can dig his hand into his pocket. A breath later, he presses a condom to my palm. Then he makes quick work of his pants, shoving them down just far enough to free his cock. "You sure?"

"Now. Hurry."

He doesn't question me again. He plucks the condom from my hand and rips it open. But his movements become less sure as he rolls it down his cock. If I didn't know better, I would think he'd never done this before. But that can't be right. I may have been a virgin when we had sex, but there's no way he was.

I almost—*almost*—tell him that the condom isn't necessary. One of the things I did during my follow-up appointment with a doctor in the upper city was request an IUD. I'm as safe from pregnancy as a person can be right now. All I have to do is open my mouth and tell him so.

But I...don't. I say nothing at all as he grips my hip with one hand and urges me back to his waiting cock. His broad head breaches my entrance, and the delicious ache takes root in my core. Even as turned on as I am, my body has to fight to take him deeper. He doesn't yank me back, though. He wants me to set the pace.

I'm not interested in going slow. I shove back onto him, too fast, too hard. It doesn't matter, because the moment I take the entirety of him, the ache inside me turns to a pulsing need for more.

Asterion is done being a passive partner, though. He hooks my thighs and guides them to the outside of his, which is a problem because my toes barely touch the floor in this position. I can't get leverage to fuck him properly. Not that he seems to care. He's too busy tugging my bra down my shoulders to expose my breasts.

"Look at you." There's something in his voice that almost sounds like wonder. "You look like a perfect little slut, taking my cock like this."

He's...right.

I stare at my reflection, at exposed breasts and the skirt bunched up around my waist, at his cock spreading my pussy obscenely. At the bite mark scarring my inner thigh. Marking me as *his*...

His eyes are dark fire as his lips curve into a tight smile. He's still speaking so softly, the sound barely reaches my ear, a mere inch from his lips. "Yeah. You like that, don't you? You've been a good girl for so fucking long. Don't you want to come all over my cock, messy and rough, where anybody can hear you?"

As if on cue, there's a knock on the dressing room door.

THE MINOTAUR

I DIDN'T PLAN ON FUCKING ARIADNE WITH MY ALLOTTED fifteen minutes. But now she's on my cock, and I'll fucking kill anyone who tries to stop us from finishing this. It doesn't matter who's on the other side of the door. She tenses, but I wrap an arm around her waist to keep her on my cock. "Answer," I breathe into her ear.

"Yes?" Her voice is a little rough, but that is the only indication that she's not perfectly composed.

She's squirms on my cock, and I don't know if she's trying to get away or if she's demanding more, but I choose to believe it's the latter. I press my hand to her pussy, creating a V with my fingers so she can still see my cock disappearing inside her but she can rub her clit against my palm.

"Just seeing how you're doing." It's Psyche, and there's no indication that she knows something is wrong. "I was right. There was a shipment of some new items."

"Oh." Ariadne rolls her hips, rubbing herself against me. She bites her bottom lip hard. Too hard. I reach up and gently tug it from between her teeth. She makes a sound that's almost a whimper. "Um...I..." She tries to gather herself, but I'm not giving her much space to do it.

Fuck, she better come fast. Being inside her is too fucking good. She's hot and tight, and I'm so damn glad I brought a condom, because if we did this bare, I'd have already blown inside her.

"Ariadne?"

"I'm not decent!" Her eyes flutter shut. "Can you toss them over the door?"

A pause that might be shock. "Oh. Of course. That's no problem at all." A few seconds later, half a dozen pieces of clothing on hangers are flipped over the door and hung on the top of it. "There's no rush, of course. Take your time. After this, we'll go get lunch."

"Sounds good."

We hold perfectly still as Psyche's footsteps retreat. Ariadne meets my gaze in the mirror and then looks down to where we're joined. She grabs my free hand in an almost desperate move and presses it to her mouth. Then she starts to fuck me as hard as she's able. I could help her, but I'm enjoying the show too much. I like watching her fight to take her pleasure, her body rolling as she grinds down on my cock, her clit rubbing frantically against my palm.

She's almost there. When she goes, she'll take me with her. But I'll be damned if I let her escape without admitting the truth. I press harder against her clit, earning a muffled moan. "You're not just any little slut, are you, Ariadne? You're *my* little slut."

She makes a sound, and I lift my palm just enough for her to speak. "No."

Her denial infuriates me. It's so obviously a lie that it would be laughable if there wasn't a kernel of doubt inside me. I was so fucking sure she knew she was mine, that our time in the maze proved it. Now? There's enough evidence to make me wonder.

"Yes," I growl in her ear. "You might be engaged to Dionysus, but it's *my* cock you were begging for. *My* cock that you're riding right now, not worrying if somebody walks in and sees you like this. I don't give a fuck about begging permission to take what's mine. You know as well as I do that the next time you see me, you're going to end up on my cock just like you are right now. And if that has to happen in the middle of a fucking party of these goddamn Olympians, then so be it. I'll claim this pussy, claim you, where everyone can see it."

Her body goes tight and her pussy flutters around me. Her eyes roll back in her head as she orgasms, and even though part of me wants to deny her, my body has its own agenda. I tighten my grip around her waist and drive up into her, chasing my own pleasure. In that moment, I promise myself that it won't be long before I'm filling her again. Watching my come leak from her pretty pussy. Claiming her in every way I can. No matter what her lying mouth says, her body knows the truth.

We belong to each other.

I'm not surprised to see slow-dawning horror bloom on Ariadne's face. It stings all the same. She practically leaps off my cock. "This can't keep happening."

There's a whole lot I could say to that, but there's no point. She's going to spin her wheels until she twists herself into knots. "Take off the skirt."

"What?"

"The skirt. Take it off." No matter what she says about other lovers, after what just happened, I'm less worried about that being a possibility. Even so, I'll be damned before anyone else sees her in the skirt. Once we get all this bullshit figured out, I plan to pull it out when she gets bratty and remind her exactly who she belongs to. But there's no reason to tell her that now.

She glares at me but she shoves the skirt down her thick thighs and kicks it at my face. I catch it easily. Some of the sting of her rejection eases as I watch her dress. She's putting on a show for me, going a little slower than necessary, bending just the right way to give me a view worth dying for. She grabs every single item of clothing and piles it in her arms. When she catches me looking, her expression goes mulish. "If Hera is paying, then she's going to damn well pay. No one else is looking out for me. I have to look out for myself."

Pride flares in my chest. I know better than to show it at this point. She won't appreciate it, not when she's standing on her own and demanding her due for the first time in her life. "I didn't say anything."

"Yes, well, you weren't saying anything rather loudly." She glances at the door. "You'll have to wait in here until we leave."

If I don't, it will be a fight. It doesn't matter that Hera all but served Ariadne up on a platter for me. Somehow, I don't think she's told her sister and brother-in-law about her plans. If Eros and I get into it, it will turn this boutique into a bloodbath, which will kill the last flickers of pleasure in me. "Go. I won't make a scene."

Her attention falls to the skirt I have fisted in one hand. She looks like she might demand it but finally shakes her head and slips out of the changing room, careful to keep the door closed as much as possible when she does.

I listen to Psyche ooh and aah over her choices and to Hera make a dry quip about her finally starting to learn. Within fifteen minutes, they're gone. I wait another five before I leave the dressing room. Then I head to the register and buy the skirt. That shit is sure as fuck going home with me. And she *will* be wearing it again. Just for me.

But now it's time to get to work.

I check my phone, cursing when I see a dozen texts and calls from Minos. He's gone from threatening to almost pleading. The man is losing it. I couldn't give a fuck about his mental state, but I don't want him to send another killer after his daughter, so I have to play the game for a little longer. I stop on the street corner and pull up his contact info.

He answers on the first ring. "Where the fuck have you been?"

"Doing exactly what you asked of me."

"And yet my daughter is still alive, whoring herself for Olympus, and that goddamn disgrace of a tower still stands. You're failing me. Again."

I have to wait several long beats to wrestle my fury out of my voice before I speak. "There's been a delay in acquiring the blueprints. We can't get into the tower without them, and I'm working on it. I expect to have them within the next day or two. I wasn't aware we were on that tight of a timeline."

He curses. "We still have a couple weeks left. The city is soft, but not quite soft enough. And there's the question of the barrier. It's turning out to be slightly more challenging to bring it down than I expected. We had intended to do it through the lower city, but that way is barred to us now."

Interesting. I won't point out that he's had his own roadblocks and should be more forgiving of mine as a result. It doesn't matter. "Want me to look into the barrier while I wait for the blueprints?"

"Do it." He hangs up.

As much as I would like nothing more than to haunt Ariadne's steps for the rest of the day, I have a vested interest in that barrier coming down. I walk a few blocks while I consider what angle to come at this from. If Theseus still held the Hephaestus title, that would be a good option, but the person who took over isn't likely to let me through the front door. Apollo already proved he doesn't have the information necessary to fix the barrier, so he's not going to be able to bring it down. Who else…

I stop short. There's one person in Olympus who likely has answers. Even better, according to the gossip sites, she's back in town.

If Minos was smart, he'd wonder where Hermes has spent the last couple weeks. She's not one to pull a long-term disappearing act, and she knows more about his plan than he's probably aware of. But he's always been an arrogant bastard, and he never stopped to wonder why she wants to know about his benefactor. About Circe. His only thought was to use Hermes to his own benefit. Just like he thought to use me.

I'll admit that when I first met her, I grouped her into the same category as Dionysus—a vapid Olympian more concerned with partying than with being useful. But I watched her at that party. She drank and flirted and made a big show of being harmless…but then she turned around and helped plot the death of two of her peers without blinking an eye.

Maybe it's time Hermes and I had a conversation.

She's not making any attempt to hide. All I have to do is check MuseWatch. Within an hour, I'm sitting in yet another bar, watching her hold court. She's like a jester in some old-world kingdom, all bright colors and irreverent attitude...with a startling wit beneath it. She's wearing leather pants, a cropped white T-shirt that looks like she cut it off herself with a pair of scissors, and a glittering bomber jacket that hurts my eyes to look at. For someone known for stealth, she's practically a walking disco ball.

I don't recognize the people around her. It's just as well; I have no intention of joining in. I see the moment Hermes clocks me, but she makes me wait another twenty minutes before she circles around to hop onto the bar next to my elbow. "If you're here to kill me, I should let you know that I won't make it easy on you." She winks behind bright-yellow glasses.

I'm getting really fucking tired of people assuming I'm going to murder them. "I have a couple questions for you."

"You'll have to get in line behind my many admirers." She flicks a hand toward the group she just left. "Though you should know, as much as I hate to disappoint you, you really aren't my type, Minotaur."

I blink. "You go from assuming I'm here to kill you to assuming I'm here to fuck you?"

"What can I say? I'm a woman who inspires a wide variety of reactions." She kicks out her legs like a child. "Are you playing obedient dog to Minos today, or are you seeking me out on your own?"

I consider the implications of telling the truth. I assumed a lot of things about the Olympians before I came here, and most of them have given me no reason to question those assumptions. But I didn't expect Hera or Dionysus. It stands to reason that Hermes may surprise me, too. There's no harm in telling her the truth. She and Minos aren't on good terms any longer, so even if she runs to him telling tales, he's not going to believe her. "I have my own reasons for seeking you out."

"Delicious." She practically purrs the word. "In that case, let's go somewhere more secluded and have a frank discussion."

I follow her to a private room located down a long hallway. It strikes me as I walk through the door that this could be an ambush, but the room is empty except for a U-shaped booth that takes up most of the space around a large table.

I fucking hate booths.

I sit across from her and watch as she fiddles with a salt shaker, unravels all the silverware wrapped up in napkins, and flips the menu over several times, far too quickly to have read anything. Finally, she folds her hands in front of her and gives me a solemn look. "I'm ready to hear your proposal."

I didn't come here with a proposal. I didn't come here with a fucking plan. I'm starting to wonder if it was a mistake. "What business do you have with Circe?"

If I wasn't watching her so closely, I wouldn't see her nearly imperceptible flinch. She gives me a bright smile. "I suppose the cat's out of the bag now that the lovely Ariadne has gone telling tales. You're aware that Circe was originally an Olympian. She and I have a history. You might call us old friends."

The statement leaves a lot to be desired. It doesn't matter. I care less about her history with Circe than I do about the future. "Are you with her or against her?"

"That question is too simplistic."

I don't have the patience for word games. I brace my elbows on the table and stare her down. "You haven't done a single damn thing to stand in Minos's way. You're not actively helping him, either. So let me ask you this instead—do you want the barrier to come down?"

Her smile is brilliant enough to light up the room. "Now *that*, my dear Minotaur, is the right question."

ARIADNE

AFTER A LONG DAY OF SHOPPING AND WATCHING MY words while a secret part of me relishes the ache between my thighs, I almost don't answer my phone when my brother calls. But that's selfish and shortsighted. Hera promised him safety, but Icarus has to get out from under my father's thumb first. He can't do that if he doesn't know that escape is possible.

"Hello?"

"Ariadne." He exhales shakily. "You're okay. When I didn't hear from you, I started to get worried."

Guilt threatens to swallow me whole. I haven't been thinking about Icarus, for all that I used his safety as a bargaining chip. I've been worried about myself and my future. Selfish. So fucking *selfish*. "I'm sorry." I swallow down the excuses that spring to my lips. That I'm overwhelmed. That I've been so busy that I lost track of time. That I've been working to keep us safe.

"It's okay. I *would* like to see you, though. If you think you can get free."

I look around the penthouse, empty once again. I'm not sure where Dionysus went this time, but he made a passing comment about not waiting up. Who knows if he'll even come home tonight? "Why don't you come here? It would be safer than meeting outside, and we can talk freely."

He hesitates long enough that I think he might say no, but finally he sighs. "Sure. I'll be there in twenty. Tell security not to shoot me on sight."

I don't think that's a real risk, but as soon as I hang up with him, I call Dionysus. Just in case. Wherever my fiancé is, there's blaring music that makes it hard to hear him. I manage to get my point across, and he promises to add Icarus to the list of approved guests. I'm a little worried that he'll forget as soon as he hangs up, but twenty-five minutes later, I get a call that my brother is in the lobby. Less than five minutes after that, he's right in front of me.

Icarus looks like shit. He was always thin, but his face has a gaunt look that worries me. And his hair, normally as impeccable as mine, hangs lank and greasy against his forehead. Even his skin has lost its luster. More worrisome, he throws himself into my arms and hugs me tight enough to steal my breath. "You're really okay."

I hug him right back, alarmed to feel his ribs. I've only been gone a couple weeks. How has he deteriorated so quickly? "But you're not. When's the last time you've eaten?"

"I had a shake this morning."

It's nearly 9:00 p.m. Gods, but this is bad. I take his arm and drag him into the kitchen. Dionysus keeps it well stocked, though I haven't seen evidence that he actually cooks. I'm not good at it myself, but even I can throw together a few simple things.

Thankfully, Icarus's favorite is easy enough. Blueberry pancakes. A quick check ensures the kitchen has the necessary ingredients, and then I get to work. My brother watches me with haunted eyes. "You look better. I'm sorry about the choices you had to make, but I'm glad that it's working out."

"It's a little too early to say for sure if anything is working out, but I'm doing better than I was." I put a pan on the stove to heat. "I want you to get your stuff from the apartment and come here. I don't know what our father is doing, but it's obviously hurting you. I'm not exactly free, but I made a deal with Hera. She'll protect you."

Icarus laughs bitterly. "You're always looking out for me. But when you needed help, you didn't even think to turn to me, did you?" He takes hold of my hand before I can formulate an answer. "I'm sorry. I've been worried and I'm indulging in more self-pity than I usually allow myself. Don't think for a second that I begrudge your choices, Ariadne."

"But?"

"But you don't have to ride in to rescue me this time. Between our father and the Olympians, you need to keep your wits about you. I don't want to become the lever that they use to control you. Maybe it's my time to play your knight in shining armor for once."

I can respect that he doesn't want me to give up anything for him, but it doesn't mean I like the direction this conversation is going. "If you have the option of Hera, why would you stay with Father?"

"I'm not going to stay with him." He shrugs. "I'm going to take a page out of your book and bargain my knowledge for safety."

I stop in the middle of pouring blueberries into the pancake mix. "What are you talking about? I already gave them everything."

"I'm not talking about the Olympians, Ariadne. I'm talking about the Aeaeans." He says it with such exhaustion that I want to hug him again, but the brittle set to his shoulders says that he won't accept it this time.

"Our people don't hold any love for us. Father made sure of that." I'm snapping at him for no damn reason, but I can't seem to stop. I worked myself into exhaustion compiling the information that I facilitated Apollo finding. It took weeks. All for the chance to get me and Icarus out. And he's dismissing it as if it means nothing.

My brother shrugs. "People whisper secrets during pillow talk that they would never put on a computer. They don't have to hold love for me to fuck me, and when they fucked me, they inadvertently gave me all the information I need to ensure their...cooperation."

I stare. I know he was free with his charms back on the island, but he kept to our peers, the adult children of the scions. Most of those operated the same way our father did—keeping all their information to themselves. The only secrets Icarus would be able to find are unsubstantiated rumors. "There's no proof that the information you have from your past lovers is true."

His mouth twists. "Ariadne, for every lover I had in public, there were two in private that wanted to keep our...activities...secret. I wasn't just fucking our friends. I was fucking their parents, too."

"Icarus," I whisper.

"Don't do that." He shakes his head sharply. "Don't pity me. Every choice I made, I made willingly. I sought them out, not the other way around. No matter how this conflict ended with

Olympus, I wanted us to have a way out. And we *do*, Ariadne. Some of the secrets I hold will pave our way to freedom, financial and otherwise."

He might have chosen this, but the only reason he was put in a position to do so was because of the trap our father created. We never possessed any freedom of our own, and if Minos had his way, we never would have. I would be married off to further his power. Since he made it clear from a very young age that he didn't intend to pass on his businesses and money to Icarus, he likely would've married off my brother as well.

But that doesn't make it any easier to hear. I would have saved Icarus from such desperate measures if I knew he was considering them in the first place. "But my deal with Hera—"

"Is just another cage." He stands and crosses to me, taking my hands in a desperate grip. "Just stay alive long enough for that damned barrier to come down and we can escape. I don't need to bargain secrets with the Olympians. I have enough blackmail secured to fund us for the rest of our lives. We can go anywhere, do anything. You've always wanted to travel. You can do it, Ariadne. Just trust me."

I don't know if I'm feeling hope or despair. The barrier coming down means my father and Circe have furthered their goals enough to take the next step in assaulting Olympus directly. It means people will die—more people. They might not be my people, but that doesn't mean I'm immune to the potential loss of life. If I was, I never would've betrayed my father to begin with. I never would have agreed to Hera's plan. I never would have done...a lot of things.

I squeeze my brother's hands and gently disentangle myself. "Icarus—"

"No, don't say anything now. I know I've shocked you. Let's just eat and spend some time together. Just…think about what I said. Please. I don't know what I'll do if something happens to you."

He's all but guaranteed that I won't think of anything else. I knew my brother was reckless and occasionally self-destructive, but this is a whole different level even for him. I don't even know how to process it.

But I can do as he asked. I can give him a safe space, at least for the moment. I feed him blueberry pancakes and then we turn on some reality television that almost—*almost*—allows me to escape the new weight pressing down on my shoulders.

At least until Icarus leaves and I'm left on my own.

Then the thoughts come too fast, too frantic. I pace around the living room, but the movement isn't enough to distract from the panic fluttering in my chest. I knew things were bad. Of course I did. I've been aware of my father's distaste for us long as I can remember. He's made no secret of the fact that neither I nor Icarus is good enough to be his child. But for all that, my brother got the brunt of our father's anger. He's the son, after all. He should be like our father: strong and brutal and ruthless to a fault. Minos never would have slept his way to secrets and used them for blackmail. If he knew what Icarus was doing, he would be incandescent with rage.

I don't consciously make the decision to pull out my phone. I don't think about the fact that I'm dialing a number I most certainly shouldn't. It's instinct driving me, the overwhelming feeling that will suck me under and drown me if I'm left sitting with it a moment longer. When I felt like this in the past, there was only one person I gravitated toward. Old habits die hard, I guess.

When Asterion answers, it isn't with threats or a reminder of the danger he is to me. There's actual concern in his voice. "What happened?"

A sob lodges itself in my chest. I've been running from feeling things for weeks now, and all it took was a single conversation with my brother to have it all come crashing down around me. I can't stay here. Not right now. Not alone. "Where are you?" My voice breaks in the middle of the question.

"Give me ten minutes and I'll be outside. Meet me at the side door that you left from last time." He hangs up before I can decide whether I want to argue.

What a joke. I was never going to argue. There's only one reason I called him, and it's because when the world becomes too overwhelming and I don't think I can fight another second, I've always found Asterion. He's created a safe harbor for me to weather the rain. At least until dawn. Until we have to go back to pretending.

I don't give myself a chance to second-guess this decision. It's child's play to hack into the security system and put the cameras on a loop. I barely pause to grab my key and then I'm rushing down to street level, retracing my steps from the other night.

Only this time, Asterion's waiting for me on the curb.

He doesn't give me a chance to speak, not that I'm able to currently. Instead, he wraps an arm around my shoulder, tucking me into his jacket. Then we walk. I know our destination even before we turn the corner and stop in front of the door to his apartment. There's no point in pretending we would end up anywhere else.

But what I didn't expect is for him to have clothing waiting for me. He barely pauses to lock the door before he strips me out of my sweats and T-shirt in simple, efficient movements. And then he dresses me in a different pair of sweats and a different T-shirt. His clothing. It's clean, but it still carries the scent of him.

I stare up at him, my heart in my throat. "Why?"

"It makes you feel better. Safe."

He's not wrong, but...I didn't think he noticed. He's never said anything about it before now. I used to pretend his shirts and sweatshirts ended up in my laundry by accident, that it was coincidence they never made their way back to him. I should've known better. Asterion notices everything.

He nudges me down onto the couch and sits next to me, draping one arm behind my back. An invitation, not a demand. I am seven different kinds of fool, because I don't hesitate to crawl in his lap and let him wrap his arms around me. This is new. This is something we've never done. Before, when the walls started closing in on me and I would seek him out late at night, he wouldn't say much at all. I'd sit on his bed while he played a handheld video game and I clutched my laptop, reading fanfic. Until the steady cadence of his breathing calmed mine and I could actually concentrate on the words I was attempting to read.

But he never touched me.

I bury my face in his throat and shudder out a breath that's almost a sob. "This has all gone so wrong. It wasn't supposed to be like this."

"I know." He strokes a gentle hand over my hair.

"I don't know how to feel about what keeps happening between us. About marrying Dionysus. About being a key part of the plot to kill a person, even if it will save other lives." I cling to him harder and he responds by tightening his arms around me. It's more difficult to speak the next bit. "I don't know how to feel about the pregnancy or the fact that it's gone. In another life, I would've been happy to have your child. But I couldn't do it, Asterion. Not when my first thought was panic, and the fear only grew with each hour that passed."

He presses a featherlight kiss to my forehead. "I know. You did what you had to do."

"That's the excuse we keep using. That we did what we had to do. That you kill people because you had to do it. That I lied and betrayed my family and country because it was something I had to do. That my brother"—again, my voice breaks—"had sex with people he never would've chosen with the intent to blackmail them so we can be free."

It's too much. I can't stop the tears from coming or the sobs from following until I'm crying so hard I can barely breathe. And through it all, Asterion just holds me, the mountain that I can crash myself against and never have to worry about breaking.

Tomorrow, I'll go back to fearing him.

Tomorrow, I'll take away all these messy emotions and put one foot in front of the other just like I always have.

Tomorrow.

THE MINOTAUR

ARIADNE CRIES HERSELF OUT AND THEN FALLS ASLEEP IN my arms. She's so fucking strong, but even strong people need a place and time to crumble. She's always come to me in the past when things become too ugly in her head. It warms my heart that she did it tonight, even with everything else going on. But I can't stop thinking about everything she said. The way the words poured out of her like poison.

I carry her into my bedroom and take a moment to strip out of my shirt that she's soaked with her tears. Then I stretch out next to her, waiting until she instinctively finds her way to me and presses against my side.

I fucked up.

I knew shit was bad with Minos. He's even worse at being a father than he is at being a person. He might not beat the shit out of his kids, but they both wear emotional scars with his name on them. It was my mistake for not realizing the depth of those wounds. If I had, maybe I would've anticipated Ariadne running to the Olympians instead of me when things got too scary. For better or worse, I'm attached to her father in her head.

Her brother didn't help. Later, I might have more grace for him. Right now, all I know is that talking with him caused Ariadne enough distress to seek me out. As much as I love that she came to me, it hurts that she needed to in the first place.

"Only a little while longer, sweetheart." I speak softly so I won't wake her, the endearment slipping out as naturally as breathing. I can't stop myself from stroking my hand down her spine and urging her a little bit closer. Someday, she'll come to me simply because she wants to be in my presence, not because she's fleeing worse nightmares.

I let her sleep as long as I can, but I wake her well before dawn. "It's time to get going." She mutters a protest and nuzzles my shoulder. Ariadne was never one to spring to wakefulness. I give her a light shake. "You've got to get back to your fiancé."

That snaps her eyes open. I can practically see the moment she registers what happened—that she came to me, that she cried herself to sleep in my arms, and that she's waking up in my bed. At least she doesn't skitter away from me. She blinks slowly. "What time is it?"

"Four."

"Damn. Okay. I didn't mean to fall asleep." She sits up and rubs her eyes, still puffy from crying. "I'm s—"

"Don't you dare apologize. Not to me. Not for this."

She pauses, her knuckles still pressed to her eye. "You say that, but you're mad at me."

I start to deny it, but she's not wrong. "Yeah. I am. But not because you came to me, and not because you got an abortion."

"Asterion. I wish you'd…" She takes a deep breath and shakes her head. "Never mind. I'll have the blueprints to you by tomorrow night."

She's retreating from me again, and the realization makes me want to snarl. For someone so smart, she seems determined not to see the truth of me. Of *us*. Again, I wonder if Icarus is right. If this has only ever been one-sided, if all she feels for me is lust and fear. "Okay," I finally say.

"Oh. I forgot." She doesn't quite shift away, but the distance between us seems to grow. "Hera is willing to clear the way for you to take down Dodona Tower, as long as you promise not to kill anyone but Zeus. It's a good deal, and it means only one person will die instead of hundreds. It protects your team, too. Less resistance and all that."

It's interesting that Hera didn't inform Ariadne of our conversation. It might simply be because they didn't have a moment alone yesterday, but I don't think so. That woman is holding her cards close to her chest. She wants her allies to think that they know everything there is to know, but she's not telling the left hand what the right hand is doing. "I'll let her know the time and day we plan to bring it down. It's on her if she wants to evacuate the nearby buildings or not." I have no interest in mass casualties. I honestly don't give a fuck if Zeus lives or dies, either. But keeping Hera happy means keeping Ariadne safe—from the Olympians, at least. It's a small enough price to pay.

Ariadne frowns at me. "Just like that?"

It shouldn't continue to sting that she thinks so little of me, and yet here we are. "The tower coming down is the important part. The rest is just details." Dodona Tower…and the barrier. I don't trust Hermes as far as I can throw her, but I'm willing to wait and see if she'll follow through on our conversation. If she does, it will make my life significantly easier. Even if it means waiting a little longer than I like.

"Oh. Okay." She slides to the edge of the mattress and stands, seeming almost reluctant to leave. That makes two of us. I'm fighting the instinct to drag her back to the bed and lose all track of time. Only the fact that staying here too long will put her in danger keeps me from giving in.

But she surprises me.

Her gaze lands on my chest, sliding from one scar to another. I have more than a few. Plenty from before I came to live in Minos's household, but nearly half of them came after. Minos doesn't believe in coddling his weapons in training. Not to mention all the assignments he sent me on that went wrong. I probably should be dead a half-dozen times over, but I always managed to drag myself back to the villa where his team could patch me up.

To drag myself back to *her*.

"Asterion…" She licks her lips. "It's like I'm addicted. I get close to you, and I lose all sense of self-preservation." She speaks softly, almost to herself.

Because part of you recognizes me as yours, even if the rest of you won't acknowledge it. I don't say the words aloud. I doubt she'll believe me. I just sit there and wait to see what she'll do next.

Again, she surprises me. She hesitates, twisting her hands together in front of her. "Thank you. For last night. For your kindness. For taking care of me."

"Sweetheart—" Again, that damned endearment slips out without my meaning to.

"I'm not ready to leave yet." She throws herself into my arms hard enough to send me back onto the mattress. And then her mouth is on mine. If I were a better man, a kinder one, I would stop this. If I had any of the self-preservation that she seems to possess in spades, I would deny her until she acknowledges the truth between us.

I don't.

Instead, I pull her closer. "I'm not ready for you to leave yet, either." There's no going slow this time, no playing with her pussy for hours, no taunting her. There's only the frantic scramble of hands shoving clothing to the side so that nothing remains between us. Desperation is thick on my tongue, twining with the taste of her.

Why is it always like this with us? Stolen fucking moments. Secrecy. Frenzy. It feels as bad as it feels good.

And then I sink into her and nothing else matters. Just her wet pussy welcoming me home, her fingernails digging into my ass, urging me deeper, her whimpering little cries that rise with each stroke. Frantic. Fast. Rough. I drive into her and she rises to meet me. I barely have the presence of mind to shove a hand between us and stroke her clit, to make sure she follows me right to the edge and then over. To pull out at the last moment and finish all over her stomach instead of deep inside her.

I stare down at my come lashing her light-brown skin. Another time, the sight might fill me with satisfaction, a temporary marking of ownership. Right now, it feels like a lie. She's still fighting the truth of us, and I'm a fucking fool, because I keep giving her exactly what she wants even though she plans to get out of this bed and leave me. Again.

I squeeze her thigh, right over the scar of my bite mark, as much to comfort myself as a reminder that it's still there. "I'm going to come to you today."

She blinks those big eyes up at me. "What?"

She won't believe me if I tell her that I'm worried about her. That I'm not sure all the power players actually have her best interests in mind. Right now, she's leading with lust, so lust is where I'll meet her. "Tomorrow night isn't soon enough, sweetheart. I need this pussy again."

"Asterion, you can't say things like that."

That I need her? Or that I called her *sweetheart*? I swallow down the questions, deciding it's better if I don't know. "What are your plans for the day?"

She worries her bottom lip and then looks down to where my orgasm marks her. Her thighs shake a little on either side of me. "Um... I think there's a dinner or something. Dionysus and I are supposed to be seen as a couple desperately in love, but it's really for the Thirteen to be seen as a united front."

The thought of her playing loving fiancée makes me see red. I release her thigh and move back. "No panties, Ariadne. I want you ready for me." If fucking her rough and dirty is the only way she'll have me, then I'll damn well do it.

"I can't. We almost got caught yesterday. There will be press there. If I'm photographed with you..."

"Then I guess you better be careful. Do you remember what I said in the dressing room?"

"That you would fuck me at a party in front of all of Olympus." Her voice wavers a little bit, as if she can't decide if she likes it or not. "But, Asterion—"

"Be ready for me, Ariadne. Or I'll bend you over the table right in front of your fiancé and all those cameras."

She squeezes her thick thighs together in response to my words. Yeah, she likes the thought of that a lot. She might not trust me entirely, but she eats up the fact that I want to claim her in front of everyone.

It pisses me off that the only thing she'll take from me is sex, but at least she's not running screaming into the early morning darkness. I'm trying to see that shit as an improvement. More, she came to me when she was upset. Just like she used to. Maybe she doesn't understand the significance of that, but I do.

I really want to believe it *is* significant and I'm not looking into things that aren't real.

I watch her walk toward the door, moving slow enough that it's obvious she's not eager to leave. "Ariadne." I wait for her to turn and meet my eyes before I continue. "Don't trust Hera. Or Dionysus. Or any of them. They're playing benevolent captor now, while you're doing what they want. The second you push back, that will change."

She smiles, but her dark eyes are sad. "I know."

It's on the tip of my tongue to ask her to stay. To say, *Fuck everyone, we'll figure this out on our own.* She's gone before I have a chance.

I sit there for a long time. I'm not one to doubt. At thirteen, I set my eyes on the girl and knew she would be mine. Knew that, in a way, she already was. As soon as I realized whose daughter she was, I knew it wouldn't be easy. But this? This feels like standing in a pit of vipers. I haven't been bitten yet, but it's only a matter of time. There's no way forward but through. The steps of the plan haven't changed. The tower comes down; the barrier quickly follows. I take Ariadne and get the fuck out of here. We can figure out the rest once we're free of this place and her family. She's not going to be content to leave her brother behind, so I guess he's coming, too. I don't exactly relish the thought of spending more time in close quarters with Icarus, but Ariadne will never forgive me if something happens to him.

It's a lot easier to kill people than it is to keep them alive.

I spend the day going through the motions. I meet with Aeacus, but his plan is heavily dependent on the blueprints that we don't have yet. I check in with Minos and sit on the phone with him for ten minutes while he rants and raves. Theseus has cut him out completely, to the point where he won't even entertain a visit. I'm proud of the fucker despite myself. He might be wearing Eris's collar now, but it seems like he welcomes it. With him gone, Minos has lost what little leverage he had with the Thirteen. They've cut him off completely. I'm pretty sure continuing to get close to them isn't part of the plan; he just doesn't like to be told no.

By the time I manage to get him off the phone, the sun is sinking toward the horizon. I send a quick text to Hermes, but she leaves me on read. Typical.

Then I change into one of my rarely used suits and head for the restaurant where Ariadne will be tonight. Pan's restaurant, the Dryad, in fact. It's a small miracle that Dionysus is still allowed through the door after what he let happen, but that's just Olympus. They take the old saying of keeping your friends close and your enemies closer to heart in a way I've never seen before. Not even on Aeaea.

I don't bother to come to the front door. I'll be turned away for sure. Instead, I slip in through the kitchens. The head chef turns with a vicious look on his face, but I hold up a wad of cash before he can order me out. He stalks to me, a tall, lean Black man with dark-brown skin and a shaved head. "I'm not giving private shows. Get out of here. I'm busy."

"I don't want any trouble." I hold up the cash again. "A friend of mine is having dinner here tonight, but she's on the anxious side, so she's not likely to eat if left to her own devices. I just want a chance to feed her."

The chef narrows his eyes. "I know who you are."

Everyone seems to these days. At least he doesn't accuse me of coming here to murder him. "Like I said, I'm not here to make trouble. You have my word."

He doesn't seem like he believes me, but he grabs the cash out of my hand and shoves it into the back pocket of his pants. "All of the individual dining rooms are claimed tonight. The only thing I have to offer you is my office."

Hardly a romantic location, but at least it's guaranteed to be private. "That will work." Guess that shit this morning did fuck me up, because I'm determined to show Ariadne that I'm good for more than fucking. That I'll take care of her better than anyone else in this fucked-up world. And if anyone dares to threaten her? Well, killing is what I do. What I'm good at.

It would be a privilege to kill for her.

ARIADNE

DINNER AT THE DRYAD IS HORRENDOUS. NOT THE FOOD.
It looks lovely and smells appetizing, but I can't bring myself to do
more than push it around on my plate. My stomach is tied in knots
and my tongue feels too thick in my mouth. Luckily, it seems my
presence is the only thing that's required tonight. They might as
well have brought a cardboard cutout for all that the people present
expect me to engage in conversation.

I try to focus on the discussions around me, swirling faster than
a raging river, but it's all white noise. Every single member of the
Thirteen is here… Well, except for Hades. He hasn't crossed over
to the upper city since erecting the barrier along the river. But the
other twelve? They're here. Even Hermes.

Some of them—Artemis, the new Hephaestus, the new
Aphrodite—watch me as if they expect me to pull a gun out and
start shooting. Or as if they'd like to push me into traffic. Demeter
and Hera lean close to each other and speak so softly that I can't
pick up their words. It's enough to make me wonder if Demeter is

aware of what her daughter's plotting. With that family, it's difficult to say.

Ares is here with her two partners, Achilles and Patroclus. The trio is beautiful enough to make my eyes hurt, and they all watch me warily. Zeus sits between his sister and his wife, and yet he might as well be on the moon for all he appears to be present. His cold blue eyes are watching something a thousand miles away.

Next to me, Dionysus and Hermes chat easily, belying the tension I picked up from him when he mentioned her previously. There are a couple of other partners here; Apollo has brought his fiancée, Cassandra, and Athena has Atalanta at her side, though I can't tell if she's there as a bodyguard or a girlfriend.

"Ariadne."

I turn my head slowly, belatedly realizing that it's not the first time Dionysus has said my name.

His dark eyes are sympathetic as he takes me in. "Are you okay?"

No. I'm not even a little bit okay. I try for a smile but give up halfway through. "I'm a little overwhelmed."

"Understandable. All of us together is a little much." His grin is crooked. "If you need some air, there's a stairway back by the bathroom. Technically, the balcony that it leads to is designated for employees taking a smoke break, but I don't think anyone will begrudge you a few minutes up there." He squeezes my arm. "Take as long as you need."

I might be trapped in a snare of my own making, but I really could do worse for a spouse than Dionysus. He's Olympian, but he's gone out of his way to try to make me feel safe and comfortable. Even when he himself wasn't feeling safe or comfortable.

"Thank you," I whisper.

"Go on. All we have left is dessert, but they're bound to get drinks and make this stretch for at least another hour before someone starts a fight."

I hastily murmur an excuse that no one listens to and slip away from the table. The bathrooms are tucked in the back corner of the restaurant, and the stairwell is cleverly hidden around the corner from there. I make it up one step when an arm comes around my waist and a hand clamps over my mouth.

This time, I don't bother to scream. I know this hand, this arm. Asterion.

He releases me after a beat. "You're learning."

I don't dignify that comment with a response. Instead I turn to face him. Even standing one stair above him, he still towers over me. I take in the sight of him, my breath stopping in my throat. Asterion always looks good, and there's a part of me that has suspected for years that he gives off some specific pheromone I'm weak for. But seeing him in a suit? It's a different experience entirely.

When some people wear a suit, it tames their sharp edges, serving them up in a more palatable form. Not so with Asterion. With his long, dark-red hair, big body, and scarred face, all the suit does is showcases his brutality. No one will look at him and assume that he's an executive. He's a warrior right down to his bones.

"Did you come to fuck me on a table in front of everyone?" I mean for the question to come out sharp and sarcastic, but my voice is a little too breathy to quite pull it off.

He gives me a long look as if I've disappointed me somehow.

Then he steps back and holds out his hand. "Those peacocks won't miss you for a while yet. Come with me."

It's nothing more than Dionysus already said, but I can't help shooting a guilty look at the hallway leading back to the restaurant as I slip my hand into Asterion's. "I don't have much time."

"You have enough."

I'm not really sure what I expect, but it's not for him to lead me down a different set of hallways deeper into the employee side of the restaurant. We pass a handful of servers, each balancing trays filled to the brim with beautiful food, and then Asterion pulls me through a door into a small and meticulously organized office.

"Whose office is this?" I look around, but the answer is readily apparent in the sticky notes with comments about different flavor profiles and appetizer ideas and the calendar with a color-coded employee schedule. This must belong to the head chef. "I'm not fucking you in some stranger's office."

Asterion's still got that disappointed look in his eyes. I don't like it. Before I can say anything, he snorts. "All I'd have to do is crook my finger at you and you'd fall to your knees and beg for my cock, so don't pretend otherwise." He turns for the door. "But that's not why I'm here. Sit down. Don't touch anything. I promised him we wouldn't fuck with his stuff." He's gone before I can pepper him with further questions.

Part of me didn't believe that he'd come tonight. The Olympians don't necessarily have a price on his head, but he's hardly safe here. I eye the rolling chair—it's a fancy wide-set one that probably cost a small fortune. It's remarkably comfortable when I sit down. There's a part of me that wonders if Asterion thought of even this, but surely that's a step too far.

He returns a few minutes later with a covered plate on a tray. It looks absurd in his large hands, and he doesn't carry it with the same grace the servers at the restaurant do. Still, he manages to place it in front of me with a little fanfare.

He removes the lid and steps back, and I'm left staring at a replica of the main course that I ordered but was too nervous to eat earlier. I don't know how he timed it so perfectly, but steam rises from the pasta, and the parmesan has barely begun to melt.

I shift my attention to him, noting the way he stands perfectly still as if he's holding his breath. As if he's not quite sure of my reception. "Why?" I finally manage to ask.

"You never eat at political dinners. Your nerves get the best of you and then you spend the rest of the night starving because you're too ashamed to admit you're still hungry."

Not that my father would have permitted midnight runs to the kitchen. When I was younger, he caught me once or twice, and I had to sit through a lecture on gluttony every time. I learned to be sneaky after that, though Icarus usually got there before I had a chance to leave my room, showing up with an armful of snacks and a mischievous grin on his face.

I look down at the plate before me and then back at Asterion. "You had the chef make me an extra plate because you knew I wouldn't eat?"

He holds my gaze even though he clearly wants to look away. "That's what I said, isn't it?"

I pick up my fork and set it down again. I'm a smart woman, for all that it sometimes takes me a while to realize certain truths. I'm a little ashamed that I misread the situation so intensely. That I misread *him* so intensely. "You were never going to kill me, were you?"

"Eat your food. You don't want it getting cold on you."

It's not an answer, and yet at the same time, it is. I don't know what this means. I don't see how it can change anything. If Asterion doesn't obey my father's commands, then he'll just find someone else to do it. If I don't marry Dionysus and get the blueprints, then it won't matter what my father wants, because Hera will demand her due. I'm still trapped.

But…maybe I'm not trapped alone? I'm terrified to even hope that's the case.

"Thank you," I say softly. This gift is damn near priceless, because it shows the depth of knowing that only exists between me and two other people. My brother…and Asterion. I pick up my fork again, determined to honor this. My stomach is still twisted up, but here in this room with only us, I relax enough to take a first bite. And then another. And another.

It's phenomenal. It tastes just as good as it looks, just as good as it smells. Asterion doesn't speak as I eat my way through the meal, but he slips out of the room right as I'm about to finish, reappearing a few moments later with a small bowl. "This isn't technically on the menu, but I saw the chef and sous chefs trying it out, so I… convinced…him to give me one to sample."

I stare at the chocolate dessert and have to fight not to cry. "This isn't going to end well for us. I don't see a path forward."

"You don't have to." He sets it on the desk in front of me. "I'll see the way for both of us."

"How can you be so sure?"

"I just am."

What must it be like to have that kind of confidence? I'll never know. I fight and scramble and do my best not to be helpless, but at the end of the day, I suffer at the whims of those more powerful than me. Truly, Asterion and I should be on the same page when it comes to that. He fought his way up from nothing, but even now, more powerful physically than anyone I know, he's still my father's man. But he's not letting that stop him from doing what he wants. For...me.

I eat the dessert slowly, and it's truly the best thing I've ever tasted. The entire dinner is. Some of that is the nature of the food itself, but a good portion of my feelings is the result of the care that went into planning this. I always knew that Asterion saw me. I just never quite understood what that meant. I'm still not sure I do.

It's over far too quickly. I know better than to try to make it last, but I still eat slower than is wise. When I finish, Asterion takes my plate and presses a light kiss to my forehead. "Tomorrow, Ariadne. Bring the blueprints to me, and then we'll talk about the next steps."

I don't tell him that I got the blueprints the morning after our disastrous meeting at his apartment. I've had them since yesterday, and not even I can explain why I hesitated to hand them over. It's not because I hold some fondness for Zeus or even really care if he lives or dies. The man might play at being a king, but he's just as much a monster as his father was. He must be for Hera to plan to kill him. Though, truth be told, she's plenty monstrous in her own right.

"I want to get out of the city."

Asterion crouches in front of me. He's tall enough that we're almost the same height. He studies my face as if memorizing it, as if for the first time in as long as I can remember, he's not entirely sure of me. "I can get you out. Not yet—not everything is in place to make it happen—but I can do it."

I want out with a desperation I don't know how to grapple with. Wanting that makes me a bad person. There's no two ways about it. "For us to get out, that means the barrier will fall."

"The barrier was always going to fall, sweetheart. Circe made sure of that."

He's right, I think. And yet I can't stop the guilt that threatens to swallow me whole. "How many people have to die for her vengeance? For my father's ambition? If the barrier stayed up—"

"It won't."

I press on, pretending I didn't hear him. "If the barrier stayed up," I repeat, "then Circe and her army would have to give up."

"Ariadne." He waits for me to look at him before he continues. "You're not that naive, so stop pretending. Even if the barrier didn't come down, the Thirteen would keep on fucking with the people less powerful than them. You've been to the lower city, to the countryside. You're a smart woman; you understand that this is not some utopian city where everyone is treated fairly. And neither was Aeaea. The world is fucked up, but it's consistent. Powerful people do awful things to maintain their power. The barrier was destined to fall the moment Circe left and took a piece of it with her. There's no stopping it. This shit is bigger than us. It always has been."

I can't tell if I want to shove his words away or hold them close to my heart in reassurance. Doing one feels just as naive as he labeled me. Doing the other feels self-serving in the extreme. If we're just two cogs in the machine and nothing we do has any long-term con-sequences, then we can do anything at all. We could bring down the damn barrier and tell ourselves that it was fate.

"That's a cop-out, Asterion."

"Is it?" He reaches out and brushes my hair back from my face. "Look around, sweetheart. Every single person in this fucked-up world is only looking out for themselves. It's time you do the same."

THE MINOTAUR

I CAN'T STOP MYSELF FROM FOLLOWING ARIADNE AND Dionysus back to his building. I stand in the shadows across the street for far too long, as if my presence there will do a single goddamn thing. For once, no Olympians show up to irritate me. I'm left to my own thoughts, and it's a strange place to be.

She's finally starting to understand that I'm not here to hurt her. I loved watching her dark eyes go all soft as she finally made peace with that reality, but there's still a jagged piece of glass in my chest. It was easy enough to anticipate her needs and take care of them tonight, but I'm *not* soft. I'm pretty fucking sure that she was just being a brat in the changing room yesterday, but it's hard to get those words out of my head. *Soft.* It might not get her off as hard as being bad does, but Ariadne deserves softness.

She deserves to be with someone whose hands aren't stained with blood and death.

Which is too damn bad, because what she has is me. I just don't want her getting the wrong idea. I don't know how to be a boyfriend. I don't know how to be in a fucking relationship. With Ariadne, just existing in her presence is as natural as breathing. I want to believe that won't change, but if I really think that, then I am as naive as I labeled her.

My entire fucking life has been geared toward claiming Ariadne. It was a goalpost that kept moving through the years, Minos always pushing it out just a little farther. Part of me honestly believed it would never happen. It still hasn't happened. But now that Ariadne is starting to understand what the fuck we are to each other, there's a very real possibility she *will* leave the city with me when the barrier comes down. That she'll choose to go without me having to twist her arm.

And then what?

I had vague ideas of traveling with her, but now that reality is bearing down on me, I don't know what the fuck that even looks like. I have money, but not an endless amount. I only have one skill set, and somehow I think Ariadne will have a problem with me taking hits to fund our lifestyle.

Oh well. I'll figure it out once we get out of this fucked-up city.

ARIADNE

I'm still reeling an hour after we returned to Dionysus's penthouse. It feels like I just took a step to one side and now my entire perspective of the world has changed. Maybe that was reality this entire time and I just couldn't see it.

A knock on my door startles me, but only for a moment. "Yes?"

"Come have a drink with me. All that pacing and stressing isn't good for the body."

I smile a little despite everything and pull a robe around me. "Okay." Maybe one day I'll stop finding it strange how much I enjoy Dionysus's company. Maybe I'll never get a chance to become used to it.

He's in the kitchen, this time with a bottle of wine. When I raise my brows, he shrugs. "It seems like you need to talk, and wine is excellent for those types of conversation."

I watch him pour the deep red liquid into large wineglasses. "I guess I never really thought about what kind of alcohol best fits different types of conversation."

"Not just alcohol, my dear." He hands over my glass. "Let's sit."

It's not until I'm curled on the couch opposite him that I really stop to think about whether this is wise. Dionysus has shown me every kindness, but that doesn't mean he's an ally. This could all be a ploy to get information and... I don't know if I care. I'm so damned tired of being worried about making missteps. "Thank you for that break at dinner. It was much needed."

"Mmm." He swirls his wine absently. "I'm glad you had a chance to eat in peace."

I freeze. Surely he's not... But when I look into his deep eyes, I realize that he knows exactly what I spent that time away from the table doing. "How did you—"

"Darling, you weren't exactly subtle, and Pan might not be my biggest fan, but he *is* a fan of Olympus, so he still passes on information he thinks is of value." He sips his wine. "Don't look so worried. I *am* glad you had a moment of peace and a chance to eat."

"A moment of peace." I shift and make a face. "I don't know if you could call it that."

"I suppose." He shrugs and settles back into his chair, stretching out his long legs onto the ottoman. I belatedly realize that he's wearing a dressing gown, which is so perfectly Dionysus that I almost smile.

We sit in companionable silence for a long time, long enough for the tension to start bleeding out of my body and the wine to warm my insides. When he finally speaks again, it's with a slow drawl that barely bruises the comfortable air between us. "You love him, don't you?"

I try to tense, but truly it's too much effort. There's a relief in hearing those words spoken aloud, in his tone having no judgment whatsoever. "Yes. I have for a long time, even if I was too scared to admit it."

He rests his head on the back of his chair, staring at the ceiling. "Thought so."

I should probably leave it at that, but words bubble up all the same, drawn out by the strange feeling of safety Dionysus has created here. "What does it matter how I feel? He owes *everything* to my father. For almost half my life, he's been doing whatever he was commanded. If I trust this—trust him—it might be the last thing I do."

Dionysus's lips curve in a sad little smile. "Darling, considering three of my people died on the first night you were here, two on the other side of that door…" He nods at the door just visible down the shadowy hallway. "I would venture to say if he really planned to commit violence against you, he would have already done it."

"But—"

"Life is short. Or long, I suppose, depending on how you look at it." He drains half his wineglass. "You've already taken astronomical risks to help others. Maybe it's time to take one to help yourself."

I inhale slowly, letting his words settle over me. It's shocking how tempting they are. The very idea of walking willingly to the cliff that represents my and Asterion's relationship, of jumping over and letting faith in him, in me, in *us*, guide me... It's terrifying. It's exhilarating. "What if it ends badly?"

"That's the wrong question." He finishes his wine and climbs slowly to his feet. "The question you should be asking is what if it ends well?" He walks over and plucks my mostly empty glass from my fingers. "Come along. I think you might be able to sleep now."

Indeed, my eyelids are already starting to get heavy. Too heavy to blame on the wine. I lean on his arm and blink up at him. "Did you drug me?"

"Only a light sedative. You need your rest." He walks me to my door and then helps me stumble to my bed. Dionysus smiles down at me, though his eyes are still sad. "You're strong, Ariadne. Strong and good and far cleverer than most people. I suspect you already know what you need to do."

I suspect he's right. Still, I grab his hand and stop him from retreating. "Thank you. For everything. You didn't have to show me such kindness. I'll never forget it."

Dionysus squeezes my hand. "I'd wish you good luck, but you don't need it. Good night."

THE MINOTAUR

The next day, I'm still trying to figure out what my next steps are when someone buzzes my front door. I hit the intercom. "What?"

"Let me in."

I blink. I didn't expect anyone to be here, let alone Ariadne. I'm not about to turn her away, though. I hit the door buzzer to let her in and have to fight down the weird-ass urge to pick up around the place. It's not messy. She's been here before. But the urge remains all the same.

She's perfectly put together as she steps into my apartment, wearing one of her new dresses, and I'm no expert in fashion, but it seems too fancy for wandering around town in the early hours of the morning, its silky texture clinging to her breasts and stomach and hips before fluttering down around her knees. The pale-purple fabric looks soft and fragile enough to tear beneath rough hands. It's also fitted in a way that makes me wonder what she's wearing underneath it...and what she isn't.

Need hits me hard enough to make my voice harsh. "What are you doing here?"

"I thought you would appreciate me being punctual." She surveys the apartment as if seeing it for the first time and holds up a zip drive without looking at me. It strikes me that she looks well rested—even more so than when she left the other night. There's no reason for the spike of jealousy that knowledge brings. I *want* her to be okay. But there is a monstrous part of me that's so damn pleased at the idea that she only sleeps well with me.

I clear my throat, trying to shake off the feeling. "This is more than punctual. You're early."

"I am. I had some questions for you, and I thought it best we talk in private."

I narrow my eyes. There's something in her tone, a new determination that I know better than to trust. "You're making it sound like you'll be involved in this beyond getting the blueprints. Get that thought right out of your fucking head. You're not going anywhere near that tower, the barrier, or Zeus."

"We'll see." She shrugs out of her jacket and tosses it over the back of a chair. Which showcases the fact that the back of the dress is made entirely of straps pressing against her skin from the top of her shoulders to the jaunty little bow at the small of her back. Two things become clear in the space of a heartbeat.

One: She's not wearing a single fucking thing underneath that dress.

And two: There's no way she could have gotten into it on her own.

Jealousy surges forward and pours out of my mouth before I can call it back. "Who tied that bow for you, sweetheart?"

"I'll make you a deal." She sets the zip drive carefully on the coffee table and turns to perch on the edge of it. Ariadne meets my gaze boldly, not a hint of fear in her dark eyes. Something's different. But before I can figure out what changed, she keeps speaking. "I'll tell you who helped me into this dress…if you answer a question for me."

I take two steps toward her before I can stop myself. And then I wonder why the fuck I bothered to stop at all. If she came here only to deliver the blueprints, she would've shown up right on time, not early. That wouldn't have stopped us from putting our hands all over each other just like we have every time we've been alone, but she could've pretended that she wasn't planning on it.

But this? The sun's barely up in the fucking sky and she's knocking on my door. This doesn't feel like that frenzied fuck on my bed, where she was looking for sex and sex alone before she bolted back to her fiancé. This is…different. She knows what this is. Me? I'm still figuring it out.

I stop in front of her, close enough that her knees bump mine. Close enough to intimidate. "Sure. I'll play your game. What's your question?"

She lifts her hand slowly and hooks her fingers into the front of my pants. One tug and I'm standing between her thighs, but she makes no move to do anything else. She licks her lips. "Asterion?"

Oh fuck. Even as I tell myself to move, to speak, to do fucking *something*, I stand there as still as a statue and watch her unbutton the front of my jeans and drag my zipper down. The moment she touched me, my cock hardened, but now it's pressing so tightly to the front of my jeans that it's a wonder I'm not losing circulation.

Did she say something? I'm having a hard time concentrating. "Yeah?"

She tugs my jeans down just a little so she can stroke my cock through my boxers. It's a light, teasing touch. It's fucking heaven. She licks her lips again, as if I'm not already possessed by the fantasy of pressing my cock into her mouth, of watching her swallow me down until tears spring to her eyes and she gags on my length.

Ariadne gives me a heartbreaking smile that's completely at odds with her fingertips coasting up and down my length. "That time in the maze. My first time."

I'm having a difficult time thinking, let alone trying to anticipate where she's going with this. "Yeah? What about it?"

She presses her thumb to the sensitive spot just under the head of my cock. "Was it... Was it your first time too?"

It takes far too long for her words to penetrate. The meaning washes over me, and I'm not a man who wastes time with regret, but it sinks its claws into me all the same. My stomach twists. I have to actually take a step back to break her hold on me. I don't want to muddy this moment with my past, but her words have skeletons I barely think about rattling around in their closets. "That's a ridiculous fucking question, Ariadne."

"Is it?" She watches me with narrowed eyes. "I don't think so."

Fuck. She's really going to make me say it. I take a step back and drag a hand over my face. I can't bring myself to look at her. "Listen, we've known each other a long time, and I don't talk about what happened before I came into your father's household, but I did a lot of shit to stay alive. To ensure I didn't starve."

She's still watching me too closely. It makes me feel like my heart is beating on the outside of my skin, exposed and uncomfortable. Vulnerable. If she looks at me with pity, I might have to leave the fucking room. But she just tilts her head to the side and seems to consider something. "Before. What about after?"

I shake my head sharply. "It's always been you. I'm not interested in anyone else. I haven't been since we met." And Minos knew better than to send me on *those* kinds of missions, if they even existed in the first place.

"You were thirteen when we met."

I swing back around to face her. There's something tight and hot in my chest. "No, I was fourteen when I moved in."

"Yes, I know that." She waves it away. "But that day in the

market. You were thirteen then, right? It was winter, so it was well before your birthday."

She remembers.

I rock back on my heels, that feeling of vulnerability threatening to sweep me away. I don't have it in me to lie. Not to her. Not like this. "Yeah. I was thirteen then." I speak so softly, it barely counts as a whisper. She hears me anyway. Of course she does.

"One last question." She seems to lean forward, gravitating toward me without moving an inch. "Would you have chosen any of those people if the alternative wasn't starving to death or some other awful outcome?"

"No," I say softly. There it is. The ugly truth. Maybe it would feel less ugly if I *had* chosen them. I don't think so. I was just a fucking kid. Trauma can make you grow up fast, but in the end, it's not a substitute for the life experience that comes with a few decades on this goddamn rock orbiting the sun. I'm grateful to the kid I was. He did what it took to survive, to bring me to her. The cost is barely worth counting.

Her lips curve a little, even though her eyes stay so incredibly serious. "Then I think the maze *was* your first time, wasn't it?"

I stare at this woman, at the shining star that has been my guiding light for most of my fucking life. I knew from the start that I would never deserve her, but I didn't give a fuck. I wanted her all the same. And yeah, there was a moment in the maze when I was sappy enough to mourn the fact that this might be her first time, but it wasn't mine. That experience had been taken from me a very long time ago, through desperation and violence. I swallow hard. "That's not how it works."

"It is with us."

The same words I said to her back in the maze. I stare at Ariadne, and there's a part of me that almost hopes she doesn't remember. That might make this experience more bearable, this vulnerability less shocking. But no. The knowledge is there in her eyes. She knows exactly what she's saying, exactly what that sentence means to me.

To us.

I clear my throat again. "Yeah." The tightness in my chest gets stronger. Hotter. "Yeah, I guess that is how it is with us."

She holds out her hand, and I move to her on pure instinct. Ariadne lifts my hand to her face and rubs her cheek on my knuckles. "If I read this in a book, I would throw it across the room in pure disbelief. But I think there's a part of me that knew you, even then."

I scrub at my chest, but it does nothing to alleviate the thickness there. "I didn't think you remembered."

"Of course I did." Her heart is in her eyes. It's the way that I've always wanted Ariadne to look at me. The foundation has been there, but it's always been overwritten with fear or guilt or lust. Even now, my mind shies away from labeling it.

I don't know what else to say, so I speak the first thing that bursts into my mind. "You never said anything. When I showed up, when he put me to work, you acted as if it was our first time meeting."

"For a little while, I did think that. You looked so different when he introduced us that I wasn't entirely sure you were the same boy I'd seen in the courtyard."

I smirk. "A bath and haircut can do wonders." To say nothing of clean, expensive clothing. Or at least the new clothes had felt expensive and downright decadent. In hindsight, I recognize them for what they were—disposable in Minos's eyes. The cost might have been world-changing to me as a kid, but they were one step above trash to Minos.

Just like me.

"I suppose so." She presses a kiss to my wrist. "It took me a couple days, but no matter what else changed about you, your eyes were the same. They're still the same." Ariadne smiles, looking almost self-conscious. "By that, I mean you looked at *me* the same."

I shouldn't ask, but I can't seem to help myself. "How did I look at you, Ariadne?"

For a few moments, I think she might not answer. But she finally lifts her chin. "Like I was your everything. Like I was some goddess who wandered into your life. It made me uncomfortable as a kid because I didn't really understand it."

"And now?"

She smiles. "I still don't really understand it. I'm no goddess. I'm human and flawed right down to my bones."

I stroke her fingers with my thumb. "Not to me. To me, you're perfect, sweetheart."

That manages to fluster her when nothing else did. She sputters a little and won't quite look me in the face. It's incredibly fucking cute. Finally, she blurts out, "I like it when you call me that."

"I like calling you that." Sweetheart. Mine. It all amounts to the same thing.

She's still shifting and not quite meeting my gaze. "How are you so good at all this? I feel like I'm fumbling my way through the sex, to say nothing of this…relationship."

It's tempting to avoid answering, but she's given me a priceless gift, and at this point, it's everything I can do not to fall to my knees before her. "I read your books."

She blinks. "What?"

"Your books. The ones you only read in your room so no one else knows." Now it's my turn to shift, my skin hot. "I was curious, so I grabbed one of them. Then I'd just switch it out for the next one. Plus, sweetheart, your favorited fanfics are public. Between the two, I got a good idea of what you might like." Both in the bedroom and out of it.

"I mean, I knew it was public, but you'd have to know my screen name and…" She snorts and shakes her head. "Of course you do. How many times have I read fanfic when we spent time together over the years? I never thought you were paying attention."

"I was." Her tastes are varied and occasionally shocked even me, but I liked the little window into her fantasies. "Even without all that, it's not like you're subtle about what you like—at least when someone knows how to read you."

She kisses my knuckles. "After all this time, you're just full of surprises."

"Yeah, I guess I am."

"Asterion?"

I swallow hard at the look on her face, at the way her eyes got hot, and she licks her lips slowly. "Yeah?"

"If we're talking about firsts, I've never sucked a cock before."

Suddenly, there's not enough air in the room. I think I make a sound, but it's hard to tell over the rushing blood in my ears. "I, uh, have never had mine sucked."

Her grin lights up the room. "Well, then. I have a brilliant idea."

ARIADNE

THIS MORNING, WHEN I WOKE UP WELL RESTED AND slightly peeved at Dionysus for drugging me, I couldn't shake the conversation we had. Or the truth within it. Dionysus was right. Doing this now, for me, might be a leap of faith, but is it really a leap of faith when Asterion will be there to catch me?

Our conversation this morning, the way he's looking at me now, has made things even clearer. He was never going to kill me. What he said in the maze is the truth between us.

And now he stands before me, as vulnerable as I've ever seen him. There is no wall of coldness and violence between us now. Only the truth. It's going to take some time to process all this. But I don't have to do it right now. Not when I can offer this experience, not when I can give us both something pure and free. All our challenges will still be waiting on the other side.

I hold his gaze and hook my fingers into the front of his pants once more. This time, there are no secrets left between us to stop things. We put them all to rest. Or at least I hope we have. I tug his pants down to free his cock. "May I?"

He huffs out a strangled laugh. "Sweetheart, I might die if you don't."

Considering I feel the same way, I don't hesitate or ask again. I simply lean forward and take him into my mouth. I've read about this act more times than I can count, have fantasized about it an equal amount. In reality, it's...different. His cock is wide on my tongue, and it feels like I barely take the tip of him into my mouth before my gag reflex kicks in. I ease back, embarrassment heating my cheeks. I have no idea what the fuck I'm doing.

But when I look up, Asterion is staring down at me just like he did that first day we met. As if I'm a goddess he fully intends on spending the rest of his life worshipping. As if he can't believe how lucky he is that I even deigned to acknowledge him.

That gives me the courage and confidence to lean forward and lick the head of his cock. He makes a sound like he's in pain. He tentatively slides his fingers into my hair, but he's not pulling me away from him—or pulling me closer. It's almost as if he's hanging on for dear life. Maybe he feels as unmoored as I do in this moment.

I lick my lips. "I don't know what I'm doing."

"You're perfect, sweetheart." He still sounds strangled.

I cautiously wrap up my fist around his cock as best I'm able to and take him into my mouth again. This time, I go slower, feeling my way. I'm able to take him deeper before my gag reflex kicks in again. His fingers spasm in my hair.

It seems to defy belief that my awkward ministrations are affecting him so deeply, but I can't deny the evidence right in front of me.

Every touch, suck, and lick results in some kind of noise pulled from his lips seemingly against his will.

Distantly, the solution comes to me. What I need from this interaction, what he might need as well. I ease off him again. "Fuck my mouth."

"What?"

I could tell him that I'm worried I won't be able to give him what he needs, that I'm flat out floundering, even as I enjoy this exploration. But the truth is simpler. He was right when he said that soft isn't the way. I can enjoy it for what it is, but it's not what I *need*. What I suspect we both need. "Please."

He clenches his jaw hard enough that I can see the muscles flex beneath his skin. His fingers twitch in my hair before he seems to force himself to ease his grip. "Sweetheart, you can barely take half my cock without choking on it. If I fuck your mouth, I'm going to hurt you."

No, he won't. Not in any meaningful way. Even at his most vicious, he's always been remarkably careful with me. He's only giving me just as much as I can handle. "I trust you."

Asterion curses long and hard, the vicious words slicing from his lips. Maybe he *should* scare me, but all it does is make me clench my thighs together. He glares down at me. "If it's too much, you slap my thigh." He wraps one hand around my wrist and mimics the motion. "Do you understand?"

"I do."

For a moment, it almost seems like he'll keep arguing or adding stipulations, but he grips my jaw and touches his thumb to my bottom lip, guiding my mouth open. His dark eyes are downright forbidding as he angles forward, and the head of his cock presses into my mouth.

I half expect Asterion to start pounding away at me. I should've known better. He eases past my lips and delves inside with one long, slow stroke. On and on, until I have to choose whether I'm going to submit or fight the intrusion. In the end, it's no choice at all. I open for him entirely.

In response, he stops. I didn't realize I closed my eyes, but when he doesn't move, doesn't seem to breathe, I flutter my lids open. He's staring down at me as if he wants to memorize every moment of this. He catches me watching him, and his expression goes harder yet. "I want to make you cry."

If anyone else had said those words to me, I would do everything in my power to put as much distance between us as possible. But with Asterion? I swear to the gods there's a gush between my thighs. I shiver. I can't nod, but I do my best to make a sound of consent. I never would've guessed that was something I wanted, but with this man, it's not a want. It's a need.

Only then does he start moving. He slides almost all the way out from my mouth and then pushes forward. Again, he defies my expectations. He's not going fast, but he's not giving me much time to adjust, either. This time, when he reaches the point of my total surrender, he pushes just past it. I gag, but he's already retreating, only to start the whole process over again.

Did I think that I surrendered before? What a joke. This. *This* is true surrender. I take what he delivers, and he gives me just a little beyond what I can manage. Tears spring to my eyes and my jaw aches.

I love every moment of it.

"What a perfect little slut you are, sweetheart. You take my cock whichever way I choose to give it to you. And now you're going to take my come, too. Aren't you?"

I've never wanted anything more in my life. I don't know if salvation truly exists on the other side of his orgasm, but it feels like it. My eyes flutter closed without any choice in the matter, but this time, he allows it. He never picks up his pace. He's never particularly rough. But that doesn't change the fact that he's fucking my mouth in a way that feels imprinted on my very body.

And then his strokes become less regimented. Desperate. "Sweetheart, fuck, I need—" He curses and shoves forward, and I gag around him. But this time, he doesn't retreat. His fingers are tight in my hair and his breathing is ragged. "Going to..."

Yes. This. I need this.

I moan around his cock. Not enough. Still not enough. But then, I know what he wants, what he needs to get him over the edge. I skate my hands around his hips to grip his ass and dig my nails in. Hard.

"Ariadne!" His whole body jerks and then he's coming down my throat in hot spurts. Asterion's knees buckle. For me, because of me. He eases out of my mouth and sinks down next to me on the couch, his body loose and more relaxed than I've ever seen him. I swallow, relishing the ache in my jaw and throat. Witnessing him completely undone is its own special kind of reward. Especially when he kisses me, his fingers tangling in my hair.

"Perfect. You're so fucking perfect I can barely stand it." He nips my bottom lip. "Pull up your dress, sweetheart. Let me see where you need me the most."

I brace myself with one hand behind me and use the other to lift my dress. The silky fabric feels decadent against my skin, and with how oversensitized I am, it's almost unbearable. Especially when I get the dress up around my hips and show him that I'm not wearing any panties.

"Thought so." He's regaining control of himself, his voice still ragged but no longer unraveled. Asterion grips my thigh, right over his bite, and exerts the slightest amount of pressure, guiding me to open for him. "You better have nowhere to be today. We'll deal with tonight tonight. Today you're mine, Ariadne. And I'm not going to rush. Not again."

"Okay."

"Say it," he snaps.

There's no misunderstanding what he means. Not anymore. Not ever again. "I'm yours, Asterion. Just yours. I've only ever been yours."

He covers my pussy with his hand. It's possessive and wondrous at the same time. He parts my folds and strokes two fingers up my center to press against my clit. "But that's not all, is it?"

Again, I know exactly what he's talking about. Because this thing between us has never only gone one way. He might've known sooner than I did, but I *do* know, don't I? "And you're mine. Only mine."

"That's right, sweetheart. So when you get to thinking too hard later, I want you to remember that." He turns his hand and presses two fingers into me, slowly enough that I can actually watch my pussy part for him. I'm so wet that it might embarrass me if I could think straight. Instead, I take it as simply another piece of evidence that this thing between us has always been fate. Or as close to fate as I can believe in.

"I'll try," I whisper.

"Do better than try. You're going to survive this bullshit we're in the middle of. I am, too." He wedges a third finger into me. "That fucking barrier is coming down, and when it does, I'm taking you away from this place. Do you understand me, Ariadne?"

I feel like I'm making promises I can't possibly follow through on, but I'm not going to let that stop me. "Yes, Asterion. I understand you."

THE MINOTAUR

I BELIEVE HER. MAYBE I'M A FUCKING FOOL, BUT FOR THE first time since the day I realized she'd run and left only a note behind, I feel something like hope. That I won't have to drag her into a future together. That we have a fucking future at all. But that shit is a concern for tonight and tomorrow and beyond. Right now, she's so wet and soft against my fingers that it drives me wild. I've touched her like this before, but never with the ability to take my time, without limits in place.

"Turn around, sweetheart. Let me get a look at that dress."

She starts to obey but pauses before she shifts. "I like this dress a lot, Asterion. Don't cut it off me." She doesn't wait for a response before she twists to present me with her back. Again, I marvel at the way the straps crisscross her light-brown skin. She's like my very own piece of art. A present I can unwrap at my leisure.

I trace my fingers lightly along the straps, enjoying the way she shivers in response. She's given me several gifts today already. I want to do my best to return them. I'm not made for softness, but I *am* made for her. I have to trust that I can give her what she needs.

"Stand up." I don't wait for her to do as I ask; I grip her hips and lift her to her feet. This is better. When she stands like this, I have her back even with my face. I gently tug at the delicate little bow until it unravels, baring the small of her back. I lean forward and press an open-mouthed kiss to the newly revealed spot.

And then I slowly undo the laces, following the path with my mouth. Ariadne whimpers and shakes, but she doesn't move from that spot until the last bit comes free and the dress flutters down around her body, leaving her gloriously naked. I palm her big ass and set my teeth against the curve. She squeaks, which just makes me do it again. I like that I make her this kind of nervous. As if she's not quite sure what I'll do next, but she still trusts me implicitly.

"Spread your legs, sweetheart." I barely wait for her to do as I say before I delve my finger between her legs and press into her. She's even wetter than before. It makes my spent cock twitch with need, but it'll still be a few minutes before I can fulfill that promise.

And we have nowhere to be.

I still can't quite believe it. There's a part of me that wants to rush this, to grab every bit of pleasure with Ariadne before something happens to stop us in our tracks. But she's here, in my apartment, and we locked the door to the outside.

I nudge her forward and slip down to sit on the floor. She moves easily as I guide her to turn to face me and lift one knee up to the edge of the couch. It puts her pussy within kissing distance, which is all I've ever wanted. I lean forward and drag my tongue up her center. Her pussy blossoms for me. There's no other way to describe it.

She's so soft and perfect against my tongue, and it gets even better when she starts shifting restlessly. I really thought it would take me several minutes to recover from that last orgasm? I'm a fool. It feels like I'll always be ready for her.

I turn my head and gently bite the scar on her thigh. "Ride my face, sweetheart. Take what you need."

She stills as if she's about to protest. I shift back to prop my neck on the edge of the couch, giving myself up to her. The sweet vulnerability on her face slowly melts away, replaced by need. For me.

Ariadne shifts closer and then her pussy is against my mouth. I kiss her thoroughly, giving myself over to the rolling motion of her hips grinding against the flat of my tongue. And then her hands are in my hair, guiding me right to her clit even as she keeps fucking my face. Her moans are the most beautiful thing I've ever heard. Especially when they go frustrated and sharp. "Your fingers, Asterion. I need them."

I don't make her beg. I press two fingers into her and curl them against her inner wall in the exact way that made her come apart so beautifully for me before. She cries out my name and then she's coming all over my face. She presses me down hard to the cushion, covering me so thoroughly that I can't draw a single breath. Good. I don't fucking need to breathe. Not as long as she's coming. Not until she's finished.

Her hips jerk one last time, and then she slides bonelessly down my chest to straddle my hips. She cups my face, her expression pleasure-drugged. "Did I kill you?" I love that she doesn't sound particularly concerned one way or another.

"Still alive and kicking, sweetheart."

"Good." She kisses me. After all the dirty face-fucking, it's sweet and light and absolutely perfect. She nips my bottom lip as she eases back. "We're not done yet." She squirms a little, grinding her wet pussy against my rapidly hardening cock.

"No, sweetheart. We're not done yet." I grip her thighs and stand. It's awkward as fuck, but I love the way she shrieks and clings to me. As if I would ever fucking drop her. "I'm taking you to bed."

Her grin is free of all the stress and fear that's plagued her steps for far too long. "I would be heartily disappointed if you didn't."

I carry her into my bedroom and lay her down on the bed, settling between her soft thighs. It's so fucking tempting to just keep going, but I'll have no regrets between us. Not anymore. Not again. I reach down and yank the bottom drawer of the nightstand open and pull out a box of condoms.

Ariadne watches with wide eyes as I rip it open. "A whole box, just for me?"

"It's sure as fuck not for anyone else." I yank a string of condoms out and toss them onto the pillow next to her head.

I start to rip one open, but she lays a gentle hand over mine. "We don't need to use them."

Need almost makes me reckless, but Ariadne was hurt by my recklessness before, and I'll be damned before she is again. "If you want kids, we'll do that—when it's safe. Not risking it. Not a second time."

"Oh." She clears her throat, shifting nervously. "No, I didn't mean *that*. I just meant that I'm on birth control. I have been since my follow-up appointment after the...procedure."

Which means we didn't need to use a condom in the dressing

room. I almost ask her why she let me put it on, but the answer is clear enough. She didn't fully trust me then. She does now. I gather her close and kiss her. "You sure?"

"Yes. Absolutely."

I don't ask her again. I guide my cock to her entrance. "Ready, sweetheart?"

"Yes." She reaches down and sinks her fingernails into my ass just like she did when she was choking on my cock. The pain makes me jerk forward, and we both moan as I enter her. Too good. It's always too fucking good with her.

Because it's her. Because it's me. Because it's *us*.

I slip an arm between her hips and the mattress and roll us. Ariadne plants her hands on my chest, steadying herself. I squeeze her hips. "You didn't think you were done yet, did you? You rode my mouth. Now ride my cock."

She opens her mouth like she wants to argue, but I thrust up into her just a little, and it seems like she forgets what she was about to say. It's just as well. I'm running out of words myself. I don't believe in the gods, but if I did, no one could convince me that Ariadne wasn't a child of them. Everything from her savvy brain to her hidden ruthlessness marks her as a person far above the rest. But this? Watching her start to ride my cock? It feels beyond good, but it's the sight of her taking her pleasure without hesitation that really does me in.

I stroke my hands up her sides, my thumbs feathering over her stretch marks, and cup her breasts. Perfect. Everything about her is perfectly made.

"If you could...see the way...you're looking at me."

"Don't need to see it. I'm feeling it." My chest is too tight. I have been in love with this woman since I was a kid, but it's never felt like this before. As if the overwhelming need I had for her, to be around her, has morphed into something infinitely stronger. As if she's pulled my heart right out of my chest with her bare hands. This pleasure is so acute, it morphs into pain. I welcome every moment of it. *Good. Take it. It was yours all along.*

Ariadne skates her hands up my arms and then down her stomach to finger her clit. Almost immediately, her strokes go jerky. I grab her hips and keep her moving at the pace that will get her there. I need to feel her come around me. I need to watch her expression in that moment of perfect surrender. I need it more than anything.

"Asterion!" She throws her head back and arches her spine, grinding down on my cock as she orgasms. "Oh gods, don't stop."

I don't stop. I keep her fucking me through the end of this orgasm and into another. And all the while, I watch her face and know that I'll seek a repeat of this moment for the rest of my fucking life.

I don't believe in the gods, no, but I believe in Ariadne. Her body is the altar I worship at, and her love is the only sustenance I need.

Then the little brat reaches back and takes my balls in a firm grip. Her nails prick the sensitive skin there, and surprise sends me hurtling into an orgasm that's so strong, my vision shorts out. I fuck up into her, needing to be closer, needing to go harder. Needing for it to never end.

I arch up and kiss her as the last wave recedes, leaving me boneless and more relaxed than I've ever been. She slumps onto my chest and starts to move to the side, but I'm having none of that. I'm not ready to let her go yet. I never will be. I kiss her lips, the bridge of her nose, her forehead. "Stay."

"I'm not going anywhere. I promise."

ARIADNE

I THOUGHT ASTERION WAS OVERLY OPTIMISTIC WHEN HE
pulled out that giant box of condoms, but even though we don't use
them, he proves my doubts to be unfounded over the next few hours.
We come together again and again, in every position imaginable,
with questing hands and writhing bodies. There's a hint of desperation to it, but neither of us comments on it. We have today, and
part of me mourns the fact that even now a deadline looms over us.

The sun sinks below the horizon, bathing the room in shadows.
As much as I want to go for another round, I don't think I can survive it. It's just as well; our reprieve is over now. "Asterion…"

"Yeah, I know." He brings my hand to his mouth and presses a
kiss to my knuckles. "This won't be the last time we spend the day
in bed, sweetheart. We have the rest of our lives ahead of us, and I
plan to take advantage of it every chance we get."

I don't understand how he can be so relentlessly confident. I'm
not sure of anything anymore. It feels like everywhere I turn, enemies are popping up to shove me into a corner I can't possibly fight

my way out of. The stakes have never been higher, and all I want to do is enjoy this time with the man that I...love.

Why is it such a revelation every time I admit it? It feels like I've loved him for years—longer even. But it's something we've never said aloud to each other. Not with words, though one could argue that our actions more than support that truth between us. I stare into his brutal, scarred face, and my throat closes before I can speak those three little words. It feels too much like throwing out a last-ditch promise on the eve of a battle I doubt we'll both survive. I didn't think I was superstitious, but apparently I am.

Instead, I say, "Can I tell you a secret?"

Asterion rolls onto his side and props his head in his hand. "I want all your secrets."

"I had the blueprints days ago. I just wasn't ready for this to end."

He strokes a thumb along my cheekbone. "I don't know how many times I have to say it before you believe me, sweetheart. This thing between us is *never* going to end. You and I were written in the stars."

I choke out a laugh. "I don't think anybody else believes that except you."

"You believe it."

His confidence and arrogance might be aggravating in the extreme sometimes, but I can't deny the comfort in them. Even when doubt makes the ground beneath my feet shaky, I can rely on Asterion to always point to my true north. To a future where the two of us are free.

"Sometimes I feel doubt." I lean into his touch. "But you believe enough for both of us."

"I'll keep doing it."

My smile falls away. "The odds aren't in our favor. We have my father on one side, Hera and the Olympians on the other. I don't see how we can thread the needle without something terrible happening."

Asterion pulls me close and wraps his arms around me. When he hold me like this, it's hard not to believe. I suppose that's the point, or maybe he just likes holding me as much as I like being held. His words rumble through his chest against my cheek. "Only for a little while longer. The timeline for the barrier coming down is quicker than we assumed."

I almost ask him how he knows that, but ultimately it doesn't matter. "And then what?"

"You know the answer to that. We can talk in circles as long as you need for you to feel better about it, but the facts haven't changed. We're getting the fuck out of here. Circe and the rest of them can fight their war without us. We've both sacrificed enough for other people, don't you think?"

I shift up to press a light kiss to his lips. "I think we both know by now that the world isn't fair."

"Where do you want to go first?"

The question startles me, but it probably shouldn't. I'm still so focused on the here and now and all the challenges between us and anything resembling freedom. But Asterion is right, in his own way. There's nothing we can do right this second to affect the barrier or Dodona Tower or any of the threats rising against us. And maybe there's a part of me that just wants to sink into the fantasy that everything really will work out.

"You've had to sit through more than a few of my prospective destinations. Which of them would you like to see first?"

His laugh rumbles against me. "Now you're just trying to get out of choosing. Fine, sweetheart. I'll play."

He strokes a hand down my spine and back up again. I don't think I'll ever get tired of this casual touching between us. It's not something we have to hide right now, and I want to melt right into him.

He considers for several minutes. I like that he's taking this question seriously. He gives me hope, even if it's undeserved. Finally, he says, "Nowhere cold. I'm fucking tired of winter. It will take some convincing to get me to go to Antarctica."

I laugh softly. "Don't you want to see the penguins?"

"There are penguins in places that won't freeze my balls off." Asterion traces abstract patterns against my skin. "You've talked about Rio and Carnaval enough times that I know it by heart. It's one of the places both you and your brother want to experience. Maybe we'll start there."

"Carnaval isn't for months yet. It's in February." I'm mostly poking at him to keep this conversation going. To keep dreaming before reality comes crashing back down around us.

"Always so difficult. Maybe we go to Canada, to the West Coast, and start driving south. We'll take our time and see some shit and circle around to Rio in time for February. How does that sound?"

My heart feels too big for my chest. I want that. I want that so fucking desperately that it makes me shake. I don't just want to visit places; I want to experience them fully. The picture he paints is exactly that. A wandering life with no true responsibilities, where we go where we want and drift as we need. The world is such a big place, and I want to see all of it.

I swallow past the lump in my throat. "That sounds good, Asterion. Really, really good."

"Then consider it done. As soon as we get our papers, that's our plan."

"Just like that?"

He brushes my hair back from my face. "Yeah, sweetheart. Just like that. No reason to complicate shit unnecessarily." He kisses me. "Stay until morning."

It's *almost* an order, but there's a lilt at the end of the last word that edges into the territory of question. He didn't have to ask, but I love that he did. "It *is* sunset."

"Then stay a little longer."

"Okay," I whisper. "I'll stay as long as I can." Until we have to go back to the real world and face the fact that we are only two people in a fight against titans. It will take a miracle for us to get out alive. But Asterion believes we can make it happen...so I will believe, too.

And in my moments of doubt, he'll have to believe enough for both of us.

THE MINOTAUR

23

AS DIFFICULT AS IT IS TO LET ARIADNE LEAVE MY SIGHT, I don't want her around for the next steps. I've got to get my hands dirty again. No matter who's calling the shots, that's one outcome I can't seem to escape. Violence comes naturally to me.

Aeacus meet me at the same apartment as last time. The place is still dingy and dirty enough that I know they're not letting anyone else in here to clean, and none of his people are doing the job. He looks like shit, too. I know what it's like when Minos is riding your ass and you actually care about what he thinks. Theseus used to get the same hunted expression.

I don't miss the guy, but there's a part of me that doesn't really know what to do without my ever-present competitor. We were never going to be friends—Minos made sure of that—but there's something about him being the only other person in the world who has the same shared experiences as me that built an intimacy I never asked for.

He's better off. Or at least he thinks he is. I mean to feel the same.

Aeacus drags a hand over his face. "About fucking time."

"I said I'd get them, and I did. If you could do it faster, you should have."

He curses under his breath but just motions me to the computer at the central table. It only takes a few minutes for his guy to get the zip drive pulled up and displaying the blueprints.

I stare at the lines. I hate this part of the process. It's all waffling and planning and no action. It's necessary, but that doesn't make me enjoy it.

Aeacus's guy does something to get the blueprints projected onto the blank wall across from us. I round the table to eye the layout. It's not great. I'd hoped there would be some kind of clear way in that would allow us to dodge security. There doesn't seem to be.

Of course it wouldn't be that simple.

Though, if Hera keeps her word and gets everyone out...

But how the fuck is she going to do that? A bomb threat might clear out the neighboring buildings, but Zeus isn't a complete fool and, to the best of my knowledge, his people aren't disloyal. They aren't going to abandon their posts, and if they leave the building, they're going to make sure he comes with them when they do.

Another of Aeacus's people, a small person with medium-brown skin and more piercings than I can easily count, comes up. They point to a spot that looks like every other part of the building. "Do we have a security layout?"

"Let me check." The guy at the computer mutters a little and then the image changes, a secondary layer appearing in green over the black lines. "There."

"This is Mars," Aeacus introduces the new person. "They're the best."

I haven't worked with them before, so I'll believe it when I see it. But I'm not usually sent on shit like this. I prefer to work alone, and I'm not what you'd call *subtle*.

Mars whistles under their breath. "They have this thing locked up tighter than…" They glance at me and swallow hard. "Well, tight."

I have a feeling they were about to say some shit about Ariadne, but I let it slide. This time. "Walk me through it."

"Everything is passcoded. Means you can't just kill some fucker and take his badge. You need the code. And I need some time to confirm this, but if Zeus is as paranoid as these plans indicate, I'd bet a month's wages that the passcode either changes regularly or everyone has their own individual one. Makes it harder to hack."

I eye the plans on the wall. "So we bust our way in."

"Not going to work." They tap the stairwells. "These are blast doors. They drop in the case of an attack, and they can be triggered remotely."

Fuck. I cross my arms over my chest and consider the plans. Blast doors on the stairwells. Elevators that will shut down the moment there's trouble. Means it's impossible to go up…but it's equally impossible to escape. "We go down."

"What?" Aeacus looks at me like I've grown a second head. "These buildings are created to be steady. It will take more than a handful of bombs in the basement to topple it. We need to take out at least the first couple floors, if not the entire bottom half. We *need* to go up."

Bringing down buildings is a pain in the ass. "So we don't do it all at once. We infiltrate and plant the bombs over the course of a couple days and remote detonate when the time comes."

"That brings us back to the problem of getting in."

"Yeah." I lean forward. "Is there a water line we can break? Some shit that will require outside maintenance?"

"I'll look." The guy at the computer types away and whistles. "Whoever got you these blueprints was *thorough*." One click and an orange layer is added to the schematic. "Water lines." Another click adds red. "Electrical."

Aeacus hums under his breath. "They'll pull in their own people to fix something that goes wrong."

"They'll try." I shrug. "Your team has done a bait and switch before. Won't take much to do it again." I'm too recognizable. Not that I want to dress up like a plumber and fix some pipes.

"It might work. Risky but it's something." He frowns. "Give us some time to run some scenarios and get things into place. Minos wants an update tonight." He glances at me. "You should probably be there for it."

It's the very last thing I want to do, but when has that stopped me? "Wouldn't miss it. Text me when you're ready."

I almost call Ariadne, but there's no reason to update her until I have the full details. I'd rather do it in person anyway.

As tempting as it is to check in on her, I head back to my apartment. She promised to stay inside today and keep her head down. She's as safe as it's possible to be in this fucking city. It will have to be enough for now.

Plus, I'm not as young as I used to be. I haven't slept much in the last week, and I'm starting to feel the effects. I need to crash for a few hours so my head doesn't get muddled. Missing shit because I'm fuzzy is unacceptable.

I'm stumbling a little as I unlock my door and slip inside. I haven't bothered to go back to the apartment Minos keeps, but I'll have to make an appearance tomorrow. In the meantime...I sigh and pull out my phone.

Minos picks up on the first ring, the eager fucker. "Well?"

"We have a plan. Aeacus is getting things lined up. I don't have a timeline yet, but we're moving as fast as is feasibly possible."

He curses. "I need it done next week."

I pause. "What?"

"Next week, Minotaur. Circe's orders. She's got something in the works, and she needs that tower to come down to make it happen. So we *will* make it happen."

Easy for him to say. He's sitting nice and safe in his penthouse, yelling commands without any comprehension of the implications. He wasn't always like this, but something about all the repeated failures has cracked his confidence. Or maybe it was Ariadne's defection. Or Theseus's. Impossible to say the specific thing that pushed him over the edge, but now I'm the one having to deal with the consequences.

I bite back my impatience. "Minos, that's impossible. It's not easy to bring down a building."

"Sure it is. Go in there. Kill everyone. Set explosives and get the fuck out."

If I do that—and it's a big *if* because at the first sign of attack, those blast doors are coming down and it will take more explosives than we have to get through them—then Hera will hurt Ariadne. She might do more than hurt her. "I'm telling you, it's impossible."

"And I'm telling you that I don't give a fuck. I'm calling Aeacus now. Figure it out, Minotaur. That's an order." He hangs up.

Fuck. "*Fuck.*"

"Rough day?"

I throw myself back, pulling my gun on instinct. I didn't realize I wasn't alone, and it takes several long beats…and Hermes's wicked laughter…for me to register *who* has broken into my house. "What the *fuck*?"

"Got to keep you on your toes." She steps out of the shadows in a completely different place than I expected. I don't know how she managed *that* trick, but even if I'd started shooting, I wouldn't have hit her. There's no such thing as magic, but this woman makes me doubt that. She's so damn sneaky.

My adrenaline is rushing in my ears and my body is tense with the need to attack after being startled so thoroughly. I have to spend a few seconds breathing steadily before I can slip my gun back into its holster. "What are you doing here?"

"Just checking on you." She bounces on her toes and then she's off, skipping the short distance to my kitchen and rooting around in my fridge. She shuts it and sends me a disgusted look. "I know you're out here living the bachelor life, but you're in serious danger of becoming a stereotype with that fridge. Don't you eat?"

"When I want to eat, I go out." I don't move from my spot. "Answer the question, Hermes."

"I did. I'm checking on you." She leans her elbows on the kitchen counter. "You're bringing down Dodona Tower."

There's no point in pretending otherwise. She'll have heard the entire conversation with Minos, and there's a decent chance she knew what the plan was even before that. The woman deals in secrets and has an uncanny knack of sourcing them. "The only thing you need to worry about is bringing down the *barrier*."

"On the contrary, my dear Minotaur, I worry about all manner of things." She examines her nails, and I catch a glint of glitter. "Like the fact that our very own Hera is instigating a rebellion when we're on the verge of a siege—if not an all-out war."

I lift my brows. "Neither of those things are my responsibility or my problem."

"No, I don't suppose you'd see it that way." She sighs. "Truly, it's like herding cats. Just when I get a few of you in order, half a dozen others start getting wild ideas about mutiny."

"Mutiny is only for ships."

"That's not actually true, but same difference." She flicks her fingers at me. "What terms did Hera give you?"

I start to feel foolish for standing across the apartment from her and slowly approach the other side of the kitchen peninsula. "If you know so much, I'm surprised you don't know that."

"Gods, Minotaur, I expected better of you." She rolls her eyes. "I don't know everything, but all you have to do is *act* like you know everything and people tell you all sorts of delicious details. It works on most."

Damn it. "Did you know for sure that Hera was instigating a rebellion before I confirmed it?"

She smiles serenely. "You'll never know."

It really isn't my problem, and I just need to remember that. I need Hermes more than I need Hera, but fuck, that's not exactly true. Hera is the key to Ariadne's safety. Shit. I can't *think*. I scrub a hand over my face. "Are you going to stop Hera?"

"I haven't decided yet."

I look at her over my hand. "What do you mean, you haven't decided yet?"

"Exactly what I said. Now, what are Hera's terms?"

No point in pussyfooting around it. She's not going to leave until I tell her, and more than that, I need her help to bring the barrier down. "Hera will keep Ariadne safe—and Icarus, too—in exchange for me not killing anyone but Zeus when we bring down the building."

Hermes whistles. "So it's gotten that extreme. That's unfortunate."

Unfortunate is one way to put it. I study her. "Now what?"

"Now nothing. Minos doesn't care what Hera wants." She suddenly looks tired. "This is a gargantuan mess. I can't let you—or him—kill hundreds of people who work in that tower. They haven't done anything wrong, and while there are plenty of sins to go around this city, the problems start at the top."

Considering Ariadne will feel similarly about a bunch of people dying for no fucking reason, I'm not about to let Minos bully us into making a shitty decision—that won't even work. "And Zeus?"

"Zeus can take care of himself. And if he can't?" She shrugs. "I can't save everyone. In a conflict with these kinds of stakes, you either come out on top or you come out six feet under."

ARIADNE

I WAKE UP TO A TEXT FROM ASTERION.

Asterion: We have a problem. Minos wants us to move forward next week. Doesn't care about casualties.

I read it, then read it again. It still takes my sleep-clogged brain another minute to process what he's saying. What it means. "No." I sit up. "No, no, no." If the tower comes down like that, without Hera and the rest having an opportunity to come up with a reason to evacuate the building, a lot of people will die, and I'm a special kind of monster because even knowing that, the first thing my mind jumps to is my brother.

Hera won't protect him if we defy her. She might throw me to the wolves, too, so I won't even have a chance to do it myself. I fling off the sheets and call Asterion. I barely wait for him to pick up to say, "I thought you had this under control."

"I thought I did, too." He sounds tired, more tired than I've ever heard him. "I'm working on it, but he's already given the command to the team. The plan is in motion. *His* plan."

My stomach lurches, threatening to revolt. "What do we do?"

"You don't have to do anything but stay safe. I'll handle it."

That's lovely of him to say, but my safety is not guaranteed. More than that, I have a skill set that might actually be useful. "I can help, Asterion. You know I can. I wasn't joking about wanting to be involved."

"If your father finds out you have any connection with this, he won't wait around for me to kill you. He'll do it himself."

I press my hand to my chest and try to breathe through my racing heart. He's right, but either I'm content to sit on the sidelines and let him take the risks or I'm an equal partner. If I don't convince him to take my help, people will *die*.

Zeus was always going to die and you were okay with that.

I ignore the snide little voice inside me. "He's going to try it soon anyway. He's not one to sit around and twiddle his thumbs when his orders aren't being obeyed. It's only because the tower has taken priority that he hasn't sent someone else after me."

"Ariadne..." He curses. "No. Absolutely fucking not. You're staying out of this. You won't be able to live with the guilt if something goes wrong."

I ignore the fact that he's probably right. "Who's working the tech side of things?"

He sighs. "You're not going to let this go."

"I'm not."

"Fine." Another low curse. "It's Mars."

I don't have much interaction with my father's people, but I have spent plenty of time going through their records. Information is power, and maybe Icarus and I are using the same playbook, because I'd had a faint thought of finding secrets to use to blackmail them if things got particularly bad. The difference is that I didn't find much. Just a few gambling debts and mistresses. Nothing my father would care about enough to give me ammunition to use against his people.

Mars doesn't have any dirty secrets. Like a lot of my father's people, they were a street kid that he brought in as a teenager. They're well liked by the others on Aeacus's team, and they do a pretty decent job of hacking and whatnot.

I'm still better. "When are you meeting with them next?"

"A couple hours. They aren't early risers, so it'll be after noon."

Not long. I would have liked a few extra days to ensure I'm not missing anything, but such is life. "Text me when you're about to leave. I'll meet you somewhere and pass you the information I find before then."

"No." He keeps going before I can protest. "I'll come to you. That fiancé of yours already knows that we're working together, so he can give me access. There's no reason for you to risk yourself."

He wants to come *here*. Again. With permission this time. I look around the ridiculously luxurious room and feel a strange stab of guilt. "I'll talk to him, but I can't guarantee anything."

"You'll figure it out." He hangs up without saying goodbye.

I glare at my phone, my irritation at the way he ends calls almost enough to override the anxiety that swells in response to this new information. Things were always dire, but now the stakes are higher than they've ever been. For once, I'm not even worried about myself.

Hundreds of people go through the doors of Dodona Tower

on any given day. Maybe upward of a thousand. Maybe more. Multiply that by every building in the immediate vicinity, and we're talking about catastrophic losses.

I can't let it happen. I refuse to.

I drag in a breath and pull a robe on. Dionysus came home sometime in the early hours of the morning. He tried to be quiet, but I haven't slept well since arriving here—aside from the night he put a sedative in my wine. It's impossible to ignore the danger I'm constantly in. I have no doubt that *he* doesn't want to hurt me...just like I have no doubt that if Hera decides I'm more trouble than I'm worth, Dionysus is going to step aside and let her people cut me down.

His room is the one part of the penthouse that I haven't investigated, so it feels strange to pad down the hallway and knock lightly on the door. When there's no answer, I sigh and bang on it. "Dionysus! I need to talk to you."

"Come in."

I hesitate, but only for a moment. His room is bathed in shadows, courtesy of the blackout blinds pulled down over all the windows. I suppose it makes sense, seeing as how he's a night owl. Even so, I'm not walking into that darkness. "Can I turn on the light?"

"Hold on." He curses and there's the sound of him fumbling around for a moment before a lamp flicks on.

Dionysus's bed is startlingly normal. I don't know why I'm so surprised. It's a standard king, and though the thread count is no doubt exceedingly high, the comforter and sheets—both gray—are downright mundane.

He rubs a hand over his eyes. "As much as I adore your lovely face, this had better be good."

Just like that, I remember why I sought him out. "It's actually really bad."

"That's what I was afraid of." He motions for me to continue. "What's gone wrong now?"

I know it's not technically my fault, but I can't help feeling guilty as I relay what Asterion told me. I finish in a rush and then swallow hard. "He doesn't want me meeting him out in public right now because it's not safe, so he requests that you allow him up here."

"*Requests.*" Dionysus snorts. "More like he gave an order and probably threw in a threat of violence for spice."

I flush because he's mostly right. "Well, uh, more or less."

"Okay." He curses again. "Okay, give me thirty minutes to pull myself together. Can you get coffee going?"

I don't know why I expected him to just hand this problem off to someone else. Dionysus might be a bit flighty and irreverent, but he seems to care more than most beneath all the intentionally distracting trappings. I back out the door. "Of course."

"Ariadne."

I stop. "Yes?"

"We'll figure this out, one way or another." He makes a face. "I doubt the solution will be one anyone is particularly happy with, but we'll ensure that building doesn't come down with all those people in it. I promise."

I want to believe him. Truly, I do. Unfortunately, I've seen what my father and his people are capable of. Even with Asterion working against him, there are no guarantees. But arguing with Dionysus won't accomplish anything. Maybe he's even right. Maybe this will all work out and there's some simple solution that I just haven't thought of.

Maybe.

I back out of the room and shut the door softly behind me. Exactly thirty minutes later, a freshly showered Dionysus appears, wearing his dressing robe and slippers. He catches me looking and shrugs. "I'm awake, but there's no reason I can't be comfortable." It takes me a few minutes to doctor his coffee just how he likes it, and then he sits across the kitchen island from me. "Okay, first order of business. If the Minotaur gives his word that he's not going to murder me horribly, he can have access to the penthouse. Today."

I don't miss the limit he puts on it, but I don't hold that against him. If I were him, I wouldn't want Asterion coming and going freely from my personal residence, either. "Thank you."

"You understand that I have to call Hera and the rest of them in. Or at least update them. We might have been willing to stand by and allow that tower to come down, but without the ability to get innocents out, this changes things significantly."

I'm also aware of that. I don't know what that means for Asterion, for Olympus, or for me. It's tempting to ask Dionysus, but I manage to hold the question inside. He's not the one I made a deal with. Hera is.

"Ariadne." Dionysus holds his coffee cup in both hands and peers at me over the rim. He's as serious as I've ever seen him. "I get that this isn't your fault, or your brother's, for that matter. But Hera is..." He sighs. "You have to understand. Your people are a direct threat to ours."

I try for a smile but give up halfway through. "I understand. My deal with Hera won't stand if I can't uphold my part of the bargain. As for our marriage—"

"It stands." He takes a long sip of his coffee and sets it aside. "Your Minotaur is fearsome indeed, but he's only one man. He can't protect you in this city. I can, at least to some extent. But depending on how things go with Hera, it might be wise to send you to the countryside until this is over. One way or another."

I stare. Of all the things I expected him to say, this wasn't even remotely on the list. "But you don't want to marry me."

"Darling, I don't want to marry *anyone*." He shrugs. "But if it has to be someone, why not you? We get along well enough, and you're not looking for something from me that I have no interest in providing."

It strikes me that, under different circumstances, I wouldn't mind being married to Dionysus, either. He asks very little of me and is incredibly generous in return. There's definitely a mutual understanding and respect between us. Marriages were built on less.

But I'm in love with someone else. After having experienced a taste of *that*, entering into a marriage that is, strictly speaking, a business partnership holds no appeal. Even with Dionysus.

"I can't leave him." I say it softly, feeling my way. "I can't leave either of them. If Asterion keeps following my father's orders, he's going to end up dead. And Icarus…" I swallow hard. "My brother needs me." I think he needs more than me, but as much as I am growing to respect Dionysus, that doesn't mean I trust him explicitly. Not with my brother.

Dionysus presses his fingers to his temples. "You're not making this easy, love."

"I know. I'm sorry."

"Fine, fine, you've convinced me. Take your wayward brother

and the monster of a man with you to the countryside. I'll spin it as removing a weapon from Minos's quiver. It's a weak argument, but by the time I give it, you'll be gone."

I don't tell him that it's a Band-Aid, and not even a good one at that. If war comes to Olympus—and it's going to—the people who reside in the countryside around the city won't be immune from the conflict. It's still a sweet offer. "Why would you do that? I know that I've helped out Olympus, but I'm still little more than an enemy."

"You are." He picks his mug back up and stares into his coffee as if it may hold the answers he seeks. "But you're also a victim of your own circumstances and birth. And enough people have been hurt in this mess."

Pan. That's who he's talking about. It's on the tip of my tongue to ask how Pan is or if Dionysus has spoken to him since the attack. I don't. It feels cruel to point out that in our own ways, we've both done plenty of harm to those who don't deserve it.

So I just say, "Thank you."

THE MINOTAUR

AS SOON AS I GET CONFIRMATION FROM ARIADNE THAT I won't be shot on sight, I head for Dionysus's place. We're in the midst of a shitstorm, and I don't see a way through. The only option we have is to cut and run, but I can't even do that until the barrier comes down. With that in mind, I try to call Hermes. Naturally, it goes straight to voicemail.

Hello, darling, you've reached Hermes. I don't know why you're calling me instead of texting. Pretty sure this could've been an email. If you're still here, I suppose you can leave a voicemail after the beep. No promises on ever getting back to you. Ta!

I curse and hang up without leaving a message. That woman is a menace. If I hadn't seen the real person beneath her chaotic exterior, I might write her off as a loss. She'll come through, though. I have no doubt about that. She's gone through too much to ensure that Circe reaches Olympus. I don't know why, but at this point, the why matters less than the fact that she's not going to fuck me over. Probably.

I walk through the main entrance of the building, fully expecting to be stopped. The nervous looks the security guards give me aren't reassuring in the slightest. But they don't stop me.

As I take the elevator up to the top floor, a distant part of me wonders at the fact that Ariadne has managed to land on her feet so effectively. If it wasn't for me, she'd be marrying a man with more money than even her father. At least if his penthouse is anything to go by.

Ariadne meets me at the door, and I can only stare at the opulence of the room behind her. It's understated, but living with Minos for most of my life means I know what to look for. Wealth practically screams from every inch of the space.

I'm not usually one to let something like this get under my skin, but on the heels of wondering what kind of life I can actually offer Ariadne, it sends a sliver of uncertainty through me. That's the only excuse I have for saying, "Are you sure?"

She blinks. "What are you talking about?"

"Us. Leaving. All of it. Are you sure you want to walk away from this?"

"I'm going to pretend you didn't just say that to me." When I don't immediately respond, she sighs and lowers her voice. "Asterion, I've had people making decisions about my life since I was born. I'm not going to stand for it any longer. I told you my decision yesterday. I stand by it. Just because things have gone off the rails doesn't change anything. Not for me."

I exhale slowly. "It doesn't change anything for me, either."

"Good. Then we can figure out what the fuck we're going to do now. Come on."

She leads me deeper into the penthouse. In the kitchen, she has a full pot of coffee brewing. There's an empty mug in the sink, but that's the only evidence that Dionysus was here. "Where did your fiancé take off to?"

"He decided it was smarter to give his report in person. I don't know that it's going to make much of a difference. Hera doesn't seem like the type to handle disappointment well."

That's an understatement. I'd like to think that I'm overstating the danger, but I know better. That woman is a monster right down to her bones. Like recognizes like. Beyond that, we haven't gotten lucky yet in this mess, and I doubt we're going to start now. "Have you had a chance to look into that stuff you talked about?"

"Sort of." She wraps her arms around herself and glances out the window. "But there's something else we have to discuss first. When I talked to Dionysus this morning, he made me—us—an offer. It's a good one, I think."

"Tell me."

I'm braced for damn near anything except what comes out of her mouth. She shifts from foot to foot. "Things are going to get ugly here very quickly. I think we both know that. He offered to send me to the countryside, to one of his residences there. It's not a foolproof plan, but it's better than walking around the city with a target on my forehead. And he offered to send you and Icarus with me."

I stare. Yeah, I didn't see that coming. Dionysus continues to surprise me. At least this time it's not with drugs or threats. "That won't end up solving anything."

"I know. Circe will still come, and the Thirteen will continue to be a threat. But it would be a reprieve." She finally looks at me.

"And it would get you and my brother away from my father. I know he's only threatening me directly right now, but that's going to change when he realizes you aren't actively working with him. He'll kill you, Asterion. I can't let that happen."

I cross to her, closing the distance between us in a single step. As soon as I do, I can't believe I stood here for ten fucking minutes without having her in my arms. It feels like a missing piece of me sliding home. I rest my chin on top of her head. "You don't have to worry about me."

"Don't be naive. Of course I have to worry about you. You're actively putting yourself in danger."

"I won't let him hurt me."

She hugs me tighter. "The alternative doesn't make me feel better, either. I know he's a monster and he's responsible for so much evil and that he's hurt you and me and Icarus and even Theseus. I know that if he pushes you into a corner, if he makes you choose between us, that it will be no choice at all. But...he's still my father."

I stroke one hand over her hair. It's small comfort that she's stopped being worried about *me* being the one to hurt her. But that doesn't give me an easy answer to the obvious distress she's in. "I'll try very hard not to kill him. For you."

She laughs a little, the sound choked with emotion. "It really says something unflattering about both us and our current circumstances that that's a sentence you have to say. But I appreciate it nonetheless. Thank you."

The sound of heels on the tile floor has me twisting to put Ariadne behind me. At least this time, Hera doesn't have a chance to sneak up on me, but from the smirk on her face, I get the feeling she announced her presence on purpose. She glances to where Ariadne peers around my arm and raises her dark brows. "Isn't this cute and wholesome. How disgusting."

"Hello, Hera." Ariadne ignores my obvious attempt to stay between her and the other woman and steps around me. "I take it you spoke with Dionysus."

"Right down to business. Good." Hera props a hip against the kitchen counter. "You have to know this is unacceptable. The number of casualties we're looking at is astronomical. When we missed our first window, I was of the belief that we'd work together to create the proper timeline. Obviously that's not the case. Unless you can give me a legitimate solution—today—I'm pulling the plug on this whole mess."

At this point, she's welcome to it. But if she interferes overtly, then what little time I have left of Minos assuming that I'm still on his leash is over. That means things will get ugly. Fast. "We're working on a solution."

"That's what you've been saying from the beginning. You stalled about the blueprints, and now Minos is in a frenzy to get results. Isn't that right?" She looks from me to Ariadne and back again. "This is a mess of your own making. Clean it up, or I'll do it for you. You don't want that. Trust me."

"Hera." Ariadne takes a step forward but stops when I hook a hand into the back of her jeans. I don't want her closer to that woman than she has to be. Today Hera is dressed in a gray pantsuit that's fitted enough to not be able to hide a gun, but that doesn't mean I trust that she isn't hiding a weapon somewhere. Whatever leverage we might've had in our favor is quickly diminishing. At this point, if she thought it would serve her purposes, I wouldn't put it past her to see us dead.

For the first time, I am really fucking glad Ariadne is on the outs with her father. And that she's given all the information she has to the Olympians already. It ensures her value to them has already been spent. They might not have any reason to actively keep her safe beyond a promise, but they have no reason to hurt her, either.

Yet.

Hera gives her a cold look. "You have done very little but waste my time. I sincerely hope you're not about to ask me a question that will waste more of it. You know the terms of our deal. If you don't uphold your end of it, don't expect me to uphold mine."

It occurs to me that the way she's speaking seems to indicate that she has no idea the offer Dionysus made Ariadne. It's just as well. It's hard to threaten someone when they're miles and miles away. The Thirteen are more than capable of committing harm in the countryside—and so is Minos—but soon they'll have bigger things to worry about.

I could offer Hera information about the barrier, but she has a vested interest in keeping it up, and that outcome is unacceptable. That shit is coming down.

Ariadne swallows hard. "I understand. We'll figure out a way through this. Today."

"You'd better."

I give Hera a long look. "You could've just called. You didn't have to sprint down here in those ridiculous fucking heels to threaten us when we already know the stakes. Now who's wasting time?"

"Don't fuck with me, Minotaur." She starts to turn away. "I was down the street when Dionysus came to me. I decided it would behoove me to have this conversation face-to-face. I need your solution by tonight or the deal is off."

We watch her walk away and listen to the front door slam. Ariadne opens her mouth, but I hold up my hand. After a quick internal debate, I say, "Where's the bathroom?"

"The bathroom?" When I just stare, she shrugs and leads the way down the hall to a bathroom nearly the size of the apartment I'm keeping. Holy fuck, but this place is ridiculous.

I grip her elbow and guide her to stand next to the shower. "Give me a minute." I move around the room, turning on the fan as well as both sink faucets and all three of the showerheads. In a normal bathroom, that would be enough, but the sound barely fills in space. With a muttered curse, I flip off the sinks. "The shower."

"Asterion, there isn't a waking hour that I don't want you, but now is not the time to be fucking in the shower."

"In. Now." I pull off my clothes and step into the large space. It's like everything else about this apartment. Wasteful. After a couple seconds of cursing creatively, Ariadne follows me. I pull her close, and as tempting as it is to forget the reason why we're here, I force myself to keep on task. "We can't run to the countryside. We need to be here, in the city proper."

If it was possible to get through the barrier in the countryside, that's where Minos and Circe would've attacked. It's all farmland out there. Easy enough to march an army right through...except for the mountains. Olympus sits in a valley between mountains and sea.

I don't think anyone has been trying to excavate the mountains, but as best we can tell, the barrier slices right through them.

Which means if we go to the countryside, we'll be just as trapped when Circe lays siege.

"I understand that you think—"

"Sweetheart, listen to me." I take her shoulders and move her back just enough that she looks up to meet my eyes. "I've been in contact with Hermes. That barrier is coming down. And the second it does, we're getting the fuck out of here. We can't do that if we're miles away."

She stares. "We'll circle back to that little nugget of information in just a second. Even if the barrier comes down, it's not as if we have a clear path to get out of here. There are only two roads and the bay. You don't think the roads will be watched?"

They will be. And we can't even get to one, because it leads out of the lower city. I don't know what will happen to the barrier that runs along the river when the external one goes down, but we can't afford to assume that it will come down, too.

"We'll take a boat. Hermes is bringing the barrier down on *her* timeline, not Circe's, so there's a decent chance the blockage won't be in place when it happens. We can slip away before anyone knows what's happening."

I can't read her expression. I can't tell whether it's filled with hope or despair. Finally, she says, "I don't have a boat tucked somewhere convenient. Do you?"

"Not yet." The marina will have plenty of pleasure yachts of the rich and bored, but I haven't had reason to spend time there. "Guess we'll just have to steal one."

ARIADNE

TOO MUCH IS HAPPENING TOO FAST. I'VE BEEN KNOWN to pivot in my time, but going from planning to bring down the tower to flat out abandoning Olympus and fleeing for our lives... It's a lot. Steam swirls around us as I stare at Asterion. "So you're just going to, what? Sneak into the shipyard and steal a private vessel? Do they even *have* private vessels in the shipyard?"

"The shipyard is only for commercial shit. There's a marina right next to it. I think most of the fuckers in the upper circles have boats there, but you never hear about them using them."

I seem to remember reading something about the marina, but it never came into play for anything we were doing in Olympus, so I didn't bother worrying about it. I suspect that most of the people who own boats in Olympus do so simply for the sake of owning them, not to spend time on the water. The barrier cuts across the bay, so theoretically there's enough room for water sports, but if you misjudge your location, you could be in for a world of hurt.

Which also applies to us.

But we can't move forward until we address what he initially said. "Hermes? The woman who betrayed her city and people? The one who will betray us too if given half a chance?"

Water runs down his scarred face, and he's never looked more beautiful to me—or more intense. "I'm not looking for her loyalty, sweetheart. She wants the same thing I do right now, and that's enough for me. That barrier is coming down. When it does, we're going to be ready to get the fuck out of here."

He keeps saying that. And maybe he's right. Maybe it'll go exactly like he plans. The barrier will come down, and we will escape before any of the enemies on either side of the line make a move. But what then?

I don't want to ask the question. I don't know if the answer even matters. Except...it does matter. To me. "What happens after that, Asterion?"

I half expect him to brush me off, but he just strokes his thumbs over my shoulders. "I have some money stashed away. Some connections that can get us new papers. I don't expect that anyone is going to be looking for us at first—or maybe even at all—but there's no reason not to cover our trail as soon as we possibly can."

Hope flickers to life in my chest, but I stomp it down. "And then?"

He curses. "We talked about this. If you don't want to drive south to Brazil, we can do whatever the fuck we feel like. You have a whole room papered with dreams of traveling. I know you don't like hearing it, but I have a skill set that can keep us in good finances for a long time. Maybe forever."

I shiver despite the heat of the water hitting my body. I know what he's talking about. Doing the same job he did for my father: murder, wet work, a whole host of sins. I've never shied away from what Asterion is capable of, but...

Maybe I'm being too precious. I can do the backflips of logic necessary to justify the violence he's committed in service of my father. But can it truly be justified? No, probably not. Which means it's not that much of a reach to commit violence for other people, to put money in our pockets and ensure that we can live the life we desire.

But I'm so tired of living in the shadows. I've been aware of the consequences since I was a small child. Isn't that why I ended my pregnancy, at least in part?

I don't want that life. Not for me. Not for him, either. Not for any children we might one day have.

"Asterion." I gently place my hands on his scarred chest. "If we're leaving this all behind, then I want us to *leave it all behind*. The violence. The danger. The strings that come attached to every action and word. I'm so tired of being afraid. I know it won't be glamorous to live a normal life, but the price of all this is just too high. I don't want it anymore."

"You say that while standing in a penthouse that costs an unimaginable amount, after going on a shopping spree and eating in a fine dining establishment that we could never hope to afford on normal wages."

I can't tell if he honestly doesn't get it or if he's being intentionally difficult. "Yes. That's exactly what I'm saying. I realize it'll take some adjustment, but I'm game to make those adjustments if you are." Truth be told, Icarus might have more difficulty with it than either of us, but he'll have to deal with it. At least we'll be alive.

Asterion seems like he's about to keep arguing. I shake my head sharply before he can. "I want to travel with you. But eventually I want to settle down somewhere—with you. Have a life. Have a family. We can't do that if we're constantly looking over our shoulders because you still deal in the shadows." I look up at him pleadingly. "Isn't that what you want, too? Isn't that why you're going through all this to get me out of this city and away from my father?"

"Yes." The word sounds like it's ripped out of his chest. "Fuck, sweetheart, but this is going to be harder than either of us realize."

"I don't care. As long as we're together. As long as we're safe."

He nods slowly. "If I trust you on this, then you need to trust me to get us out of here. That means no trip to the countryside. You need to stay out of trouble and stay safe until the barrier comes down."

I don't know how I'm supposed to do that when Hera seems one step away from violence. Our time is disappearing, slipping through our fingers like sand. We can only delay so long, but... "The tower. You can't let it happen. Hera thinks she can stop them, but I *know* you can. Please, Asterion."

He slides his hands down my arms and then takes my waist, pulling me back to tuck me against his body. "Ariadne, I know you. You were never going to be able to live with those kinds of losses. I'll take care of it."

I recognize the hypocrisy in telling him that I want us to leave the violence behind, then asking him to do violence in the next breath. This is how it works, though. You make deals with yourself, consider what losses are acceptable and what aren't. This is the life we're living currently. The one I want to leave behind. I don't want to have to weigh a handful of lives against thousands. I don't want that decision to be in my control.

"I love you."

He goes so still that I'm not certain he's breathing. We stare at each other, the only movement the water cascading around us. Asterion's fingers flex on my hips. "Say it again," he whispers.

"I love you." Speaking those three words feels a little like throwing myself off a cliff and waiting for gravity to take hold. Inevitable. I don't need to tell him that it's been true for years. There are no secrets between us. Not anymore.

He strokes my hips like he can't quite stop himself. His frown is downright fearsome. "I'll be a shit dad, Ariadne. I might be a shit husband, too. I don't know what the fuck I'm doing. You deserve better."

I slide my hands up to cup his square jaw. "We'll figure it out. We'll figure all of it out. Together. I'm hardly a paragon of, well, literally anything. We'll fuck it up and we'll make it right and we'll learn and do better." I smile a little, though it doesn't feel happy. "We can't do any worse than my father."

"When you say it like that, the bar is on the floor." He exhales slowly. "Okay, sweetheart. We'll do it your way. I'll play hero long enough to get us out of here, and we'll only keep our connections to the shadows until we get those papers and disappear properly. Deal?"

I should have learned a long time ago not to lean on hope. The world has a way of kicking you in the teeth when you least expect it. I may have been protected from some of those consequences by virtue of my birth, but that doesn't mean I am fully immune. The challenges before us are astronomical. Asterion is the most fearsome and capable man I know. But with both my father's team and the Olympians working against him...

I don't know. I just don't know. We're so close to getting something I barely allowed myself to dream of, and we've never been more in danger of having it snatched away. "Be careful. If anything happens to you—"

"Don't worry, sweetheart. This is what I do." He presses a kiss to my forehead, the bridge of my nose, my lips. "I love you, too. It feels like I've spent my entire life doing nothing but loving you."

I'm not sure which one of us moves first. He tenses, I go up on my toes, and then I'm kissing him properly. We don't have time for this, and yet we've never had time for this. Our entire relationship has been stolen moments. What's one more?

Asterion lifts me, and I barely have a chance to worry about slippery bodies in the shower before he pins my back to the cool tile wall and steps between my thighs. Did I really think there was even the slightest chance I would fall? Silly me.

He'll never let me fall.

His hard cock presses directly to my center. I tangle my fingers in his hair and kiss him with everything I have, letting my desperation take hold and drive me. It's nothing so simple as lust between us now. It never has been. I just want us to be okay. To make it through and have a chance at the life I've barely allowed myself to dream about. I never thought I'd get it. I still might not. So many things can go wrong.

But we have right now. And we have each other.

He rolls his hips, dragging the length of his cock up and down my center, through the wetness of my desire and over my clit. It's perfect and nowhere near enough, both at the same time.

He thrusts into me slowly, the angle absolutely perfect, each stroke winding me tighter and tighter. "When we're out of here. When we're safe. I'm going to put a ring on your finger and a baby in your belly. We're going to have that family, Ariadne. But not till we're ready. No more regrets between us."

My head falls back against the tile, and I'm helpless to do anything but take what he gives me. Pleasure, yes, but it's so much more than that. He's taking care of me in his own way. He always has. "Promise me."

"I'll promise you anything."

I tug on his hair, pulling him back to me. I speak my next words against his lips even as my orgasm starts to pull me under. "I want that, Asterion. The ring. The baby. All of it. Promise me. Promise me we're going to get through this and we'll have that one day." I know I'm asking for the moon, but I don't care. If he makes a promise, then I'll believe him.

"I promise, Ariadne." He keeps fucking me as I orgasm, as I pull him tighter against me, as he loses control and grinds into me, driving me to new heights and coming deep inside me. Asterion rests his forehead against mine, both of our chests heaving. "I'm not going to let anything get in our way, sweetheart. Not Hera. Not Circe. Not even the gods themselves."

"I believe you. I love you."

"I love you, too." He eases me back to my feet, and a comfortable silence falls between us as he grabs some soap and washes the mess away from our bodies. Everything is changing and yet nothing has changed. The future may be promised, but it's still far too nebulous to bet on.

There are so many barriers in our way, from the mess with the tower to the barrier coming down. As fear tries to take hold, I draw forth Asterion's promise and hold it close to my heart.

We'll get through this. We have to.

THE MINOTAUR

27

I DON'T WANT TO LEAVE ARIADNE ALONE, BUT AT THIS point, standing by her side will do more harm than good. Knowing that doesn't stop dread from taking root inside me as we dress after the shower. Too many things can go wrong. Too many things already *are* going wrong.

"Stay in the penthouse today." I hesitate. "Please."

Ariadne looks like she wants to argue but finally nods. "I already planned on staying here and seeing what I can find on my computer. That's where I'm the most useful right now. It also can't hurt to be out of sight, out of mind, for my father."

I don't tell her that that sort of thing only works when she's playing the obedient daughter. Over the years, Minos only pulled her out when he wanted to use her to make an impression on someone. When it comes to punishments? He knows how to hold a grudge; he seems to love them more than he loves his children.

Saying as much will only hurt her. Besides, she already knows.

She's a smart woman, even if she has a hard time acknowledging just what a monster her father is.

I brush a kiss to her lips. "I'll update you as soon as I have information."

"I'll do the same for you."

I don't want to leave her alone, but there's nothing else to do. I have to see what Aeacus is planning, and the fact that Minos has left me alone overnight instead of demanding more answers has me fucking worried. As I step out onto the sidewalk, I weigh which route is the better option.

In the end, it's decided for me.

My phone pings with a text from Icarus, of all people.

Icarus: You better get back here. It's bad.

It must be for him to reach out to me for... Is this a plea for help? I don't fucking know. And I can't forget that he might want Ariadne out of the city and free, but in his perfect vision of the future, I'm not involved. That fucker wants me dead. Which means this could be a trap.

But I don't think so. It doesn't feel like a trap that *he's* put together, at least. It takes me barely ten minutes to walk to Minos's apartment building. He's not as close as he wants to be to the center city, but he's too close for my peace of mind.

I head up the stairs, but instead of going to the main penthouse where the family lives, I stop the floor below and go to the apartment that Minos likes to pretend doesn't exist. It's not much of a secret these days—both Ariadne and Icarus are aware of it, and Theseus found out about it before his falling-out with Minos.

Theseus. I don't spend much time thinking about that fucker. He was always just another flavor of enemy. The competition that Minos liked to play one against the other. He's not a friend, no, but spend more than a decade with a person and you build a kind of intimacy through shared experiences.

Or maybe Ariadne's softness is rubbing off on me. I don't fucking know why I pull out my phone, but when I realize my body's moving on autopilot, I make no effort to stop myself from dialing him. I don't honestly expect him to pick up. We haven't talked in weeks. He might not be Hephaestus anymore, but he stayed married to that Olympian wife of his. Last I heard, he and Pandora had moved in with her. One big, happy, complicated family.

Something curdles in my stomach, and I'm surprised to find it's jealousy. He's living in a city that's about to be ash, married to a woman I wouldn't willingly turn my back on, and yet the asshole seems so happy it's sickening.

I am so distracted by my thoughts that I don't register that the call hasn't gone to voicemail until Theseus curses and says my name again. "What the fuck do you want, Minotaur?"

That's the question, isn't it? I don't know what I want. Or at least I don't know why I called. I glance at the closed door to the apartment and take a couple steps back. "We aren't friends."

"No shit."

"But if we were friends, I'd give you the courtesy of letting you know what's coming." I don't know what the fuck I'm doing. I should just hang up and be done with it. But I don't.

He's silent for several long moments. "You're right. We're not friends. But I'm listening."

"It doesn't matter what the Olympians do or what plots and schemes they put into motion. The barrier is coming down. There's no stopping it. If you're smart, you'll take you and yours and be ready to leave the moment it does. Escape in the chaos before either side has a chance to settle into a siege."

He laughs, the sound filled with bitterness. "I honestly can't tell if you're being genuine or not. But I'll give you the benefit of the doubt this time. My wife is a Kasios. She might have relinquished her title at the same time I did mine, but she's never leaving the city. Which means neither am I."

I exhale slowly. Once Theseus sets his mind on something, nothing can dissuade him. Sure as fuck not me. I don't point out that this decision puts Pandora in danger, too. I don't ask what Adonis thinks of the situation. Their little poly knot is filled with fools with stars in their eyes. Eris might be ruthless to a fault and vicious as the day is long, but as Theseus said, she's a Kasios, as are her siblings Zeus and Ares. That family is baked right into the foundation of Olympus. "It's the wrong choice."

"Without a doubt. But I'll gut anyone who comes for her. Including you."

I snort. "Your wife and lovers are safe from me. I have other priorities." I hesitate, but there's nothing more to say. I've delivered my warning. Whether he chooses to ignore it or do something about it is up to him. And yet I can't stop myself from saying one last thing. "It's going to happen soon. Be ready."

"I will."

I really am going soft, because I don't leave it at that. "And, Theseus? Stay away from the city center for the next week or so. Especially Dodona Tower."

The dark amusement is gone from his tone. "What do you know?"

I hang up without answering. With the Thirteen fracturing, there are clear lines forming. Zeus's siblings will fall in with him. Hera only seems to want Zeus dead, but she doesn't seem like the type to let a little collateral damage get in the way of her desires, especially if she sees them as the enemy too. Theseus's wife is in nearly as much danger as Zeus himself.

Ideally, the Olympians will keep chasing their tails until the barrier comes down and they have bigger enemies to worry about. But nothing has gone to plan to date, so I won't place any bets on it.

There's nothing else to do but walk through the door.

Or at least I try. My key doesn't work. I stare down at the lock, my brain struggling to catch up with reality. "Well, fuck. It's a trap." My time of playing both sides against the middle is over. It was inevitable, but it's fucking inconvenient.

I almost turn around right then and there. Minos has no reason to take me alive. If he knows I betrayed him—and all evidence points to exactly that—then he's going to attempt to kill me when I walk through the door upstairs. The smart thing would be to turn around and get out of here. Ariadne isn't safe with Dionysus. If I could get to her, whoever he sends to replace me will be able to as well, even with the increased security.

But there's Icarus to consider. He called me, which means he's with Minos now. Ariadne won't leave without her brother, and this might be my only chance to get him out. "Fuck. *Fuck.*"

There's no choice. I head upstairs to the penthouse that Minos keeps with what's left of his family. It's almost humiliating to have to knock on the door and wait for entry. Or it would be if I gave a shit what he thought of me.

It's Icarus who opens the door, and he looks even worse than the last time I saw him. The bones in his face stand out starkly, and if he's still beautiful, it's tempered with his obvious despair. He looks me up and down without much interest. "So the dog still comes when he's called."

I stare. I know Ariadne wants to bring him with us when we leave, but I doubt he's going to come peacefully. It seems far more likely that he's going to make our lives miserable, intentionally or not. But leaving him behind will hurt her. That I won't allow.

I grab the front of his shirt and pull him close enough to smell the alcohol on his breath. It's a layered scent, both stale and fresh, which indicates he's been drinking long enough for it to start seeping out of his pores. Damn it. It's going to be a nightmare getting him out of here. "I need you to sober up, and do it quickly."

Icarus's head lolls on his shoulders. He blinks at me blearily. "What are you up to?"

I don't care if he loves his sister or if she loves him right back. Icarus is weak—a liability. But I love Ariadne and she loves him, so I'll make it work. "We're leaving."

"The fuck we are." He tries to pull away but only succeeds in swaying in my grip. "Let go."

"Your sister needs you." I give him a shake, my frustration causing me to be a little too rough. Or his drunkenness causing him to be too boneless. "Prove that you're worth something and sober the fuck up. If you don't, she's going to get hurt, and it will be *your* fault." It's not the truth, but I don't fucking care.

After this morning, it feels like the damned walls of the city are closing in around us. There's not enough time and too many things to do... Too many things that could go wrong.

Icarus shoves ineffectively at my chest. He's like a child throwing a fit. "You don't get to talk to me about my sister. Not when you want her dead."

I shoot a look around the penthouse, but Minos is nowhere to be found. That won't last long. We're wasting valuable time, but I need Icarus to cooperate if I'm going to get him out of here. I fight to keep my voice even. It would be so much easier if I just knocked him out and hauled him from the building, but I need my hands free to ensure we make it out. "If I wanted her dead, she would be dead."

I feel the air change in the room before Minos steps around the corner. The last time I spoke to him, he seemed to be unraveling, but there's no evidence of it now. He stands tall and proud—and absolutely furious. He looks at me just like he did that first day when he brought me into his household—as if I'm shit on the bottom of his shoe.

The truth. Not the faux fatherly charm, not the disciplined commander. He thinks I'm garbage, and now he's not even bothering to hide it.

"Minotaur. I see you finally decided to grace us with your presence." He shifts, and I catch the dull metal gleam of a gun held at his side. "Come in."

Yeah, that's not going to happen. The door's behind me, only a few feet away. I'm nearly certain I can get there before Minos can plug me full of bullets. I look at Icarus, and though his eyes are still hazy with drunkenness, the seriousness of the moment seems to have penetrated. He shifts a little closer to me—and farther away from his father. Too little, too late.

"You changed the locks." I grip the back of Icarus's shirt, out of Minos's sight, and tug him back a few inches. Closer to the door. This is a clusterfuck, but I'll get him out of here. For Ariadne.

His grip shifts on the gun. "You know how it is in the city, boy. Can't trust anyone."

I ease back a step, pulling Icarus with me. "I am—"

"No, *I* am done with your lies." Minos lifts the gun and points it directly at my chest. "You said it yourself—if you wanted to follow my orders and kill my traitorous daughter, you would've done it by now. I've been distracted, so it took me a little longer than normal to figure it out. That's done now. I've passed the order to someone more capable and loyal than you will ever be."

Fuck. *Fuck.* It's exactly like I suspected. Worse than I suspected, because I would have preferred Minos attempt to kill me before he sent someone else after her. There's no time. We have to get out of here. Now. "Who did you send?"

"You won't live long enough to figure it out."

Icarus moves first, tearing himself from my grip and throwing his lean body in front of mine. I see the exact moment Minos decides he doesn't care if he shoots his son in the process of shooting me. *Damn it.* I grab Icarus around his waist and shove us against the wall as Minos pulls the trigger. He's so skinny. It's easy to shield him with my body.

I scramble for the doorknob, my hand closing around it as fire explodes in my shoulder. That motherfucker shot me, and not even well. I've been moving through pain for my entire life; a shoulder wound sucks, but it's not the worst I've experienced. It's nothing to get the door open and shove Icarus through it ahead of me.

We hit the hallway at a dead sprint, or as close to it as we can manage with him stumbling drunkenly and pain flaring with every step I take. The elevator will take too long to get to us, and we'll be sitting ducks while we wait. Instead, I hook him around the waist and haul him through the doorway to the stairwell.

He tries to stop three flights down, but I grab his arm and keep him moving. Blood is a hot, wet cascade down my back. My head feels a little woozy. That isn't a good sign. When my adrenaline crashes, I suspect it will be a crash in more ways than one.

On the second floor, I tighten my grip on Icarus's arm and hold him back. "Need to go through a side door."

He's panting and his sweat is more alcohol than water, but he already seems a little more sober than he was a few minutes ago. "You think he called security?"

"He doesn't have to when he has his own people to call." I take the chance and grab my phone. We need to keep moving, but I can't stop thinking about what Minos said. Ariadne is in danger. I don't know who the fuck he sent, but I'm not with her to protect her.

She answers immediately. "Asterion? Is everything okay?"

I'm sure as fuck not about to tell her that in the time since she last saw me, I've gotten myself shot. There are more important things in play currently. "Your father called in someone else to take over the job. Your brother and I are on our way to you. Be ready when we get there. We're getting the fuck out of here."

ARIADNE

ASTERION HANGS UP BEFORE I CAN ASK ANY QUESTIONS, but it's just as well. There's no time. If he was anyone else, I might assume that he was overstating the danger. He's not. I knew that there was a good chance I'd have to escape in a hurry, so I already have my bag packed. I'm just vain enough to mourn leaving so many of my gorgeous new clothes behind, but I have to be able to move quickly, and I can't be weighed down. Asterion might be a machine, but Icarus and I are hardly people capable of long-distance cardio. Better to plan to carry my own shit.

It's tempting to start for the street, but with Dionysus's security in place, the penthouse really is the safest place for me to wait. Maybe. Hopefully. He did mention increasing security after...last time. Surely it's enough to deter whoever my father has sent.

If Asterion has my brother, that means he's coming from our father's apartment. It's a good ten-minute walk, give or take, depending on if they're running or trying to move stealthily.

I drop my bag on the floor near the chair by the entrance and pull out my laptop. It takes seconds to let myself through the back door I created in the building's security system. I make a mental note to tell Dionysus about it after I'm gone so that he can fix the problem—or to just fix it myself—as I pull up the feed from the security cameras.

I may not have had much interaction with my father's people aside from Theseus and Asterion, but I know most of them on sight, thanks to my research. I click through the feeds of the entrances, wondering who my father will send to kill me. There's a small possibility it will be one of Circe's people they snuck into the city, but I don't think so. Admitting his daughter turned traitor and that he needs help to deal with her is far too much weakness for my father's liking. No, he'll deal with this in-house.

It's entirely possible that I'm being paranoid. A smart assassin will try to draw me out from my defensible position or simply wait for the perfect opportunity. But my father is frustrated with his recent failures, and he'll be looking for a win. Since Asterion and Icarus are together, that means... Honestly, I'm not entirely certain what that means.

Asterion went to the apartment to keep my father happy so that he can maintain access to the team planning the bombing of Dodona Tower. If he is warning me off, it means something went wrong. It means he took my brother and they're running, and he wouldn't have done that unless he had to. There was a fight, maybe. Definitely a confrontation with my father.

If that's the case, then my father knows he's lost his pet monster and likely both his children as well. He won't want to wait. He'll send his pet assassin now, and it won't be with some clever ploy to pry me out of the penthouse.

Tension courses through me as I flip through the security screens again. Maybe it's paranoia, but I'm certain I can feel the hunter closing in. The desire to run is almost overwhelming. I breathe deeply and slowly, but it only makes my brain buzz harder.

I catch a familiar face just as I'm clicking away from the current screen of the hotel lobby. I click back and lean closer. The cameras are only slightly higher end than what you can find in generic buildings, which means zooming in will cause too much pixelation to see the person clearly.

They walk across the lobby in a loose, ambling gait. I click through the cameras situated around that space, but they always seem to have their face averted.

As if they know where the cameras are and they don't want to be seen.

The small hairs on the back of my neck stand on end. The sensation only gets worse as they chat with the security guard and pass over what appears to be an ID. There's nothing overtly wrong, and yet I can't shake the feeling that I'm staring at a predator.

The security guard laughs at something they say and waves them toward the elevator. The person turns, and I finally get a proper look at their face. All the blood rushes from my head. *Phaedra.* They grin at the camera and give a little salute.

As if they know I'm watching.

They don't hesitate in their path to the elevator. It's only when the doors slide shut behind them that I realize what's happening. They're taking the damn elevator directly to the penthouse. "Shit!"

I slam my computer shut and shove it into my backpack. I can't afford to assume that Phaedra doesn't have access to the penthouse. Asterion sure as fuck did.

I have to get out of here, and I have to do it now. The elevator is now closed to me, and the main stairwell doesn't go all the way to the penthouse. But there has to be another way. Fire codes are a thing, and they require there to be an emergency exit with stairs on every floor.

In the hours I've spent in this place, I've been over every inch of it, and I've seen no sign of a staircase or a door that leads where it shouldn't. The only room I *haven't* explored is the primary bedroom.

I rush into the room now. I only got a glimpse this morning, and I don't slow down enough to appreciate the cool and soothing space Dionysus has created for himself. There's no door to be seen, just an open archway leading into the bathroom. With nowhere else to go, I step through it.

The bathroom is lovely, decorated in the same cool gray tones, but what catches and holds my attention is the door I can see peeking through the clothes in his closet though a second archway. "Thank the gods." I hurry to it and shove the clothes to the side. It's fancier than any emergency exit has a right to be—and it's locked. "*Shit.*"

I turn around, panic flaring, and stop short. Dionysus obviously never expected anyone to come in here, because the key for the door hangs on a hook tucked right inside the archway. "Fuck the gods; thank you, Dionysus."

I grab the key, but my hands are shaking so much, I can barely fit it into the lock. I just manage to slide it home when, in the distance, I hear the front door crack open.

Phaedra is here.

As if thinking their name summoned them, their melodious voice rings out. "Ariadne. I know you're here, love. I have no interest in hide-and-seek. Your father would like a word."

I bet he would. But if they think dangling my father's orders in front of me is going to do anything but cause me to flee, they have another think coming.

I turn the key as silently as I can. The penthouse is large, but it's not *that* large. I'd expect Phaedra to systematically clear the space, which means they'll reach the primary bedroom last. That only means the difference of a few minutes, but it's all I have. There's no time to go back to lock the bedroom door. It won't slow them down much anyway.

Bless Dionysus or whoever maintains the door, because it opens soundlessly on greased hinges. I slip into the dim stairwell and ease it shut behind me. There's a lock on this side, too. I've never seen that before in an emergency exit door, but then I've never seen one that leads directly into the bedroom of a penthouse. I force my hand steady and lock the door behind me.

If I'm lucky, Phaedra will assume that I slipped out without them realizing it. If I'm not, they'll simply be waiting for me on the ground floor when I finally make my way down this narrow stairwell. And it *is* narrow. It's nothing like the wide public one. There are no cameras in here, either.

In fact, as I descend flight after flight, I realize there are no other doors in here to the other floors. Which means this isn't an emergency exit for the entire building—only for Dionysus.

I send a quick text to Asterion telling him that I had to leave the apartment and then I'll meet him when he gets close. He doesn't answer, and the text doesn't switch over from delivered to read. Worry worms through me. He's okay. He has to be. But I can't spend any energy worrying about him right now. My own life is in danger.

I force myself to listen over the pounding of my heart as I descend the stairwell. Dionysus living on the top floor meant great things for the defensiveness of his penthouse, at least in theory. It also means that I have dozens of flights to conquer. If Phaedra comes through that door at the top of the stairs, I'm fucked.

Worst of all, I have to keep pacing myself, because my thighs are shaking and my breath is harsh daggers in my lungs. And still, Asterion doesn't text me back.

Halfway down, I pause to catch my breath, and guilt has me texting Dionysus a warning. He's not the target, but that doesn't mean he couldn't end up as a casualty. He's taken great care with me, and he might be one of the Thirteen, but that doesn't mean he deserves to be cut down for being in the wrong place at the wrong time. Naturally, he doesn't respond to my text, either. Because of course not.

I nearly weep at the sight of the door that leads out of the stairwell. It has another lock that I assume matches the key in my hand. It's tempting to unlock it and run for my life, but I force myself to sit down and pull out my laptop. I have a pretty good idea where the stairwell leads—to an exit on the north side of the block—but there's no reason to get sloppy now. The lack of cameras in the stairwell suggests there should be a lock on the exit, but if there's not, I'm practically jumping around and waving my arms until someone notices me.

Not to mention I just pushed myself to the edge of exhaustion coming down the stairs. I'm not going to be able to outrun anyone in this state. I'm in the process of pulling up the security feeds when my phone buzzes at my hip.

Asterion: We're a block north. Where are you?

I make a sound perilously close to a sob. He's okay…unless something's happened to him and his killer stole his phone.

No. Damn it *no*. I can't afford to believe that—but I can't afford to ignore the possibility, either. I glance at the security feeds and go still. Phaedra stalks through the lobby, their casual ambling gait turned into something fierce and angry. I hold my breath, but they don't exit. Instead, they check themselves, seem to recenter, and wave cheerily at the security guard. Then they head down the hallway deeper into the first floor.

In my direction.

Damn it. I have to move now. I shove my computer back into my bag and rush for the door. I type a quick text as I unlock it.

Me: Meet me where we had a special meal.

It's a risk. The Dryad is farther away from my current location than Asterion is right now, but I have to believe that he'll know what I'm talking about and meet me there. If it's really him. I take a deep breath and pull open the door.

I expected it to lead into a hallway or maybe the basement. It doesn't. Instead, I am on a little landing just below street level. I can see slices of pale-blue sky in between skyscrapers and hear traffic and people walking. My legs almost can't conquer the twelve steps it takes to get to street level, but I force myself forward through sheer willpower alone.

I couldn't run if I wanted to. It's smarter not to anyway. Instead,

I fall into step with a group of what appears to be college girls. One of them shoots me a strange look, but there are enough people out and about that they don't say anything about it.

It takes everything I have not to glance over my shoulder every other step to see if Phaedra is following. If they were savvy enough to realize I managed to escape through the stairwell, then it's only a matter of time before they start tracing my steps. Calling a car might be smart, but it would require waiting in one location for it to arrive. As exhausted as I am, it's still better to keep moving on foot.

The group I'm walking with splits off after two blocks, and only then do I allow myself to look behind me. The sidewalks are busy at this time a day. It's hard to pick out just one person from the crowd. Phaedra could be ten feet behind me and I'd never know. The thought makes me shudder.

My phone buzzes in my hand, and it startles me so intensely, I almost drop it. My breath catches in my throat when I read the words there.

Asterion: Go through the door on your right.

I turn to my right. At first glance, I have no idea what the store sells. The windows are clogged with everything from wine to blankets to stuffies. Olympus doesn't get tourists because of the barrier, so I don't know why they have what appears to be a souvenir shop here, but I duck through the door all the same. Inside, it's even more claustrophobic. The aisles between racks of clothing and other paraphernalia are so narrow that my body brushes them as I pass.

There's no one at the counter, and I don't know if that's

comforting or worrisome. Again, it strikes me that someone could have taken Asterion's phone. But the only reason I would be on this street at this time is if I was heading from Dionysus's building to the Dryad. And the only way they would know *that* is if they understood my reference earlier. There's no reason to think someone who isn't Asterion would know. No one saw me with him that night.

I think.

When a familiar shadow falls across me, I almost sob in relief. "Asterion." But then I get a good look at him. He's wavering on his feet a little, carrying himself with a brittleness that would be familiar if I could just focus long enough to understand. "What happened?"

"Not here," he rumbles.

I swallow down the questions bubbling up in my chest and follow him deeper into the store. He has an even harder time with the narrow aisles than I do. But at least with his bigger body knocking the clothing racks out of the way, I'm brushing against fewer of them.

We duck into an employee break room. There's no employee to be found, but my brother sits in one of the folding chairs with his head in his hands. He looks up as we walk through the door, and a storm breaks across his expression. "You made it."

My knees choose that moment to buckle. Asterion sweeps me into his arms before I have a chance to make contact with the floor. His grunt is almost silent, but it goes through me like a rocket. "Put me down. You're hurt." *That's* why he's moving so stiffly. I should've recognized it. I would have if I wasn't so exhausted.

"Hurt." My brother gives a mirthless laugh. "That's one way to put it. He got shot. By our father."

THE MINOTAUR

WE MAKE QUITE THE TRIO AS I LEAD ARIADNE AND ICARUS through the back door and into the car I called. Doing so is a calculated risk, but I'm still bleeding, and the other two look dead on their feet. If the taxi driver tries to fuck with us, I'll just kill them. I start to rattle off the address for my apartment, but Icarus laughs and interrupts me. He holds Ariadne's hand in a white-knuckled grip, but his expression is relaxed. "Come now, Minotaur. My father has known about that apartment since the beginning. He allowed you to have that freedom, but don't think for a second there aren't people waiting for us there."

I wasn't trying to be overly secretive with the apartment, but I didn't advertise it, either. It's irritating as fuck that I didn't realize how closely Minos was having me watched. "We have nowhere else to go."

Ariadne stirs. "That's not true." She leans forward to catch the cab driver's eye. "Do you want to earn a huge fare with one hundred percent tip?"

He laughs a little. "Sure, lady. Where are we headed?"

The address she gives doesn't sound familiar, but from the driver's response, it's some distance. He holds out his hand. "Listen, if you want to go there, I'm going to need half up front."

She sends me a pleading glance; I'm already pulling out my wallet. The amount the driver requests is absurd, but there's no point fighting now. The longer we stay in one place, the easier we are to track. I still don't breathe a sigh of relief as he pulls from the curb and enters into traffic. "Where are you taking us?" I murmur.

"Dionysus has no fewer than three houses in the country." She speaks softly, matching my tone. "They're going to expect us to scurry to your apartment or one of our allies in the upper city. It will take them longer to figure out we've gone outside the city proper. Long enough that we should be able to figure out our next steps and anticipate theirs."

It's hardly a foolproof plan, but it's better than what I have. I lean back against the seat and hiss out a breath when my wound makes contact. The bleeding has slowed, but I'm pretty sure the bullet is still embedded in my muscles. It sure as fuck feels like it. My shirt is plastered to my back; it's going to be a bitch to get off.

We've barely gone six blocks before my phone starts buzzing. I need Ariadne's help to pull it out, and when I see the name flashing there, I curse. *Hermes.* "Now isn't a good time."

"That's quite the hostile greeting, and when I come bearing gifts, too. How thoughtless."

I almost hang up then and there, but our list of allies is rapidly shrinking, and while I would never be foolish enough to list Hermes among them, she's the only chance I have to bring the barrier down. Or, more accurately, to bring it down on my schedule instead of Circe's.

"Being shot puts some motherfuckers in a bad mood. You didn't answer when I called earlier."

"I was busy," she says blithely. "But now isn't a good time for you to leave the city. I need you here. I found the last component we need to bring down the barrier. We can do it. Tonight."

Tonight.

I thought I wanted it to happen soon, but now that it's on the horizon, I feel so unprepared. I don't have my shit. I don't have any weapons beyond a single gun with a single clip. I have an exhausted Ariadne and an Icarus who's likely in shock with me. Bringing them is out of the question, but I have nowhere to put them, either. "It's going to have to wait."

"Can't wait. This is our chance. I can probably do it myself, but you said you wanted in, and I'm not above using the tools available to me."

Telling her why I'm hesitating means trusting her in a way I'm not prepared to do. But I don't see how I have any other choice. "I have Ariadne and Icarus with me."

"Ohhh." She manages to stretch those two letters into three syllables. "Why didn't you just say so? Easy-peasy answer there. They can hide out while we get this done. I'll text you an address—or rather, two. One for you. One for them. See you in an hour." She hangs up before I can think of an argument.

Within seconds, two texts come through. Two addresses, just like I was promised. One is on the north side of the theater district.

The other is to the east, tucked in the outskirts of the shipyard. I stare at them for several beats too long and curse.

Me: Which is which?
Hermes: You, shipyard. Them, other. Code is 69420.

Fuck, but I don't trust her. Unfortunately, I don't have any other choice. I catch the cab driver's eye. "Change of plans. Keep the change, but I need you to drop me here and take them to this address." I rattle off the one in the theater district. As much as I want to go with them, if I only have an hour, I need to get to the other location—and fast.

Ariadne grabs my arm. "What are you doing? You've been *shot.*"

"We might not get another chance like this. If I'm with Hermes when she brings the barrier down, then I *know* when it's coming down. If we don't escape in the direct aftermath, we might not be able to do it at all."

"Then I'm coming with you."

Fuck no. My woman isn't trained the same way I am, and if whatever Hermes has planned is dangerous at all, it means *Ariadne* will be in danger. She's not ruthless like I am. She's not a fucking killer like I am, either. If she came with me, she'd be a walking target, and that I can't allow.

I open my mouth to shut this shit down but pause. She's staring at me with shining dark eyes and worry written across her pretty features. She's not demanding to accompany me because of some arrogant reason—she's afraid *for* me.

I take a ragged breath and fight the pain from my voice. "No, sweetheart. We're going to do this quick and dirty, and if you come, you could get hurt."

"Or you could distract him so *he* gets hurt," Icarus pipes in.

I glare at him. He's trying to help, but fuck if I want her to worry any more than she's going to. "I am not going to be hurt."

"You've been shot."

I swallow down my frustration and pain. "I'll get patched up before doing anything else—*if* you promise to go directly to this address and stay there."

Ariadne searches my face. "Come back to me."

"I will. I promise."

"Okay." I don't like the way her shoulders slump in defeat, but she nods and that has to be enough. "I'll go to the house. I'll stay there. I promise, too."

"Thank you." I hook the back of her neck and drag her into a quick kiss. "I'm going to text you the code. Do your best to get in without being seen. I'll call you—not text—as soon as I have a timeline."

"Stay safe. We haven't come this far for you to sacrifice yourself nobly."

I force myself to smile because I know it will reassure her. "Haven't you figured it out by now, sweetheart? I don't have a noble bone in my body." I point at the curb. "Drop me here. You've been paid, so get them where they need to go." I let my tone deliver the threat I don't speak explicitly.

The driver holds up his hands. "I've been paid. You got nothing to worry about from me, mister." He pulls to the curb too fast, the movement throwing me back against the seat. My wound screams in agony, but I just grit my teeth and push through it. There will be time to bandage me up later. Hopefully.

I step out onto the sidewalk and watch as the cab pulls back into traffic. It takes no time at all to send the code to Ariadne. She responds with a string of emojis, which don't mean a damn thing except that she's trying to reassure me in her own way. I hate letting her out of my sight, but there's no other way.

It takes longer than I'd like to flag down another cab, and as a result, it's almost exactly an hour later when I walk through the door of the address Hermes gave me.

At first, I think I'm in the wrong place. This little building is dingy in a way that suggests no one has walked through it in a decade or two. Dust is coated thick on the floor, and the ceiling is more cobwebs than not.

Did she set me up?

"I bet you're wondering if I set you up." Hermes's laughter fills the space. "Come into my parlor, said the spider to the fly."

I almost turn around and walk out right then and there. Working with Hermes wouldn't be worth the headache if not for the proven fact that she can take care of business. But I don't have a choice. One by one, my avenues have been closed to me. Minos is hunting us. It's only a matter of time before the Olympians are, too.

There's nothing to do but walk deeper into the building. I get the sense that it was an office space at one point, but it's hard to tell. "I thought you said time is of the essence. Why are you playing games?"

"Life is too short, Minotaur. You have to get your kicks where you can. And I like when people underestimate me. It allows me the element of surprise."

Impossible to determine where she is. The open space makes sound bounce strangely. I resign myself to this experience and keep moving. "I don't fuck with that. If people underestimate you, then they're always trying you. If they're scared of you, they don't try you at all."

"A difference of opinion." She steps out of a shadowy doorway on the other side of the room. And promptly sneezes. "Gods, I know Poseidon likes to stay in his hidey hole, but would it kill him to send a maid through these outbuildings from time to time?"

I look around again with renewed interest. "This is one of his buildings?"

"It was. Long time ago. This isn't the city center or the shipyards or the university, so people like to pretend it doesn't exist." There's something in her voice, something that sounds almost like memory. She beams at me before I can confidently nail it down. "You look like absolute shit. Rough day?"

"You could say that."

"Well, I need you in tiptop shape, so get in here and let's patch you up. We have a little bit of time before we can move anyway."

I reluctantly follow her through the doorway into a room that makes me question what the space I just left was. Because it's set up like a dorm room, with two faded twin beds pressed up against opposite walls and a doorway that leads into a bathroom. At least the dust isn't as bad in here. "What is this place?"

"It doesn't matter anymore." She grabs my arm and I allow her to lead me into the bathroom. Hermes crouches down and pulls a sparkling new first aid kit from beneath the sink. At my look of confusion, she shrugs. "You never know when you might need something like this. A smart person would keep them stashed around the city so they're never far away."

I shake my head. "You're Hermes, party girl and irreverent trickster. According to MuseWatch, you've never been in a proper fight." There have been some drunken brawls, but the videos of those events seem like she's having the time of her life, not intent on hurting anyone.

"You did your homework on me. Cute." She lays out various tools from the first aid kit. It's far more loaded than any first aid kit I've ever seen before. She points at my shirt. "That's dried to your wound, hasn't it?"

"Stop dodging my questions."

"Maybe you should start actually *asking* questions instead of just making statements." She tugs my jacket off, and I consider fighting her, but I really do need this taken care of. So I hold still while she peels my shirt off and whistles under her breath. "You're lucky. A couple inches either way, and he would've shattered your scapula. Or your shoulder. Messy, messy."

I let her guide me to a stool I hadn't noticed before. "Why do you have first aid kits stashed all over the city, Hermes?"

"I'm only going to answer you because you're about to be in excruciating pain and I don't need you to flinch away or punch me. Ready?" She doesn't wait for a response before fiery pain shoots through me as she starts digging out the bullet. But true to her word, she starts talking. "Everyone thinks that I'm practically magic. It suits me for them to believe that I can come and go from any place at any time."

I grunt, but there's not enough air in my lungs to form a reply. Thankfully, she doesn't appear to need one.

"It takes a lot of work to look so effortless, and it's not easy to live a life of sneakery. Sometimes I get hurt, but I wouldn't be a very good mysterious Hermes if I was constantly going to the hospital to get patched up. So I do it myself."

It makes sense. And yet I'm left with more questions than answers. "Why do it at all?"

"No one tells the truth in Olympus. Only a fool takes everything at face value and doesn't delve deeper for the secrets. They're more valuable than money."

The pain of her digging around my back has black spots dancing across my vision. I take several deep breaths until they retreat. "How do you know Circe?"

"Got it!" There's a clink as she drops the bullet into the sink. "You didn't even pass out. The first time I had to take a bullet out, I passed out twice before I managed it. Granted, I was doing it to myself, but you're still impressive." She pats my shoulder.

I could press her on the Circe question, but the truth doesn't really matter. I plan to get the fuck out of the city before whatever secrets are revealed and sins are called due. "What now?"

"Now, my dear Minotaur, we're going to take a trip to the catacombs." I start to twist to face her, but she smacks the back of my head. "Hold still. I know what you're about to say anyway." Her voice drops, and she does an eerily accurate mimicry of my voice. "Hermes, I didn't know that Olympus *has* catacombs."

I open my mouth, but apparently she doesn't need me to hold an entire conversation by herself. She answers in her normal voice.

"Most people don't know that Olympus has catacombs, Minotaur. There's been a lot of knowledge about this city lost over the years... Unless you know where to look for it."

ARIADNE

I HONESTLY EXPECTED A TRAP, EVEN WITH ASTERION'S reassurance. But when the taxi drops my brother and me off in the theater district, the street is deserted. We're a few blocks off the main avenue that has the theater, so I suppose that makes sense. It's the middle of the day, after all. Most people are at work, and it's not time for the lunch rush.

I lead my brother to a strange gate between two tall buildings with the address molded into the iron of the arch overhead. The only part of the setup that looks remotely modern is the keypad over the knob. It clicks open the moment I type in the code that Asterion gave me. *So far, so good.* Without meaning to, my hand finds my brother's, and I link my fingers through his. Just like we used to do when we were children and facing something scary.

I glance at him. "How are you holding up?"

"I'm not." He gives me a brief smile. "Let's get inside before someone else tries to kill us."

We're going to have to talk about the fact that our own father shot at him. Somehow that's so much worse than him ordering me dead. At least with me, he wanted to avoid doing it himself. Icarus doesn't look well, but I doubt I do either.

We slip through the gate and walk down a narrow cobblestone path with plants in pots hanging from the walls on either side. Most of them are dead, and the one bright-green fern I see looks fake. It creates a strange atmosphere. As if we're entering another world. It was kind of like that when we first moved into the manor house our father bought from Hermes. He did his best to sweep away any strangeness and modernize everything, but hints of it remained. Even if I didn't know this was a house that belonged to her, the vibe would be telling.

The door at the end of the path looks normal enough, and it opens under my hand. I can't help tensing in response. Nothing else has gone right, so why should this? But as we step into the house, it's cool and dark and has the energy of a building long abandoned.

"What is this place?" Icarus moves deeper into the large open room we've entered. I think it's a living room, based on the shapes underneath the white sheets covering the furniture. There appears to be art on the wall, but it's also covered. For all that, there's not a speck of dust to be found.

"I don't know," I say slowly. "Obviously she doesn't live here full-time." Or at all. It's weird, though. Because I would bet good money that if I went to one of Dionysus's houses in the countryside, it would look like he just stepped out for a minute. He has a full staff at all of his residences, with the sole exception of the penthouse, and only because he values his privacy. He has a cleaning service come in once a week, but that's it.

I would expect the rest of the Thirteen keep their various holdings in the same standing, ready for them at a moment's notice. So why not Hermes? Or why not in *this* place specifically?

"Let's look around." Sandwiched between two larger buildings, the windows offer little light. Either the person who built this home has a spiteful nature, or the house was here before the apartment buildings.

We walk through room after room, finding more of the same. All the furniture is covered. In the kitchen, there are some nonperishable items in the pantry, but the fridge has been wiped clean. I stare at a can of spaghetti. "Are you hungry?"

"Not particularly."

"Me neither." I glance at my phone again, but not much time has passed, and I don't have any messages from Asterion. He said he would call, not text, anyway. I don't know why I'm checking, except yes, I do. I'm worried about him. About us. About all this. "This has all gone to shit."

"Of course it has." Icarus stirs, giving me a wan smile. "I would've liked to slip out of the city gracefully instead of running for my life, but we work with what we have. Let's sit before you fall down."

I'm tired, but even with the frantic descent down the stairwell, it's more stress than anything else to blame. The pounding headache starting behind my left eye is testament to that. It's a relief to follow my brother to one of the bedrooms and watch as he pulls the sheets from a fainting couch, the bed, and the dresser.

When I raise my eyebrows at him, he shrugs unrepentantly. "I'm curious. So sue me."

I almost sit on the bed, but even with how frazzled I am, if I go horizontal, it's very likely that I'll pass out. I don't want there to be any chance I miss Asterion's call.

Icarus digs through the dresser, muttering under his breath. I don't bother to tell him that any secrets Hermes has won't be hidden in the house she sent us to. Besides, we're going to get out of here, and then we'll never see any Olympians again. I lean back against the chair and let my eyes drift closed. "You're wasting time."

"We've got nothing but time to waste." He opens the drawer and curses. "But even I draw the line at pawing through someone's panties."

I open my eyes and give myself a shake. I've had my phone in my hand the entire time, but I still glance at the screen and make sure it's not on silent. "We're going to get out of here."

"Maybe. Maybe not." He finally gives up on the dresser and comes to flop down next to me on the fainting couch. "It wasn't supposed to be like this."

"I know." I study my brother's face. I know the planes and angles almost as well as I know my own, but there's something in his expression that makes him almost a stranger to me. "Are you hurt?"

He shakes his head sharply. "Your big brawny monster of a man threw himself in front of me. I don't think I'm allowed to hate someone who took a bullet for me. It's really fucking inconvenient."

The reminder that Asterion got shot sends my heart racing. "He's in no shape to be running around, doing whatever the fuck it is Hermes has him doing. If he gets killed for this—"

"He won't."

I give my brother the look that statement deserves. "You can't just declare something to be true and expect the universe to conform to it. That's not how any of this works. He's only human." And he's been missing sleep. Running himself ragged as he tries to find a solution to get me out of Olympus. I want to believe that nothing on this earth can slow Asterion down, but that's the dreamer in me talking.

"If someone was lucky enough to kill him, he'll probably fight his way back to the land of the living to return to you." Icarus shakes his head. "It's scary the way he wants you, but there's something reassuring in it, too. Anyone who tries to hurt you will have to go through him, and he's a hard fucker to put down."

It's natural for my brother to prioritize my health and wellness over anyone else's, but he's looking at Asterion the same way our father does. As meat to be thrown into a grinder to serve a higher purpose. Asterion is worth more than that to me. He's worth *everything*.

Icarus throws an arm around my shoulders and gives me a firm side hug. "Just rest, Ariadne. That's the only thing you can control right now."

"My phone—"

"I'll keep watch. It's the least I can do. We won't miss his call."

I don't mean to close my eyes again. Really, I don't. But the next thing I know, my brother is shaking me gently awake. I startle up, but he puts his hand over my mouth before I can speak. The light has changed in the room, the shadows longer and darker.

Once Icarus is sure that I'll be silent, he slowly lowers his hand and speaks softly. "I thought I heard something."

We sit on the couch in perfect silence except for our soft inhales and exhales, listening with everything we have. I don't tell my brother that he's being paranoid. It's impossible to be paranoid when multiple parties are out to get you. No one should know we're here, but that's a fool's hope. We're in the middle of the city. There are cameras everywhere, and we took a cab ride to this address.

It still should've taken Phaedra longer to find us. They aren't some magical tracker, and my father doesn't have access to the network cameras in the city. Even as the thought crosses my mind, I curse myself for my shortsightedness. *Of course* they have access to the network. They have Mars. It still should've taken longer, though.

Except that's not the truth, is it? I could track someone within a few hours, and it's been at least that since I escaped Dionysus's penthouse. I hold perfectly still and listen intently, waiting to hear whatever put the fear in my brother's eyes.

Just when I'm on the verge of telling Icarus that he must've imagined it, I catch the sound, too. A faint whisper of movement. The footsteps of someone trying to walk silently.

I share a look with my brother. Fight or flight? He shrugs. If there's only one person, technically we outnumber them, but neither of us is a fighter. We don't have the training for it—something our father insisted was completely unnecessary—and we don't even have a weapon to our name.

Flight it is.

My legs feel like wet noodles as I push to my feet. I'd like to sleep for twelve more hours, to wake up and have this all be a bad dream, but that's not how life works. Asterion won't show up to save me. I have to save myself—and Icarus, too.

The only thing in our favor currently is that this house isn't an open concept. It's a warren of rooms connected to each other with only a small hallway here and there to break up the confusion. The sound came from somewhere close to the front door. We could try to avoid them as they move through the house and then escape out that door, but I don't think it's a good idea. I doubt whoever it is came alone. If I were trying to trap or kill us, I would send several people into the house and leave the rest of the team to block the exits.

"Is there a back door?" I whisper. I was distracted when we arrived, and all the rooms started to look the same after a short period of time.

"Yeah, but there's no exit back there." My brother matches my tone, the volume barely more than a whisper.

Fuck. "Then we have to hide." And hope that they assume we've left. It's a shitty plan, but it's the best I have with those footsteps creeping closer.

For a moment, it looks like Icarus is about to start arguing, but then he gives a jerky nod and grabs my hand. There's no need to speak anymore. Without meaning to, I fall back into the habit we created during our late-night wandering in my father's house as children. Being caught meant a lecture if we were lucky and the belt if we weren't. We were almost never caught. We'd slip out of the house and go to our spot on the roof where no one else visited.

When did we stop doing that? I don't know. Only that our nightly escapes happened less and less as we got older. Until they stopped altogether.

My body still remembers, though.

My brother leads the way through room after room. Several times, I almost question if he actually knows where he's going or if he's about to lead us directly into whoever is pursuing us. I manage to swallow down the question every time. The desire to run, to sprint, to put as much distance between us and danger, is almost overwhelming. Only habit keeps me moving slow and steady.

But I can't hold on to my silence as Icarus leads us through a door and into the cool night air. I look around in a panic and hiss. "You said there was no exit back here."

"They don't know that." He tugs on my hand, pulling me out onto a patio. Where the entrance of this house reeks of abandonment with dead plants and cracked flagstones, the back is a completely different story. There's more light back here, and even in the growing darkness, I can see full trees and hedges and bushes that fill the space with their scent. It's lovely enough that I almost pause, but Icarus keeps me moving.

He guides me to a particularly large plant that's part bush and part tree. "It's not going to be comfortable, but hide back here."

"What are you—" I bite off the question as he darts away. He has a plan, and I have to trust that he knows what he's doing. I wedge myself between the brick wall of the building bordering this courtyard and the scratchy branches of the plant. It's not quite late enough in the year for them to have shed their leaves fully, but there are a few sparse spots that I can see the back door through. I crouch down and battle the urge to pray.

A rattling sound snaps my head around. I watch in horror as my brother rips vines from the iron fence that closes the backyard off from a short alley that leads to the street on the other side of the block. He yanks down several more handfuls, enough that I can clearly see through the iron fence. Not an exit, no, but it could be for someone who is desperate enough.

I have the horrifying thought that my brother intends to leave me, but he ducks to the side and takes up a position almost opposite me behind a similar-looking bush. Understanding dawns as my heart races so hard, it creates a rushing sound in my ears.

He wants them to think we climbed the fence and escaped out the back.

It's a desperate play, but it's the only one we have. I open my mouth to say something, but the creak of the back door stops me short. I turn slowly to see the outline of a person standing in the doorway. It didn't seem that dark a few minutes ago, but now it feels like midnight. They step out into the courtyard and look around slowly.

Instinctively, I close my eyes and duck my head, letting my hair fall over my face. Willing myself to melt with the shadows behind the bush. Without my eyesight, every sound feels amplified. Their soft footsteps over the cobblestones are as loud as gunshots.

They stop less than five feet from me and curse softly under their breath. A few seconds later, they speak in a normal tone. "Atalanta here. I searched the whole place. They were definitely here just like you saw, but they must have escaped out the back at some point." She moves to the fence and rattles it a little. "I can see two side entrances from here and not a single damn camera. If they got into one of the apartment buildings, they could be anywhere now."

I press my lips together and hold my breath, willing Icarus to stay just as silent. *Atalanta*. That means she's here at Athena's behest. And that's bad news for us. With Ares, we might have a chance at a public trial or just be tossed into a cell somewhere. If Athena is sending her people after us, then she wants us to disappear. Permanently.

Atalanta listens for several beats. "We'll keep eyes on both entrances going forward. I doubt they'll come back here, but there's no reason to be foolish about it. Yeah, I'll meet you up front." She turns and stalks silently back to the door.

Even so, I don't move. I barely breathe as the seconds tick into minutes. I finally gather the courage to lift my head and look out through the space between branches. The courtyard is empty. She obviously did exactly as she said and went back through the front door. There's still a part of me that's certain this is a trap. That as soon as we come out of our hiding places, we'll be killed.

Eventually, Icarus makes the choice for me. He slips out of his hiding spot and crosses silently to me. "Well, we're fucked."

"Probably."

"What do we do?"

That's the question, isn't it? We're trapped here, but even if we weren't, we shouldn't be rushing around Olympus and hoping for the best. I take Icarus's hand and let him pull me out of my spot. "We do exactly what we were planning on doing. We stay here and wait for Asterion's call."

THE MINOTAUR

"DO WE NEED TO GO OVER THE PLAN AGAIN?"

I hang on to what's left of my patience with everything I have. "What plan, Hermes? All you've said is that I need to walk through the front door."

She beams at me. "Exactly. Now you're getting it."

I resign myself to not getting any further information and check my phone one last time. There's nothing from Ariadne, aside from letting me know that they got to the address Hermes provided safely. That should be enough to reassure me, but everything about this feels rushed and wrong.

I don't even know where the fuck we are. Hermes drives like an erratic old person on a Sunday outing, weaving and making wrong turns and circling back. I don't know how the fuck she has a license because she's an absolute terror. We're somewhere near the edge of Olympus, but I can't begin to guess where exactly. I keep having to tell myself that this isn't a trap. If she wanted to ambush me, she's had plenty of opportunity to do so.

The building we stand in front of looks abandoned. The glass on all the windows is foggy with dust and grime. The brick walls need a good power washing. I wouldn't look twice at it if I was walking past...unless I noticed that the door has a brand-new lock or that there's a camera tucked up in the eaves.

Someone really doesn't want anyone to notice this place.

Hermes fiddles with her phone. "Give me just a moment... Oh. There we go. You can walk in now. Remember, I need ten minutes."

"To do what?" I'm speaking to empty air. She's melted into the shadows behind us. I stare hard at them, trying to divine where she went, but there's no way to tell. I know she said it's pure athletics that allows her to do this, but I can't stop myself from shuddering. That shit is freaky as fuck.

I glance around, but the street is just as deserted as it was when we first arrived. It's not late, but this place has even less to offer than the warehouse district. There isn't a single soul around as I cross to the front door. It feels absolutely absurd to try the door, but it swings open soundlessly in response to my touch.

She really did hack it. It should be impossible with this tech, but when have the rules ever applied to Hermes?

I curse myself for getting into this mess and walk through the door. The outside of the building might lean more toward office, but inside is all military. There's a foyer with a booth on the other side. Two people stand inside it, their shocked faces showing through the glass.

Well, shit.

Hermes could've given me some warning. As the guards and I stare at each other, I notice that their black uniforms don't have an expected crest on the shoulders. It's not Athena or Ares or even Artemis. It's the gears and tools that denote Hephaestus.

She really was right. There's something important pertaining to the barrier here.

"Hey."

They stare at me. One is tall and nearly as broad as me, their skin the sickly kind of pale that comes when white people spend too much time away from the sun. The other one is nearly an identical build, but with warm medium-brown skin and a shaved head.

How long has it been? A minute? Two? I guess we could stare at each other for the next ten minutes while Hermes does whatever it is that she's doing. But surely there are more people here than just this pair. If they're going to such lengths to keep this place hidden, they would leave more than two people here to protect it.

I have the distant thought that Theseus had never mentioned this place, but he was a really shitty Hephaestus. His people hated him, and he hated the job. There's probably a lot of really important stuff that he just never noticed or knew to even ask about. The irony that he held the position that we needed to actually bring down the barrier is almost too much to bear. I can't even hold it against him, though, because neither one of us are cerebral. That's not the kind of weapons Minos trained us to be. If he wanted us to be brainiacs, he should've gone about shit a different way. That's on him.

All at once, the guards snap out of their shock. They draw their guns and start shouting. "What are you doing here? How did you get in? Who are you?"

The last one almost makes me laugh. For once, my reputation hasn't proceeded me. Typical that it's the one time it would've been useful. I hold my hands up slowly, skating my gaze around the room once more. There's not a lot to work with here, but I don't need much to make shit happen. "I'm just a tourist looking for a good time."

They exchange a look of disbelief. The white guy starts to lower his gun. "Dude, you're in the wrong place."

His friend narrows his eyes. "He's lying. There's no way he could've got through the door unless he was trying to." He points his gun right in my face. "Put your hands behind your head."

"Sure, sure." I do as he asks, but my shoulder screams in protest and the movement is jerky.

The white guy jumps back a step and grabs his radio. "Intruder at the front! We need more people up here."

Well, fuck.

The other guy curses and hurries toward me, out of the relative safety of his little booth. Another mistake in a long line of them. People get guns in their hands and think they're invulnerable. If they were trained properly, they would know better. It's super fucking easy to take a gun from someone when you're in close proximity.

Which is exactly what I do the moment he reaches for my hands. I spin and deliver a sucker punch to bend him in half. From there, it's child's play to grab the pistol. I kick the back of his knees, sending him flailing to the floor, and aim the gun at his friend. "Drop your weapon."

I don't wait for him to decide what he's going to do before I move forward and slam my pistol butt into his temple. His eyes roll back in his head and he slips to the floor. I take the opportunity to grab his gun, eject the clip, and toss it across the room.

The first guard has a couple of zip ties, so I use those on both of them. He sputters threats that I ignore because the door deeper into the building opens and eight more people emerge. "*Fuck.*"

Ariadne would want me to not kill them, but I promised her I'd make it back to her safely. Their lives versus my promise? It's no contest. Even so, I shoot the first one in the kneecap instead of the head. They topple into the person next to them, making *their* shot go wide.

Two strides and I'm in the middle of them. Shittily trained or not, they hesitate to use their guns in such close proximity for fear of shooting each other. I use that to my benefit. I ignore my wound shrieking in pain and slam two of their heads together hard enough that I *feel* the sound the contact makes. They drop with twin groans. Three down.

The fourth tries to shoot me in the face, but I jerk their pistol up, peppering the ceiling with bullets as they pull the trigger wildly. I count the rounds in my head as we struggle. Eight, nine, ten. The gun clicks. I step back and punch him in the face hard enough to make him stagger back... Right into the bullet spray of the person behind him. Blood spatters me and the floor and he goes down.

The fifth one and I look at each other. Their eyes are wide, probably because they just murdered their companion. Not my problem. I shoot them in the shoulder, the impact spinning them away from me and sending their gun flying.

Three more.

My back is one fiery block of pain. I can't keep this up indefinitely. Ten people is several too many to fight with my current injury. Still, I can't help picturing Ariadne's disappointed face when she finds out I killed just under a dozen people. I'm a fool. A gods-damned bloody fool.

Take out both kneecaps of the sixth, punch the seventh in the throat, and kick the eighth in the balls, breaking their nose with my knee when they bend over in agony.

My breath saws in my lungs, and I spin around, fully expecting another attack. None comes. They're all groaning and moaning on the ground, except for the dead one. From there, it's quick work to find zip ties in the booth and secure them all. The seventh tries to give me trouble, but I punch them in the throat again, and then it's easy enough to get their hands tied together.

I straighten and stretch carefully. Fuck, I'm sore. "By my count, I only have a few minutes left, so sit there and don't make me kill you." They glare and curse, but they're mostly helpless.

I step into the booth and am pleased to note they have security cameras rolling. As I previously noted, the rest of the interior does little to match the abandoned vibes of the outside. It takes me several long seconds to realize what I'm looking at—a massive machine that seems to disappear into a tunnel heading toward the perimeter of the city.

Is this the barrier? Or at least part of it? When we came into the city, passing through the barrier almost felt like magic. It shimmered in the evening lights in a way that felt odd even to me. To see that reduced to gears moving in a seamless rhythm feels a little bit like peeking behind the curtain of a magician's trick. It was never magic. I knew that, but apparently part of me was still clinging to that awe. I should really know better by now.

Movement on one of the screens draws my attention. I watch in fascination as Hermes rushes through the space, light on her feet and moving at nearly a sprint. There are a few guards who maintained their position instead of coming to fight me, but they don't stand a chance against her. I don't see exactly what she does to them; the only thing I know for sure is that they fall to the floor as she passes them. It's seamless on a truly overwhelming scale. I knew she was a menace, but this display of competence puts her into an entirely new category in my brain.

Hermes is *dangerous*.

Once she's dispatched all the guards, she ducks into the tunnel the machinery descends into. When she reappears a few moments later, the backpack she had been carrying is nowhere in evidence. She hurries through the corridors and walks through the door into the foyer. She's not even breathing hard.

"Ten. Well done. You were an excellent distraction." She raises her brows at me. "Why are they still alive?"

I raise my brows right back. "I did mention that your plan wasn't explicit. You didn't say you wanted them dead."

"You're the Minotaur. I thought it would've been readily apparent." She plucks a fallen gun from the ground and fires at each guard without looking. A perfect headshot each time. And she does it without a single bit of remorse on her pretty face. "No witnesses."

"Hermes."

"Hold, please." She turns back to the door and places a small charge on the frame at the top. "We need to get out of here. The building is coming down."

"And the barrier?"

"That will be a little later." She turns back to me. "It will take you some time to collect Ariadne and Icarus and get to the marina. I'm giving you that time." She flicks her fingers at the charge. "But no one will be able to get down to that room to stop the bomb from going off. Come on."

I don't ask her how she knows my plans. It doesn't matter. But I appreciate it all the same. "Thanks."

"Don't thank me. I take no joy in any of this." She casts a single look at the dead bodies and marches through the front door, leaving me to follow on her heels. "Olympus needs to be focused on the outside threat, not on worrying about what I'm doing."

It seems to me that the *only* thing Olympus should be worried about is what Hermes is doing. But her actions are serving my purpose, so I keep my mouth shut and follow her out the door.

We walk a block in silence before a roar sounds behind us and a cloud of dust kicks up as the building comes down. Just like she planned. She turns abruptly to me. "Pleasure doing business with you."

I stare at her outstretched hand. "You used me as bait."

"Only a little. I knew you could handle it and, look at that, you handled it. Now, you're wasting time." She rolls her eyes and wiggles her fingers until I take her hand and allow her to shake mine. "Good luck with the rest of your life."

"Just like that?"

She extracts her hand from mine and gives me a narrow look. "Literally nothing from the start of this situation has been 'just like that.' I'm cleaning up a mess generations in the making. Now stop wasting time and get out of here."

I watch her walk away until she turns the corner and disappears.

If I gave a shit about Circe or the Olympians, I would tell them all to watch out for Hermes. But I don't, so I pull my phone out of my pocket and dial Ariadne.

"Hello?"

I frown. "What happened? Why do you sound like that?"

She laughs but not like anything is funny. "We had a close call with some Olympians. Athena's people. They know we came to this house. We managed to trick them into thinking that we left, but I don't know how long that will hold before they circle back. We're kind of trapped."

Alarm floods me. "I'm on my way."

"Okay." The relief in her voice only makes me worry more. "Did you do what you needed to with Hermes?"

I glance back at the remains of the unassuming building filled with dead guards and then turn the corner and head deeper into town. "We have maybe an hour or so before the barrier comes down. I'm going to come for you, and then we're going to the marina. Stay inside until I get there. I'll call you when it's safe to come out."

"What are you going to do?"

"The same thing they were going to do to you if they caught you." I take a deep breath and keep going before she has a chance to protest. "I'm going to clear a path. We don't have time for a messy confrontation, so it will be a quick getaway."

She takes a sharp breath like she's about to argue with me and then exhales shakily. "Okay. We'll keep our heads down until you get here. Please be safe."

"I haven't failed you yet, sweetheart." It feels like a lie. Safety is the one thing I can't guarantee. Actually, there's not shit I can guarantee right now. I'm going to do my damnedest to get her and her brother out of here, but with both Minos and the Olympians gunning for us, that's a tall order.

It's only as I'm hot-wiring a car to head toward the address I sent them to that I wonder if this was all part of Hermes's plan from the beginning. She doesn't want Olympus or Circe looking too closely at her, so she's offered us up as sacrificial lambs to keep their attention. It seems like something she would do.

Fuck that. I'm done sacrificing for other people, and I'm sure as shit done letting Ariadne do it. We're getting out of here, and the rest of them can murder each other and raze the city to the ground for all I care.

ARIADNE

WAITING FOR ASTERION IS A SPECIAL KIND OF AGONY. I keep analyzing our short conversation and trying to decide if I actually detected exhaustion and pain in his tone or if he's really okay. He was *shot*, for gods' sake. And in between obsessing over that, I jump at every creak and groan the house makes. We can't see the street from any of the windows, but every time a car passes by, I'm certain that the Olympians are returning to murder us.

For his part, apparently all the excitement exhausted my brother, and he passes out on the couch. It's just as well. I'm not fit for company.

It's happening. It's finally happening. The barrier is coming down, and we're going to be able to get out of here. Hope and elation twine with guilt and fear. Because our success means bad things in the future of Olympus. It's not my city and they're not my people, but that doesn't make their lives any less valid. I don't think Circe is intent on whole-scale slaughter, but it's not like I sat in on any of the planning meetings. The only information I have is what I was able to hack and deliver to Apollo. There's nothing in that correspondence about a massacre, but that doesn't mean it represents the whole of her plans.

It's guilt that has me reaching for the phone. I shoot a look at my brother, but he's still dead to the world. I know what he'd say if he knew what I intended. It doesn't matter. I'm doing it.

I dial Hera.

She makes me wait until I think it's about to click over to voicemail, and only then does she answer. "I truly hope you're calling with a solution."

I almost laugh when I realize what she's talking about. Dodona Tower. My father's team. Our deal that no longer stands. "You have bigger problems to worry about now."

She's silent for a beat. "Are you threatening me, Ariadne?"

"Not in the slightest. But I have it on good information that the barrier is coming down. Today. It's too late to stop it. The only thing you can do is be ready."

"What?" Her cool confidence falters, and actual worry worms its way into her tone. "Surely you can't be serious."

"I wish I wasn't."

"Fuck," she says quietly. "I have to... I need to..." She stops short. When she speaks again, she's back to being the cold woman I've dealt with to date. "Thank you for the information. Our deal is off. Your father's team will be eliminated. Good luck." She hangs up.

I've done as much as I can. What happens next is up to her. I have sympathy for her, even if I don't like her much. I don't know who will win in a contest between Hera and Circe. But hopefully I'll be long gone before I have the chance to find out.

"Good luck to you, too, Hera," I whisper. I grip Icarus's shoulder and give him a shake. "Get up. Asterion is on his way. We need to be ready to move when he gets here."

"Ariadne?" His voice is still thick with dreaming. "I was having the most awful nightmare. We..." He blinks, shakes his head, and looks around. It hurts to see the innocence of sleep fall away from his expression and be replaced by the hardened exterior my brother has cultivated. "Not a nightmare, then."

"It's a nightmare. It's just not confined to the sleeping world." I vow right then and there that it doesn't matter what it takes, I will see Icarus happy. His dreams were never the same as mine. He doesn't look at the horizon and imagine all the possibilities it holds. He's only ever wanted acceptance. Acceptance from our people, acceptance from our father.

Icarus smiles, and though it seems to warm his eyes, I know it for a lie. I hate that he feels like he has to be dishonest with me, but now isn't the time to call him on it.

I put my backpack on and head for the front of the house to be ready for when Asterion calls. It seems like a small eternity before my phone buzzes in my hand. I almost drop it in my haste to answer. "You're here?"

"Yeah." He sounds more tired than I've ever heard him. "There's a car parked across the street with two people in it. I clocked them when I drove by the first time. I'm not really in the mood to murder more people tonight, so we're going to time this carefully. I'm driving around the block. You and your brother need to run out and jump in the back when I pull up, and then we're going to take off."

Later, we'll talk about his statement about murdering *more* people tonight. What the fuck were he and Hermes doing? There's no time now, though. "Okay. There's not a good place to hide in the front, so we'll have to come out the door."

"Get to the front door. Now."

"We're there." I grab my brother's hand, keeping the phone to my ear. We'll be sitting ducks the moment we exit and start the sprint to the front gate and street side. If the watchers are under orders to kill us, they have plenty of time to do it.

Asterion is silent for several seconds. "I'm at the corner and about to turn. Run, sweetheart."

I hang up and shove my phone in my pocket. "Now." As much as part of me doesn't want to release my brother's hand, I have to in order for us to move efficiently. He opens the door, and we sprint out down the cobblestone pathway of dead plants. The door doesn't have a lock on this side, so I thrust it open without slowing down. I catch sight of the car across the street that Asterion must've been talking about. The people inside throw open the doors, but it's too late. Asterion slams to a stop at the curb, and Icarus shoves me into the back seat and dives in behind. We barely get the door shut before Asterion is veering back into traffic and away from the house.

My brother lets out a breathless laugh. "Never a dull fucking moment."

Asterion glances at me in the rearview mirror. "Are you okay?"

It's such a strange question given everything going on. I'm not okay. I don't know if I'll ever really be okay again. There's something about being hunted by people who intend to kill you that shifts a person's perspective. Maybe permanently. I guess time will tell, but it feels too hard to contemplate the future when we're in such a crisis currently.

Instead of answering his question, I ask a question of my own. "What happened with you?"

He curses under his breath. "Let's just say that Hermes isn't someone I want to cross. She set a bomb that will go off in…about thirty minutes from now. We have to get to the marina and get to a boat as quickly as possible."

I have a dozen follow-up questions, but ultimately it doesn't matter. The barrier will come down or it won't. If it doesn't, there's a good chance we'll end up trapped at the marina. But at this point, we're trapped no matter where we go. The barrier has made sure of that.

So I sit back and try to regain my breath. Traffic thins out as we head north toward the shipyard and marina. It's the one part of Olympus I haven't spent any time in whatsoever. It reminds me a little of the lower city. The buildings get smaller and older, but they're all in decent repair as best I can tell.

No one seems to come up here except for those who deal directly with Poseidon, or I guess those who plan to use the marina for a day trip. We've been in Olympus for several months now, and I've never heard about anyone doing that, though.

I twist to look out the back window, but I don't see anything. "Are they following us?"

"No." Asterion doesn't sound happy about it. "They never even pulled away from the curb."

I don't ask why they wouldn't follow us. It's not for any benign reason; it's because they don't need to. Which means either someone else is… Or they think they know where we're going.

It's everything I can do not to huddle in the back seat as Asterion carves our way through the city to the north. The marina stands out against the rest of the buildings in the area, shiny and polished in a way that feels brand-new, not like it's been standing here for years. Half a dozen docks stretch out into the bay, holding space for entirely too many sailboats and yachts.

As Asterion pulls into the parking lot, dread weighs me down. "Do you even know how to work a boat? I'm not even talking about just a sailboat."

"I can sail."

Icarus scoffs. "Just because you think you can do something doesn't mean it's true. I know you're formidable and all that shit, but that doesn't mean you can do anything."

"I'm aware." Asterion doesn't sound irritated. "In this case, I know what I'm talking about. Your father gave us a small amount of downtime over the years. I used mine to learn to sail."

Shock steals my breath. "I had no idea." I thought I knew everything about him. I certainly watched him closely enough over the years. But there were times when he'd disappear without a word, only to reappear hours later. Back then, I assumed he was meeting up with a lover, so I didn't pry. It would hurt too much to know for sure. After the revelation that he hadn't been with anyone since meeting me, I should've stopped to wonder what he was actually doing during those mystery absences.

"I find it relaxing. But that's not why I started learning." He glances over his shoulder at me. "We lived on an island, sweetheart. It pays to have an exit strategy in place."

Next to me, Icarus rolls his eyes. "Why not learn to fly a plane, then? It's a faster getaway."

"Because I didn't want anyone to realize I was planning a getaway. Lots of people sail recreationally." He clears his throat. "They shouldn't have been able to beat us here, but we're going to act like they did. I'm parking, and we're getting the fuck out of here. Stay close and do as I say."

"Sir, yes, sir."

I smack my brother lightly. "This is serious. He already got shot for you once. Let's not make a habit of it."

My brother instantly sobers. "I didn't forget." He rubs the back of his hand over his mouth. "Thank you, Min—Asterion. You didn't have to protect me, and you didn't hesitate. So, uh, thank you."

Asterion's shoulders hunch, just a little. "If you died, it would make Ariadne sad."

"Good to know where I stand. Won't forget it again."

I don't curse them both out, but it's a near thing. "Let's stay focused."

It's only as we're jumping out of the car and hurrying toward the docks that I think to wonder if Asterion knows what boat we're trying to steal. I've never stolen a vehicle before. It looks easy in the movies, but I'm not foolish enough to think that's reality. It's too late for questions, though.

Full darkness has descended, and I can't stop myself from huddling close to Asterion's broad back. The soft creak of the dock moving in the water feels upsettingly loud in my ears. It could be covering up all manner of sins. There could be dozens of people waiting for us to step onto the docks, intent on our murder.

I'm trying to watch all the shadows at once, so I shouldn't be surprised when one detaches from a nearby building and starts for us. And yet somehow I am. That surprise quickly turns to horror when I recognize the shape of the shoulders, the height, and the angry cadence of the footsteps.

"Father," I breathe.

The word is barely more than whisper, but Asterion hears me anyway. He moves in an instant, one arm sweeping me and Icarus behind him as he twists to face the new threat. "Minos."

My father steps into the light, and I've never seen him as angry as he is now. The veins stand out against his temples, and he's practically shaking with rage. "You've ruined it. You've ruined everything. And now you're going to fucking pay." He moves his right hand, and I go cold.

He's got a gun.

THE MINOTAUR

I DON'T KNOW HOW THE FUCK MINOS KNEW THAT WE were coming here, but the *how* matters less than the fact that he's here. Threatening us. Threatening *Ariadne*. She and her brother try to stop, but I keep them moving, inching us backward toward the middle dock. During one of my and Theseus's recon missions, we cataloged every single vessel in the marina. Minos had been playing with the idea of sinking them all before ultimately realizing the same thing we did—no one uses or cares about these ships. They're jewels in a crown that no one wears. Polished and perfect and useless.

My goal is the sailboat near the end of the row. The *Daedalus*. It's owned by Apollo, a gift from the last Zeus when he took the title ten years ago. It looks brand-new, and knowing what kind of man Apollo is, I'm certain it's kept in the best working condition, even if it's never used.

But none of that is going to help us unless we can fucking get there.

I keep a wary eye on Minos as I back his children away from

him. "You got what you wanted. The barrier will come down in less than thirty minutes. You don't need us anymore."

I can't see his eyes in the low light, but his movements are jerky with rage. "You don't get to walk away from me, boy. Theseus must've given you the wrong idea. Just because I couldn't touch him doesn't mean I'm going to watch you leave with my traitorous bitch of a daughter and my pathetic excuse for a son. Better you're dead than betraying me."

That's what I was afraid he would say.

The boat we're aiming for is positioned at the end of the dock, perfect for a smooth getaway, but there's too much open space between our current position and the cover it offers. Even if Minos doesn't have another clip, he has more than enough bullets to put all three of us in the ground.

I keep inching Ariadne and Icarus backward. "When I say run, you run. You don't look back. You don't hesitate."

"Okay."

Ariadne grabs a fistful of my shirt. "No, Icarus, *not* okay. We're not leaving you to get shot again, Asterion."

I don't see how we have another choice. The barrier is close to coming down, which means our window of escape is rapidly shrinking. "For once in your fucking life, listen to me and obey."

A gunshot makes us all flinch. Minos stalks toward us, his expression falling into cold lines. "Even now, you're not taking me seriously. That's fine. I'll ensure you take me seriously after this." He aims the gun right at the center of my chest. "Get on the ground."

Absolutely fucking not. He's liable to execute me on the spot. The fact that he hasn't started shooting at us yet... I look over his shoulder. "Shooting a gun in Poseidon's territory? You really don't want to get out of here alive, do you?"

"What's that big ginger bastard going to do? Scowl and wring his hands? Don't make me laugh. And don't make me ask again. Get on the ground."

Ariadne's grip on the back of my shirt shifts. I tense, but twisting to face her will leave her exposed. I'm fucking trapped, and I know down to my very soul that she's about to do something reckless. I have to end this and do it now.

I start to step forward, but Icarus gets there first. He moves several wide steps to my right. Far enough that Minos will have to pick a target. Did I think Ariadne was going to be the reckless one? I should've known better. Her brother makes her look downright biddable.

Icarus's expression is terrible to behold. He looks utterly hopeless. "I did everything you wanted. Everything you ever asked for. And it was never good enough."

Minos sneers. "If that was true, then I wouldn't have needed *him*." He motions violently toward me with a gun. "You're pathetic. Weak. A sad excuse for a son that no one would be proud of." He turns that ugly expression on me. "And *you're* not even a son at all. You're just trash I picked up off the street, and instead of being grateful, you stole the most precious thing I own."

"You don't own me. You never did." Ariadne steps from behind me, smoothly evading my grasp for her. It's not until she lifts my gun in a two-handed stance that's only slightly off that I realize she took the damn thing in the first place. Tears stream down her face, but her hands don't shake. "I'm not going to let you hurt anyone else ever again."

"Ariadne—"

She doesn't look at her brother. Or at me. But when she speaks, it's for us. "You've both done too much, sacrificed too much, and for what? Someone else's war. Someone else's gain. I'm not letting either of you get your hands dirty any longer. You deserve better."

Minos, the fool, actually laughs. "Put that thing down before you hurt yourself."

"Strange that you're still worried about me hurting myself when you sent someone to kill me."

He's still not taking her seriously. He shakes his head, laughter trailing off slowly. "Phaedra wasn't there to kill you. She was there to retrieve my wayward daughter. I found a use for you, after all. One of Circe's generals needs a little reassurance to cement his loyalty. And he's not too concerned about the goods being tarnished."

Even after all this time, he still doesn't know his daughter at all. Ariadne was never going to allow herself to be traded for her father's game. Her gun doesn't waver. "Let us go. I'm not your bargaining chip any longer. And if Icarus and Asterion are so worthless to you, then you won't feel their loss at all."

"You've lived your whole life in my household, and you still haven't learned. If it is no longer an asset to you, you put it down so it can't be used against you." As he speaks, his focus swivels toward Icarus, his finger moving to the trigger.

I don't think. There's no time for that. My body takes over, flinging itself toward Ariadne's brother. The one person in this world she loves even more than me. If he's murdered by her father...

I hit Icarus hard enough to take us to the ground as two gunshots scream into the night. Icarus groans, but I don't have time for him. He's fine. I lurch to my feet, my brain belatedly categorizing a number of scrapes and cuts from the rough ground. But no bullet wound.

The scene hits me in flashes. Minos and Ariadne sinking to their knees with mirrored expressions of shock and pain. They've never looked more like father and daughter than they do in this moment. My brain scrambles to understand what the fuck I'm seeing. Minos was going to shoot Icarus. Did he shoot Ariadne instead?

I rush to her before I finish the thought. "Sweetheart? Sweetheart, talk to me. Where are you hurt?" If he got her in the chest or, fuck, the stomach—

"I'm not."

I keep patting her down, barely registering her words. "Yes, you fucking are. He shot you. Where is it, sweetheart? We need to get you to the hospital." Fuck the boat if it means she dies at sea.

Ariadne catches my wrists in a pathetically weak grip. "Asterion." She squeezes me. "He didn't shoot me. I shot *him*." Her voice is wrong, distant and almost peaceful. She's going into shock. My woman has never hurt a fly, and she just shot her father.

"Dad?" Icarus's voice breaks. "Dad, talk to me."

"Let me up," Ariadne murmurs. She's still too calm. It's freaking me out. "Asterion, move. Please."

I don't want to. Bad enough that she pulled the trigger, but to actually watch the life leave her victim's eyes... I've seen it happen more times than I can count. So often that I'm immune to it. There are scars on my heart from the first couple of them, though. I would save her from that if I could.

Too bad she won't let me.

Ariadne pushes me to the side, and I let her. I follow her as she stumbles to her fallen father's side. He's a monster. All three of us know that, and yet even my chest sinks at the sight of the blood bubbling up from his lips. He was the only father figure I ever had, and he might have been a shitty-ass father, but he was ours. He gasps, sounding weaker than I've ever heard him.

That doesn't stop me from moving his gun out of reach. Just in case.

Icarus is openly weeping, clinging to Minos's hand like a child. But Ariadne kneels there, her expression cold and contained. Later, she'll break down. I'm certain of it. But right now, it's almost as if she's bearing witness.

We don't have to wait long. Minos's breathing becomes weak and soft and then stops altogether. I'm the one to rise first, urging Ariadne to her feet. Then we both have to drag Icarus off his knees. "Come on, Icarus. We have to go. We can mourn later."

"You shot him," he whispers. "I can't believe you actually shot him."

Ariadne flinches, the reaction so slight, I doubt her brother notices. Not that he would anyway. He's too lost in his own fucking world right now. I want to shake him and yell in his face. To point out that the only reason she shot their father was to save her foolish brother's life. Neither of them will thank me for pointing it out. Not now. Not like this.

So I simply wrap my arm around Ariadne's waist and give her a squeeze. And then I keep it there, ready to catch her if her knees buckle. "There's not much time left. We have to go."

"You're not going anywhere."

I start to spin around, but the voice isn't coming from the land.

It's coming from the dock ahead of us. A mountain of a man moves out from the shadows of a particularly large yacht. I recognize him instantly. Poseidon.

"*Fuck*," I breathe as people melt out of the shadows on either side of us. There are five—no, six. Too many to fight without risking Ariadne or Icarus. Damn it, I should've come to the marina earlier and cleared our way. Not that it would've helped, because I would've had to leave to deal with Hermes and retrieve Ariadne and Icarus. Fuck, my brain is running in circles. I don't see a way out of this.

"It's too late, Poseidon." Ariadne sounds more tired than I've ever heard her. More defeated. "Minos is dead, but you have bigger things to worry about. The barrier will fall and Circe is coming for you. Taking us won't do a damn thing to stop either."

"So you say." He shrugs. "We're going to lock you up all the same until we know for sure. Now isn't the time to let enemies of Olympus run rampant." He motions at his people. "Take them."

ARIADNE

I DON'T KNOW IF I BELIEVE IN CURSES, BUT NOTHING HAS gone right since we came to Olympus. Since before that, even. Maybe things started to go wrong the moment my father threw his ambitions in with Circe and turned his eye on this city.

And now look at us. I have my father's blood literally staining my hands. My brother will never forgive me, even if he doesn't realize it yet. And for what? Our escape from the city is closing before my very eyes.

Poseidon's people approach slowly, cautiously. It's then that I realize I still have the gun in my hands. I start to lift it, but Asterion gets there first. He plucks it from my hands as if taking a toy from a toddler. I thought I had a good grip on it, and he doesn't hurt me in the taking, but one moment the metal warmed by my palms is a comforting weight, and the next it's gone.

This time, at least he doesn't push me behind him. But he does step forward to face Poseidon, raising the gun to point at him. "Not another step."

Poseidon ignores the order and moves forward. "Shoot me if you must, but my people will open fire on your companions the moment you do."

Asterion glances at me, his eyes wild with the desperation coursing wildly through my body. He shifts his stance to point at the person to the right of Poseidon, their body clothed in black with his distinctive crest on their shoulder. "Maybe you're willing to die, but are you willing to let *them* die? You care about them more than the others. Every one of them can walk away from this confrontation if you make the right choice. Stand down."

I search Poseidon's face for some sign of weakening resolve. There is none. "Every one of them knew what they signed up for and agreed to the risks."

Fuck, fuck, *fuck*. We're not getting out of this. My brain scrambles, frantically spinning in circles, but there are no answers to be found. There's no clever way out of this. "Please!"

Everyone is so focused on me and Asterion that they don't see Icarus move. Truth be told, I don't either. It seems like one moment he's cowering on the other side of Asterion, and the next he darts forward, too quick to stop. Poseidon doesn't see him coming.

He kicks out the bigger man's legs and then slips behind him. We all freeze at the metal glinting in the low light cast by nearby boats. My brother is holding my father's discarded gun to Poseidon's throat. His eyes are wild and reckless, his voice panicked. "No one move or I blow his head off."

"Icarus, no!" I lurch forward, but Asterion catches me around the waist and pulls me back to his chest. I'm struggling and I can't seem to stop, but he holds me effortlessly.

Poseidon's people have frozen. The man himself seems shocked by the turn of events. My brother has a fist in his dark-red hair, and he's holding the gun so closely that the muzzle dents the skin at Poseidon's temple.

Icarus looks around wildly at the black-clad people gathered around. "No one move or he dies." He jerks Poseidon back a step, closer to us. "I mean it!"

This has all gone so wrong. "Icarus…"

But he's not listening to me. "Throw your guns away. *Now*."

Poseidon's people don't hesitate. There is true fear on their faces as they carefully set their guns down and kick them away. Asterion might have been right about Poseidon caring about his people, but it's obvious that they care about him just as much.

"Move, Ariadne. We don't have much time." Asterion tugs me back a few steps, and Icarus follows, muscling an unresisting Poseidon along as we retreat down the dock. Poseidon's people carefully shadow our steps, but they keep well back. Too far away to help, and yet…I don't see how we're getting out of this. Even if we make it to the boat.

Eventually, the dock runs out, and Asterion pulls me close to a white sailboat with *Daedalus* written across the bow. "Up."

I'm afraid of what will happen if I leave the dock. "But—"

"Trust your brother." He lifts me and all but tosses me onto the boat, quickly following behind.

I stumble and scramble to the edge. The deck is a little higher than the dock so I have a perfect view of the standoff happening below.

"Give me a few minutes, Icarus." Asterion takes my shoulders.

"I know you're scared, sweetheart, but I have to focus on getting this thing running. I need you to untie the lines keeping us at the dock. Can you do that for me?"

He's coddling me, but I can't stop shaking. "How much time do we have?" Surely the barrier is about to come down. If it does before we're ready...I don't know what happens.

"The lines, sweetheart." He lifts his voice. "Icarus. Get Poseidon up here. We can toss him into the water once we've made a clean escape, and he can swim back to shore." A neat solution. One that doesn't require yet more deaths tonight.

I scramble to the first line on the side opposite where my brother is. The boat seemed absurdly large standing next to it, but now that I'm onboard, I wonder how we'll manage the seas on it. I have to trust Asterion. He said he can sail, and I believe him. We just have to get the fuck out of this marina.

My fingers are clumsy with fear. It takes me three tries to get the first knot undone. I can't see what's going on. Someone is shouting, but it's hard to tell who over the roaring in my ears. I want nothing more than to rush back to the other side of the boat and see what's going on, but doing that won't help. It won't get Icarus and Asterion and me out of this alive.

Resolve steadies me. There are entirely too many things that I can't afford to think about right now. Action is easier. I get the second knot undone on the first try and then rush back to the other side of the boat for the last two.

The third knot is just as easy as the second, but on the fourth, I pause. If we're entirely unmoored, how likely am I to drift away before they can jump aboard? I don't fucking know. I don't know a goddamn thing about boats. If I do something to fuck up our ability to escape, I'll never forgive myself. And I already have more than enough to never forgive myself for.

Movement draws my attention just as I unravel the last tie. Poseidon elbows my brother hard enough to send him stumbling back a step. It's all the opportunity the big man needs to spin and level a punch to my brother's stomach, folding him in half. Even though he doesn't say a word, it's as if his people heard a rallying cry. They rush down the dock toward us.

"Icarus!" I scream.

Asterion rushes to my side. "Fuck!"

Poseidon turns to us. He's as composed as ever, as if he wasn't just held hostage by my brother. "Surrender. There's no need for more violence."

I can see Asterion weighing the growing distance between the boat and the dock. The engine hums softly behind me, but it's the water itself to blame. We're drifting. If he jumps, the space will increase dramatically, and I don't know how to sail. He could probably swim back to me, but it's a risk.

It's one I'm willing to take.

I get one foot on the bottom rung of the railing before Icarus sways to his feet behind Poseidon. "Go, Ariadne," he shouts. "I'll find you when this is all over." He ignores my scream of protest and takes Poseidon down in a flying tackle that sends them over the edge of the dock and into the dark water.

They surface almost immediately and then go under again, fighting in the water. My brother knows how to swim, but he's not a fighter, and he's nowhere near as large as Poseidon.

He's going to drown.

"Asterion! We have to go back for him."

But Asterion isn't listening to me. He grabs my arm and pulls me away from the railing toward the steering wheel or whatever it's called on a boat. "He made his choice, sweetheart. He'll find us when this is all over."

I stare at him in disbelief. "You can't be serious. My brother—"

"Made his choice," he repeats firmly. He does something to make the engine's sound increase, and suddenly we're moving with purpose away from the dock. "Just like you did when you made your deal and left us wondering what happened to you. Let him have this, Ariadne."

My knees give out and I sink to the floor. "But..." But he'll be hurt. Maybe killed. Even as the thought crosses my mind, the boat eases around the dock so I can get a straight line of sight to where Poseidon hauls himself onto the dock, dragging a soaked Icarus behind him. My brother falls to his hands and knees, his head bowed. But he's breathing.

A sob wrenches from my chest. He's alive, but for how much longer? "This is a mistake."

"Trust him." Asterion guides us away from the docks and out toward the bay. Even in the dark, I can see the faint shimmer of the barrier still in place.

It makes me laugh, the sound gaining a hysterical edge. We've come so far, sacrificed so much, and yet we're still trapped. "What if it doesn't come down?"

"It will."

We sit in silence as we cut through the water, sailing closer and closer to the barrier. I don't know how much time has passed, but surely we're beyond the hour Hermes promised. It defies belief that so much tragedy could be packed into such a short time. "I killed my father."

Asterion looks down at me, his dark eyes sympathetic. "You were saving your brother. He was going to shoot Icarus. Maybe I would've got there in time. Maybe not. But you made sure your brother was safe."

My throat goes tight and hot. I hadn't been thinking when I pulled the trigger. I just wanted all this to stop. "Only for Icarus to end up hurt anyway."

"*His. Choice.*" He crouches down in front of me and grips my chin. "I would've done the same damn thing to protect you if he hadn't gotten there first. You're allowed to have your feelings about that, Ariadne. But at least they have reason to keep him alive. Poseidon's too smart and cautious to kill him out of hand. Icarus is smart enough to work any situation to his advantage eventually."

I don't know if he's telling the truth or giving me a comforting lie. I don't know if it matters. Going back now defeats all the sacrifices my brother made. Asterion is right about that, at least. "I'm not happy about any of this."

"I know, sweetheart."

I don't know what else I might say because I never get the chance. There's a rumble, too low for me to determine whether it's a sound or a feeling. It grows and grows, making my teeth ache. That's when I notice that the waves have gone choppy and angry.

Asterion grips the wheel with white knuckles and puts his other hand on my shoulder, keeping me in place. As if I'm about to do anything. I wouldn't be able to stand without falling. It's as if a storm rolled in, but the skies are clear and there isn't so much as a hint of wind.

And then the barrier comes down.

It's more energy than physical reaction as the glitching rainbow of light cascades down toward the surface of the bay, as bright as fireworks but in an almost uniform pattern. It's...beautiful. I start to stand, but the boat heaves violently beneath my feet.

"Fuck. Shit. *Fuck*. Get down!" Asterion grabs my shoulder and shoves me into the small space between him and the half wall by the wheel. I understand why a breath later when it feels like we're sucked down into a crater. My stomach heaves, and I press myself as tightly to the wall as I can.

Asterion somehow manages to keep his feet, his expression fierce as if he can will us to stay afloat. Somewhere in the back of my mind, I'm laughing hysterically at the thought of surviving to this point, only to capsize and drown in the very event we worked so hard to make happen.

The boat veers sideways, tipping violently, and then swoops up, sending my stomach in the opposite direction. Oh gods, I think I'm going to be sick.

"Almost there, almost there." It's strange how I can hear him clearly. It seems like there should be screaming wind and roaring rain, but for all the noise of the waves themselves, it's still remarkably quiet.

The next dip the boat battles through is smaller. The next smaller yet. By the fourth, it's mostly choppy water that's sickening but survivable. Only then do I fight to my feet and look back the way we came.

The barrier is no more.

Olympus is sprawled out along the coastline, a glittering, poisonous creature that's caused so much grief for so many people. A creature that still holds my brother in its clutches.

Asterion barely waits for the boat to steady further before he's moving. He rushes around the deck, doing stuff to make the sails come down and then returning to the wheel to guide us farther out to sea.

There's barely any sound at all as we cut through the waves. I half expected us to angle to follow the coastline, but Asterion cuts a direct line toward open water. I understand why after about thirty minutes. There is a trio of massive ships heading toward the bay of Olympus. I don't have to see the banner they're flying to know that they belong to Circe. It's notable that they're flying her colors, not Aeaea's.

Bitterness bubbles up inside me. "All this loss. All this violence and destruction, and for what? I know she was hurt by Olympus, but she's hurt so many others."

I want to hate her for the man my father was, but that poison resided inside him long before he ever met her. She gave an avenue to his ambitions; she didn't create them. I have so much anger and nowhere to send it.

We pass through the ships without conflict, and only then does Asterion turn south. He glances at me, and I know him well enough to read the worry there. "There are no easy answers, sweetheart. Olympus has had a reckoning coming for generations. Maybe as far back as its founding. The way they run shit is fucked up, and you can't deny it. They would've hurt you just as quickly as Circe did."

He's right. I know he's right. But I can barely focus past the loss of my father...and my brother. I want to ask Asterion for reassurance that Icarus will be okay, but any words he gives me would feel like a lie. He can't guarantee my brother's safety. Even if we turned around right now and went back, it would be for nothing.

Without thinking, I pull up my phone and type out a text.

Me: You have to be okay, Icarus. We always promised we'd meet in Rio for Carnaval someday and I'm holding you to it. I'll be there waiting.

Even knowing that his phone went into the water with him and there's no way for him to respond to my text, I stare at my screen until light peeks over the horizon. Only then does Asterion wrap a blanket around me and ease my phone from my grip. He doesn't take it far, though. He sets it on the seat right next to me, screen up.

Then he pulls me into his arms and hugs me close and tight. For the first time in hours, I draw a full breath. "Am I going to be okay? Are we?"

"Give it time, sweetheart. You haven't had the space to feel your shit for a very long time. It'll probably come in waves. I'm here and I'll ride them with you. Whatever that looks like."

For someone who acts like he's not good with words, he sure knows the right thing to say. I wouldn't have believed a promise that everything would be okay. But a journey? That I understand.

I nestle tighter against him and bury my face in his throat. "I love you."

"I love you, too." He presses a kiss to the top of my head. "We have a couple stops to make to get money and our papers in order. But then we have the whole world in front of us, sweetheart. Where do you want to go first?"

My smile is faint and feels bittersweet. "Everywhere."

EPILOGUE

ICARUS

EVERYTHING HURTS. POSEIDON WASN'T GENTLE WHEN HE hauled me out of the water and onto the dock, and my body feels like one big bruise. That doesn't stop me from turning to watch the boat disappear into the distance, even though it wrenches my shoulder to do so. My sister is safe. My father is dead. I don't know what the fuck to feel.

Being left behind—*choosing* to stay behind—feels strangely inevitable.

At least I'm finally good for something.

Poseidon shoves me to my knees at the end of the dock. People mill around, not sure what to do in the wake of the barrier coming down. They better figure it out and fast. Circe isn't going to go easy on them. The thought almost makes me laugh.

At least until I look up as a woman strides toward us, someone who wasn't on the docks previously. Athena looks as untouchable as always. Her black suit doesn't have a speck on it, and neither does the gun she's holding loosely at her side. She stares down at me as if I'm the most worthless piece of shit on this planet.

This time, I do laugh. She'll have to join the club of people who hate me. It was down a member with my father's death, but now it's right back up to where it should be. My laughter takes on a hysterical edge. "You'll never catch them now."

"There are larger things to worry about than your traitorous sister." She turns to Poseidon, and my laughter dies in my throat.

He's as soaked as I am, and his clothing leaves little to the imagination. I easily trace his obscenely broad shoulders and thick gut that looks like it would break the hand of someone who tried to sucker punch him. His features are rough-hewn but handsome enough, and the motherfucker has freckles.

He glares down at me as if he wants nothing more than to kick me over the edge of the dock and let me drown for real this time. The thought should bring panic, but I'm all panicked out. All I have left is a blessed numbness that cascades down my body and offers relief.

"Are you going to kill me?" I'm rather proud that my tone sounds completely disinterested, despite my heartbeat fluttering in my throat.

Athena shifts her gun at her hip as if she's considering it. "We might as well. If we had shot the lot of you the second you arrived at Olympus, none of this would've happened."

It's cute that she thinks so, even though she's wrong. If my father failed, I'm sure Circe had half a dozen other plans in place. She was always coming for Olympus. They're fools if they think otherwise. "If you say so."

Athena lifts her gun, but Poseidon reaches over without looking and grabs her forearm. She sneers at him. "Touch me again without permission, and you'll regret it."

He releases her immediately, but he angles his body between me and her. "There's been enough death today, and there will be plenty more in the near future. He doesn't need to die. He's not a threat."

I look at him with more interest. He's a fool, but most people are when it comes to me. They value physical strength and violence, and even if you accomplish your goals in another way, it's seen as less valuable. All that means is he'll be easier to manipulate.

Athena huffs out a breath. "Fine. Then *you* deal with him." She turns and stalks back to her team, Atalanta easily falling in one step behind her.

Poseidon and I watch her go and then turn back to each other. I offer him my best charming smile. "Is this the part where you let me go, handsome?"

It's hard to tell in the shadows, but I think he might be blushing. I have the space of one heartbeat to feel victorious about getting under his skin so quickly before his expression shuts down and goes cold. "And let you run amok in the city even more than you already have? Absolutely not." He grabs the back of my neck and hauls me to my feet. "You're going into a locked room where you can't cause any more trouble."

"Kinky. You can be the sexy jailer and I'll be the sexy inmate." I don't know why the fuck I say it. I'm usually better at knowing when to keep my mouth shut. But fear has a way of undercutting all my strategies.

Poseidon uses his hold on the back of my neck to turn me to face him. He might've blushed for me a few minutes ago, but now he's all business. All threat. "Let's get one thing clear, Icarus. Your family has brought the city that I care about nothing but pain and suffering—and now war. Just because I don't want you dead doesn't mean I want to spend even a second longer than necessary in your presence. Do you understand me?"

The strange elation I felt drains away, leaving behind the very familiar weight of understanding that I will always be a disappointment. To my allies. To my enemies. To my fucking family. I don't have it in me to keep fighting. Not today. "Yeah. I read you loud and clear."

But tomorrow is another day.

I'll make Poseidon regret taking me captive if it's the last thing I do.

YOU'RE INVITED TO THE BLACK ROSE AUCTION...

Dive into a series of three exciting spicy modern fairy tales centering around an elite, ultra-exclusive auction holding court in upstate New York's most luxe manor house.

Coming Soon!

ACKNOWLEDGMENTS

There are some stories that just imprint on your soul for one reason or another. The Troy Game by Sara Douglass is one of those for me. This book wouldn't exist without that series. So thank you for the cursed content!

Thank you to Mary Altman for trusting me with what is arguably the most "dark romance" dark romance of the series. As always, this book is a thousand times better for your input and ideas. Dark Olympus wouldn't be what it is without you!

Endless appreciation to Pam Jaffee and Katie Stutz for championing this series like rock stars. Your support and pushing me when I need pushing is everything.

No book is brought into the world in a vacuum, so my deepest thanks to the Production team at Sourcebooks: Stephanie Gafron, Diane Dannenfeldt, Deve McLemore, and India Hunter, for supporting this book and this series across all stages of development.

Thank you to Jenny Nordbak, Asa Maria Bradley, and Melissa

Taylor for being the best support system a chaotic person like me could ever ask for!

Speaking of support systems, Tim, my god, I would be lost without you. You keep the wheels on this bus and the bus on the road.

Thanks and apologies(?) to my children. We all know how deeply uncool of a mom I am, but you weather the uncoolness most excellently. B, stop menacing your teachers with my books.

ABOUT THE AUTHOR

Katee Robert (she/they) is a *New York Times* and *USA Today* bestselling author of spicy romance. *Entertainment Weekly* calls their writing "unspeakably hot." Their books have sold over two million copies. They live in the Pacific Northwest with their husband, children, a cat who thinks he's a dog, and two Great Danes who think they're lap dogs. You can visit them at:

Website: kateerobert.com
Instagram: @katee_robert
Facebook: AuthorKateeRobert
TikTok: @authorkateerobert

DESPERATE MEASURES

ONCE UPON A TIME, I WAS A SHELTERED PRINCESS. NOW HE OWNS ME, BODY AND SOUL.

One night and my entire life went up in flames. All because of him. Jafar. As my world burned around me, he offered me a choice: walk away with nothing but my freedom…or rise to his challenge and win my fortune back.

I bargained. I lost.

Now Jafar owns me, and even as my mind rails against him, my body loves the delicious punishments he deals out. It's almost enough to believe he cares. But a gilded cage is still a prison, and I'll do anything to obtain my freedom. Even betray the man who captured my heart.

"Deliciously inventive."

—*Publishers Weekly* STARRED review for *Neon Gods*

For more info about Sourcebooks's books and authors, visit:

sourcebooks.com

COURT OF THE VAMPIRE QUEEN

THREE POWERFULLY ALLURING VAMPIRE MEN AND ONE QUEEN TO RULE THEM ALL.

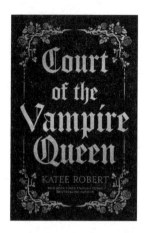

All Mina ever wanted was to escape her father's control. Half human, half vampire, she lived eternally torn between two worlds, never fully experiencing the pleasures of either—until her father chose her as the pawn in his latest political move, gifting her to the darkly powerful and dangerously seductive Malachi Zion.

Malachi is not a vampire to be trifled with. But the longer Mina spends with him, the more she realizes he's not the monster she first thought—and as fear bleeds into lust, then trust, then something more, Malachi opens Mina up to a world she never knew could be hers for the taking: including the love of Malachi's two closest friends and companions. Now surrounded by all three men, Mina may finally have the power to face down her father and take back the life—and crown—that by all rights should be hers.

"Addicting [and] delicious."
—*Oprah Daily* for *Electric Idol*

For more info about Sourcebooks's books and authors, visit:

sourcebooks.com